Traitor's Curse

by

Beth Trissel

The Traitor's Legacy Series, Book 3

Traitor's Curse

Cover Art by *Debbie Taylor*

The Wild Rose Press, Inc.
PO Box 708
Adams Basin, NY 14410-0708
Visit us at www.thewildrosepress.com

Publishing History
First American Rose Edition, 2015
Print ISBN 978-1-5092-0153-2
Digital ISBN 978-1-5092-0154-9

The Traitor's Legacy Series, Book 3
Published in the United States of America

"Turn back. A man watches you."

Again, the warning carried from the unseen source.

What man, and how did she know Stuart was observed? He could barely discern anything.

"Who are you? Show yourself." Uneasiness lent indignation to his demand.

Through the haze, he spotted the figure of a young female dressed all in white. A death shroud?

Pray God, it wasn't. His gut knotted, and he stood staring at her.

Ethereal, ghostly, she seemed to float toward him, but must have walked.

Must have.

A cold shiver stood the hair on the back of his neck on end. Was she flesh and blood, or spirit? Had she crossed the divide between the two worlds?

He scarcely dared to breathe.

Still, he stood rooted to the trail. And not only from fright. Fascination.

Despite fear of being haunted, an aura about her drew him. He waited, every muscle taut, poised betwixt heaven and earth, the scent of crumbling leaves in his nose. At least, that was real.

Whiteness swirling around her, she neared.

Then he spotted it, an ivory coverlet draped over her head and around her slender shoulders pinched together in front with pale fingers.

No shroud.

The blanket reached to her ankles and trailed behind along the ground. Mist muted the flowers stitched into the cloth. This accounted for him not spotting her sooner. She'd blended in with the vapor.

Dedication

To my lovely friend Joyce D'Ottavio,
whose insight helped inspire the completion of this
story—and who throws a terrific book launch party.

~

And to the fine folk of Halifax, North Carolina,
dedicated to preserving their rich heritage.

Chapter One

Late November, 1783
Cemetery in the Town of Halifax, North Carolina

"Master Stuart, do not venture here."

Master? Apart from the servants, Stuart Monroe hadn't been called by that title since he was a boy, and better deserved to be addressed as Captain.

Taken aback by the strange caution, he stopped on the hazy path and peered through the cloudy vapor for the disembodied voice uttered in feminine accents. Frost coated the slick leaves beneath his boots and cloaked the bare tree branches and gravestones, faintly illuminated in the silvery predawn light.

No one. Only his chilled breath bore evidence of a living soul. This place was eerie enough without the odd warning.

"Who speaks?" Probably a townswoman, he reassured himself. Though why she'd be here at this hour was beyond him.

"Turn back. A man watches you."

Again, the warning carried from the unseen source.

What man, and how did she know Stuart was observed? He could barely discern anything.

"Who are you? Show yourself." Uneasiness lent indignation to his demand.

Through the haze, he spotted the figure of a young

female dressed all in white. A death shroud?

Pray God, it wasn't. His gut knotted, and he stood staring at her.

Ethereal, ghostly, she seemed to float toward him, but must have walked.

Must have.

A cold shiver stood the hair on the back of his neck on end. Was she flesh and blood, or spirit? Had she crossed the divide between the two worlds?

He scarcely dared to breathe.

Still, he stood rooted to the trail. And not only from fright. Fascination.

Despite fear of being haunted, an aura about her drew him. He waited, every muscle taut, poised betwixt heaven and earth, the scent of crumbling leaves in his nose. At least, that was real.

Whiteness swirling around her, she neared.

Then he spotted it, an ivory coverlet draped over her head and around her slender shoulders pinched together in front with pale fingers.

No shroud.

The blanket reached to her ankles and trailed behind along the ground. Mist muted the flowers stitched into the cloth. This accounted for him not spotting her sooner. She'd blended in with the vapor.

He relaxed his tense vigil slightly.

The wrapping parted in front, exposing a long white shift, more fitting for the bedchamber. Where leather shoes were wanted, slippers damp from the wet clad her feet. Like him, her breath showed in the sharp air. Her face, an exquisite oval outlined by the fabric, captivated him. She possessed rare beauty, with a hint of the exotic. But something was amiss. And not only her attire.

Blue eyes, like a clear wintry sky, searched his, their expression troubled. Circles smudged the creaminess of the skin below her seeking gaze, and her eyes seemed a little too bright, her cheeks abnormally flushed. Lengths of hair as dark as the rain-wet branches overhead escaped her coverlet and tumbled to her waist. If the wind stirred, these tendrils would blow about her, but the air was still. Only an occasional birdcall broke the silence.

Expecting solitude, he'd chosen this early hour to visit the site his sister Claire and her husband, British Major Vaughan, both in England these past two years, had determined held not a body but considerable treasure. Rather than lying in the grave with the headstone bearing the name John Monroe, his father's final resting place was said to be in Bruton Parish, Williamsburg.

Stuart recoiled from unearthing anything in this holy place, but must before many more days passed. The Monroe family estate was sorely in want of fortune. Disquiet had stayed his hand from bearing the shovel, left in the carriage. He'd ventured uneasily into the cemetery for a look, and now these ungodly tidings.

What did it all mean, or was this merely the ranting of a mad woman? She had a different look than any lady of his acquaintance, and reminded him of an Irish or Indian woman the way she held the blanket around her head and shoulders.

Her eyes invited him in, and he plumbed their depths. "Who are you?"

She waved aside his question as if it were of no consequence. "Beware. You are watched."

Insistence in her face, she gestured toward the graves encircled by haze. Here and there, a raised stone table tomb took shape in the vapor. Beyond these lay the family plot, outlined by an iron fence.

"A man, dressed in black, waits for you." Her voice a hushed whisper.

A chill crawled down his spine. "How do you know this?"

"There were two. One left. He spoke your name."

Stuart clasped her shoulders. She was flesh and blood beneath his grip, yet seemed not of this world. "What did he say?"

"To watch for your coming."

"How could they possibly anticipate my visit?"

"That has not yet been revealed."

Her answer baffled him, as did she. "Why did you call me master? Are you a servant?"

"No."

He'd doubted she was in anyone's employ. Her smooth hands, opulent coverlet, and refined manner, all bespoke gentility. And she smelled of violets, a costly scent.

He gazed deeply into those mesmerizing eyes. "Why are you here?"

"I seek the living among the dead."

A peculiar reply from the haunting stranger. "Who?"

"You. Stuart Monroe."

Again, the sensation of ants scattering down the nape of his neck. "How did you know I would come?"

"I was told. In a dream."

She spoke like one in a dream. The cold mist, the woman—an apparition in the fog—seemed unreal. Yet she was no ghost.

"You can foresee events?" A sense of dread possessed him.

"In glimpses. Your father appeared to me." Her barely perceptible voice faded entirely, and her eyes fluttered, then closed. She swayed against him, any further explanation muffled by his coat.

Stuart held her fast and kept her from sliding to the cold earth. What did his father have to do with this visitation? Was the woman in his arms some sort of witch?

He pressed his palm to her forehead. *Afire*. She was deluded by fever.

But who on earth was she, and why had she dreamt of his father? Had she been acquainted with the late Captain Monroe? More than two years had passed since he'd fallen.

All questions must wait. Stuart would gain no answers from one in a feverish swoon. Going from house to house, knocking on doors, in search of her home would cost precious time. If he didn't swiftly fetch her back to Thornton Hall and Ezekiel's skillful care, she mightn't live to speak again.

A pang of regret knifed through him. He'd just met the most beguiling woman ever, and whether a witch or enchantress, he must preserve her life. For reasons known only to God, she had fallen into his care.

He swept her up into his arms and glanced around. No one stirred. Late night revelers from the *Sign of the Thistle* or *Dudley's Tavern* up the road had staggered to their beds, and it was too early for townsfolk to be out and about.

As far as he could tell, the misty green Market

Square was deserted. If unseen eyes did look on, Stuart hoped the bystander wouldn't think the senseless woman was being abducted. He wasn't in the habit of waylaying hapless females, if that's how his actions appeared. This was urgent.

Lengthening his stride, he bore her back to his coach left on the verge of King Street where Jim waited with the horses, as he'd instructed the young Negro. Time enough to discover who she was and where she belonged after she was firmly back in the land of the living. If anyone could work that cure, it was Ezekiel. Stuart prayed the old man wouldn't fail him now. Surely, Divine Providence hadn't placed this fascinating female in his path for him to watch her perish.

Dark eyes wide, Jim opened the door. "You want any help with the lady, sir?"

Stuart shook his head. Clutching her in his arms, he bounded into the coach. "I'll get her settled. She's faint with fever. Home with all speed, Jim."

Jim bit back the question that must be on his tongue, shut the door behind them, and mounted the driver's seat. With a slap of the reins, they cantered off into the whiteness.

Stuart nestled the limp bundle beside him, holding her in place as the carriage jostled on the dirt road. Chills shook her slender frame despite his efforts to warm her.

Uncertain if she'd hear, he offered reassurance. "I'm taking you to Thornton Hall, Miss, to the best healer in North Carolina."

"Bless you." Stuart barely caught her reply. At least, she'd made one.

"We played there as children, you and I, and Claire," she added in a soft voice.

Realization struck him like a cannon ball. *Hettie Fairfax.* So changed he hadn't recognized her.

She'd visited from Virginia one summer and stayed with her uncle, the prominent Halifax merchant Mister Ezra Jones. She must've returned to town while Stuart was away fighting in the war. The Jones' outstanding home stood not far from the cemetery. Stuart could have borne her to the spacious, two-story house, covering several lots in the crowded town.

No. Everything in him said he wasn't meant to go there, that without his help, she would perish.

The close proximity of the Jones' residence wasn't why she'd come to the graveyard, though. She'd been there for him.

None of this made sense. Her strange assertions must be the fever talking.

Must be.

But how had she known to seek for him at the cemetery? Was she so near to death, the veil had thinned enough for his father to communicate with her?

"Faster, Jim!" he shouted out the window.

They might all break their necks, but the sturdy pair of grays couldn't tear over the ground rapidly enough for Stuart. These horses were among the finest teams in the county. Pray God, they outdid themselves now.

As for Hettie's uncle, he'd send word later this morning. He couldn't trouble over that powerful man at present. His will was bent on saving the woman slumped beside him. If he was berated for his action, let the furies roar.

He'd endured raging battles. Even triumphed. This was simply a different sort of fight.

Chapter Two

A man's pleasing voice summoned Hettie Fairfax from a sleep so deep she had no recollection of tumbling down the black well of oblivion. Nor had she any idea how long she'd slumbered in this dark recess, or in whose bed she lay.

She opened heavy eyes. *Not hers*. And the man who'd roused her wasn't within her chamber. His low tone seemed to carry from an adjoining room.

A second male rumbled in reply, but her ear was tuned to the first speaker. She couldn't fathom his identity, only that she liked the ebb and flow of his voice, and his speech held a familiar quality. She knew him, in the depths of her soul…just couldn't think who he was. Thinking at all was difficult.

Senseless of the hour, she noted the candle on the walnut stand beside her wasn't lit. Gold light stole through windows draped in rich blue damask that matched her bed curtains. The fabric was drawn back, allowing the glow to bathe her face.

Did it herald early morning or late afternoon? How strange not to know if the sun were recently up or soon going down.

Blinking against the yellow rays as might a mole fresh from its burrow, she turned her head and stared straight ahead at the hearth. Orange flames blurred before her vision. She shifted her gaze to the black marble and Greek Key molding inlaid around the fireplace. Carvings of children at play with forest creatures lent whimsy to the frieze.

The cheery blaze in the hearth dappled the green armchair tucked before it. A plump woman dozed in the upholstered seat, her capped head nodding to one side of the tall back, striped petticoats and a white apron engulfing the base. Soft snores escaped her.

Reluctant to rouse her companion, Hettie slid her gaze past the figurines on the mantel to the high chest of drawers and chest on chest standing against one cornflower blue wall. A dressing table situated near the tall chest of drawers held a beautiful wooden toilette case painted with floral scenes on a green background. Beside it was a scent bottle embellished with an elegant lady in a flowery garden and a carved ivory hair brush.

Charming.

Spicy fragrance wafted from a brightly painted apple shaped vessel made of fine porcelain, a kind of pomander ball. All these lovely things were reflected in the mirror above the table. Though the décor was different than her own bedchamber, the tone was distinctly feminine.

This room surely belonged to a woman, or an effeminate macaroni dipped into the pots and bottles of scent, cream, and makeup the toilette case contained. She trusted the former had occupied this chamber before her, not some dandy with his white face, rouged cheeks, reddened lips, and artificial beauty patches. She loathed such men.

But the slumbering female couldn't possibly be mistress of this chamber. Her dress was far too simple. Likely, she was a servant in this home, whoever's it was.

Hettie struggled to remember under the heaviness weighing her mind and body. Where on earth was she, and how long had she been here?

Letting her gaze wander, she sought to recall the hazy events that led to her coming. Cantering horses charged through her mind. A team of matched grays.

Whose were they?

She dipped her eyes to the walnut washstand in one corner. A porcelain basin, pink with flowers and filled with water, rested on its top, a folded cloth draped over the brim as if in recent use. The matching pitcher beside the basin kept company with a collection of green and brown glass bottles. Corked and capped with leather, these phials held amber and ruby-red tinctures.

Medicine. Someone was ill.

All of this she absorbed in moments, and it occurred to her that she must be the patient.

What ailed her?

Fever, she assumed. She'd had remittent fever on and off since a midsummer's visit to Carter's Grove Plantation on the James River exposed her to *bad air.* Cycles of racking chills, alternating with sweating, 'to the bone' aches, and deep weariness accompanied these feverish bouts.

Had illness assailed her again?

Yes, it must have done. And struck even worse this time.

Disjointed images returned of a misty cemetery, ominous men, and a warning she must convey. To whom?

Like hazy tendrils, her thoughts circled around the handsome face of a young Revolutionary War Captain, with eyes the color of deep woods fern, and sun-streaked brown hair. His name floated out of reach.

She snagged it. *Stuart Monroe*, the adored boy of her childhood. Brave and adventurous, even then.

No wonder he'd fought with such dedication for the revolution. And yet, he also possessed a tender streak, especially for his younger sister, Claire. He hadn't noticed Hettie, until…

She vaguely recalled the hasty carriage ride to Thornton Hall. That's where she'd seen the grays. Stuart supported her over the jolting road, whispering encouragement and pleas for her to hold on.

Had he even uttered her name?

The delicious sense that he had tugged at the corners of her mind. But she couldn't be sure.

She'd faded, awakening to the elderly Negro with gentle hands and the bitter brews he'd tipped down her throat, followed by reviving sips of barley water. His wrinkled face swam in and out of her memory.

Women had also ministered to her. Though not Claire Monroe, now Mrs. Vaughan. Or was she lady something?

Wed to a British officer and future lord, Claire resided in England. This must have been her chamber. Unless it belonged to Stuart's mother, also said to be abroad. Or had Mrs. Monroe returned?

Hettie's mind swirled in a fog of partially recalled people and events. Did fever still addle her, or was it one of the potions she'd been given?

What in God's name was in those bottles?

She startled as the woman in the chair gave a loud snort and jerked awake. Her round face creased in a smile upon meeting Hettie's scrutiny.

"Back with us at last, are you, dearie?"

"How long have I been absent?"

"Three days."

"*That* long?"

"Aye, Miss. I daresay you have no recollection, but I can see yer better."

The amiable female clambered to her feet and hastened to where Hettie lay. "We were that afeared fer you, but Ezekiel saw you through, right enough. Bless him. Gave you tinctures of boneset, willow, and Peruvian bark. A bit of laudanum and valerian to sooth you. My, how you tossed and railed, like the devil himself chased after you."

"Did I?" She had no memory.

An emphatic nod of her capped head. "Indeed, you did. Most piteous. Ezekiel had us sponging yer forehead and cracking the window so you had fresh air. All the while, keeping the fire going. Wouldn't let no leech bleed you neither. Said it wouldn't do no good."

How the woman prattled on. But Hettie had her answers. "Pray accept my deepest gratitude. I am heartily grateful for your ministrations. 'Twould seem I owe Ezekiel a debt for his care, and Captain Monroe for bringing me here." Her heart fluttered at his name and she had to know. "Has the captain been in to see me?"

Like a mother for her son, pride shone on the woman's broad face. "Captain Monroe visits nearly every hour the good Lord sends, when he's not required elsewhere on the estate, or in town. He's across the hall in the upstairs parlor now."

"Thought I heard his voice." Pleasure rippled through Hettie, and strength pulsed in her like the returning beat of a silent drum.

"Keeps an eye on you, he does. Had a time persuading yer uncle to leave you here," the woman added.

"I can well imagine. Uncle Ezra gets in rather a huff when crossed."

Her companion nodded vigorously and tucked stray auburn curls beneath her cap. "'Twas Mister Jones as wanted to bring in the doctor to bleed you, but Ezekiel said *no leech,* and Captain Monroe insisted Ezekiel be heeded. Yer uncle was in a right temper I can tell you, but allowed as how you were faring better in the old healer's care, you might stay here under his watch until you are truly well."

This gave Hettie hope. More than anything, she wished to remain near Stuart, and, if possible, be of help to him in return for all he'd done for her. It might have been the fancies of a fevered mind, but she could swear he was in danger.

"Now then," the woman said briskly, "I'm Mrs. Jenner, housekeeper at Thornton Hall and kin to Mrs. Monroe. Captain Monroe, too. Fifth cousins, maybe. Not sure of the connection, but blood is blood, I always say. You lie comfortable like, while I fetch you some supper."

The genial flow of words washed over Hettie like a soothing stream. She shifted among the bedclothes. Someone had changed them beneath her; the linen smelt fresh, not stale from sweat-soaked fever.

"Wait—so, it's evening?" she asked the housekeeper.

"Oh. Aye." Her pale blue eyes crinkling in sympathy, she settled into the upholstered chair by the bed as though for a good gossip, which suited Hettie.

"Poor lass. You don't know which way the sun's headed, but 'twill soon be down, and Ezekiel in with yer next dose afore long. He'll be right pleased to see you awake."

"What of Captain Monroe?"

"I dare say he'll be along after a bit."

"I must be a sight." Hettie patted her tousled tresses spread over the coverlet.

The woman called Mrs. Jenner cocked her head to one side, leveling a perceptive gaze at Hettie. "You mustn't think of moving from that bed yet to dress. Still wobbly as a newborn foal, no doubt. I swore to look after you like m' own flesh and blood. And I aim to keep that vow, you hear?"

Hettie nodded meekly. She appreciated Mrs. Jenner's devotion and wasn't about to wrestle her bulk to try and get to her feet. Neither did she want to present a disarrayed figure for Stuart's inspection. For reasons known only to her heart, he mattered to her, as did his good opinion. He mattered a lot.

"Our Miss Smith will be along to see how you fare." Mrs. Jenner spoke as if this were a common occurrence.

"Who?"

"The ward of Captain Monroe's widowed aunt, Mrs. Peyton, of Williamsburg. You know the Virginia Peytons?"

"Certainly," Hettie fibbed. She knew a great many things she couldn't immediately recall, and it was an effort to follow the conversation.

Mrs. Jenner plowed on. "Mrs. Peyton sent Miss Smith to Thornton Hall to lend a hand. As agreeable a young woman as you'd care to meet. Willing to help wherever she's needed. Captain Monroe praises her highly."

Now, the housekeeper had Hettie's full attention. A twinge of what could only be described as jealousy needled her. Was this most *agreeable* young woman also fair of face and figure? Had she, even now, captured Stuart's affections? Hettie had assumed he lived at Thornton with his relations, not a potential rival.

Visions of intimate suppers shared with him while she convalesced winged out the window, and the sunlight dimmed. Uncle Ezra, Hettie's guardian since the death of her parents, had urged her to marry soon, vowing if she didn't choose a suitable husband before the New Year he'd select one himself. Hopes that Stuart Monroe might be that man plummeted. But all was not yet lost.

Fighting for control, Hettie summoned a smile to her lips. Weakness had left her emotions close to the surface, and she strove to mask her vulnerability. "Miss Smith sounds most worthy. I'm sure we shall be friends," she asserted, not at all inclined in that direction. "Thank you for your aid, Mrs. Jenner. Please send a girl to help me freshen myself."

The charitable woman laid a plump hand on Hettie's slight shoulder. "There, now. You mustn't fret over how you look. Yer fever just broke not long ago."

Which meant she must resemble a ghost, eyes ringed with circles, face the hue of death, tresses like the tail of an unkempt mare. "Only a quick wash, clean shift, and my hair brushed. I will remain abed. I promise."

A grudging nod from Mrs. Jenner. "I'll send

Maddie up. She's an able girl. Her twin sister, Minnie's, got little more sense than God gave a goose. And he didn't give 'em much."

She waved dimpled fingers at a corner of the room and the leather-bound trunk embedded with brass studs Hettie used when traveling. "Some of yer belongings were brought round, and Captain Monroe says you kin use whatever you fancy in here."

"Most generous of him."

"Only too glad to see 'em enjoyed. His mama sent that toilette case and scent bottle from England as gifts for Miss Smith, but she'll have none of it. Like a Quaker, that girl. No use for fashion. Finery's wasted on her. A shame, really."

Not entirely. Hettie smiled with rekindled hope. This gave her an edge, unless Stuart preferred plain women.

A gentleman of his position might be inclined to take a wife who'd make an elegant appearance in society. Hettie was keenly aware of how far off the mark she was at present. Still, she'd been considered a beauty once. Surely, she could attain that standing again?

Mrs. Jenner beamed approval. "See, there. Yer right bonnie when you smile."

"Good of you to say."

Hettie had also been called *a bit odd*, but never plain. If nothing else, she had the inheritance she'd come into on her twenty-second birthday. Her face and fortune were her only lures to tempt Stuart Monroe. The notion that he might love her for herself seemed exceedingly unlikely, especially when he hadn't even remembered her upon their meeting.

No. That was soaring too high.

Perhaps she could gain a proposal from him if she concealed her *peculiar little ways*, as Uncle Ezra termed them.

Ms. Jenner patted her arm. "Never you fear, Miss. We'll soon have you fresh as a new morn, and back on yer feet afore long. I aim to take good care of you."

Tears of gratitude blurred Hettie's sight. The woman's charitable demeanor meant she was unaware of the rumors surrounding her, or she'd discounted the talk.

But they were true.

Hettie sometimes received messages from the departed. She'd made no effort to summon the dead and had no control over when a spirit might appear to her, usually in a dream as the late Captain Monroe had done. But not always.

Once an apparition of her grandmother had greeted her at the bottom of Uncle Ezra's stairs. She was accused of sleepwalking at the time, making it difficult to discern reality from the dream world. Some folk thought her odd, so she endeavored to keep this *gift*, as her mother had kindly declared it, a secret.

Mrs. Jenner fished in her apron and passed Hettie a handkerchief. "You rest up, dearie, and mop them bonnie eyes."

Her thoughtfulness only made the tears flow.

Shadows and echoes of the past were all Hettie had left of her family, apart from the occasional visitation. And her gruff, but goodhearted uncle, of course. His lump of a son, her cousin Jonas, she didn't count. Nor did Uncle Ezra consider him in planning for her future.

Thumping his chest and coughing for emphasis,

he'd insisted. "I'll not live forever, Niece, and you daren't rely on Jonas. I'm getting bronchial. Got to find you a good man."

Hettie had no objection to marriage, given the right suitor. The longing for a husband and children of her own ached deep within her. Could Stuart possibly be the one who would make her his wife?

If not, she was fated to Uncle Ezra's choice. His notion of *a good man* might take the form of a grizzled male old enough to be her grandfather. But opposing the indomitable force that was Uncle Ezra required more strength than she possessed. Though possibly not more than Mrs. Jenner, if Hettie won her over.

The battle for hearts and minds was on.

Chapter Three

A rap on the cracked door of the upstairs parlor broke into their neighbor's earnest discourse. Mister Ellis halted in mid-flow. Tensing at the interruption, Stuart glanced up from the hearth. "If that's another meddlesome tradesman come to badger me, I'm hurling the fellow bodily down the stairs and the consequences be damned," he muttered.

Confound it. He fully intended to pay his debts.

From the adjoining armchair upholstered in crimson, Mister Ellis lifted a cautioning hand. His eyes were equally solemn beneath the gray wig matching his grizzled brows and drab charcoal suit. "You're sorely tried, sir, but show some restraint. I beseech you."

The older man was an honest soul, and fair in all his dealings, but he acted and dressed like a damn Puritan.

Grinding his teeth, Stuart waved aside their nervous neighbor's fears. "I shall conduct myself with decorum, unless taxed beyond endurance."

Unlike the puffed up, bewigged merchants feathering their nests, Stuart had been away with the army serving his fledgling country. Scorning wigs, he wore his own hair pulled back, and had for the duration of his service in the Virginia Light Dragoons. He'd supported General Washington, helped suppress a mutiny among the ranks, and hadn't returned until the

Treaty of Paris was well and truly signed in September, officially ending the American Revolution.

For all the gratitude he'd received.

Clearly, he'd been gone too long. The drawn-out war had taken a toll on the Monroes, in more ways than one. He'd had a long day, riding his neglected estate and taking stock. Much remained to be done, and the funds were insufficient—nonexistent—unless he sold some land to Mister Ellis, which he was loathe to do.

Again, the rap at the door. "Yes?" Stuart bit out, not bothering to rise from the chair.

Fortunately, no tradesman entered, jowls furrowed in a frown, demands on his lips. Rather, Mrs. Jenner swept into the upstairs parlor, her plump face wreathed in smiles.

"Forgive the interruption, sir, but I thought you'd like to know Miss Fairfax is awake and her fever down!"

"Oh, these are glad tidings." Stuart sprang to his feet, his spirits lifting like a bird in flight.

Their neighbor grunted appreciatively. "Indeed, Captain Monroe. Her uncle will be pleased. Mister Jones feared to lay the young lady in her grave."

So had Stuart, to his core.

"Happy news is always welcome." Mister Ellis rose stiffly, the hint of a smile on his lips. Full-blown mirth would never suit his reserved demeanor.

He grasped his brass-headed cane, the etchings in the handle worn from heavy use. It pained Stuart to see how age lay upon his neighbor, but he was a tedious fellow. Perhaps his nephew, Brinkley, Stuart's close friend and fellow officer, would come and assist the older man with his estate. After all, the war was over, as folk incessantly reminded Stuart, and Brinkley the Ellis's sole heir.

Leaning on his walking stick, Mr. Ellis cleared his throat. "I shall bid you good day, sir, and allow you to attend to your guest. I trust you will consider my proposal?"

Stuart sidled impatiently in the black riding boots he still wore. "Yes, yes. We shall speak again. I should like to discuss this matter with my grandfather first."

Ellis arched graying brows. "Is it wise to trouble him? After all, the elder Mister Monroe is rather…ill."

The word Mister Ellis politely avoided was mad. "He may not be the man he was, but he's still master of Thornton Hall and ought to have some say."

"If you insist."

"I do." Grandfather had an occasional day when his mind was clear, and the wait bought Stuart a little more time. If he had to let land go, he'd rather it was to Brinkley.

Besides, he couldn't dwell on Thornton's fate now, as distracted as he was by Hettie's welfare.

Never one to remain silent, Mrs. Jenner broke in. "I'll see Mister Ellis out, and have Jim alert his driver to bring the carriage round, then fetch Maddie to give Miss Fairfax a hand. She's wanting to freshen up. When a cat starts grooming herself, mark my words, she's on the mend."

The countrywoman's comparison was slightly offensive, but Stuart let it pass. "I'll stop by her chamber after she's been seen to. Pray caution Miss Fairfax not to overtire herself."

"Save yer breath to cool yer porridge, I did so at once." With a bob of her capped head, Mrs. Jenner turned and skirted from the room. Their bemused neighbor trailed behind her.

Stuart had long since grown accustomed to the outspoken woman, more family than mere servant, and relied on her.

Mister Ellis paused in the doorway. "The offer for the mare still stands."

"Not one I care to accept, sir."

Frown lines deepened the crags in his brow. "Needs must, at times, Captain Monroe."

Needs shouldn't rob Stuart of such a rare horse. "I shall never find her like again."

A grudging nod. "You are fortunate the renowned Captain Jordan of Charles Towne graciously allowed you to keep the mare when Major Vaughan left her behind."

"Vaughan did considerably more than that. He enhanced her training, made her what she is. The blood lines were there, but La Belle was green when he took her."

After the surrender at Yorktown, his brother-in-law, British Major Vaughan, had left La Belle in Stuart's charge before sailing from the Chesapeake Bay. With Patriot Captain Jordan's blessing, he'd bred the mare to a superior stallion, and she'd borne a promising filly. The pair formed the foundation of what would be an outstanding line of horses to race and sell—eventually.

He flicked a bit of chaff from his nut-brown coat. "I decline your offer, sir, but shall bear it in mind."

"It stands as long as the mare thrives." Mister Ellis disappeared down the hall, no doubt frustrated by Stuart's reluctance on all fronts.

His neighbor's fruitless visit didn't trouble him. Despite the welcome news about Hettie, he remained concerned over a possible relapse. She'd been gravely ill. Ezekiel hadn't spared him the possible outcome. He'd dreaded conveying grim tidings to the powerful uncle who'd reluctantly entrusted her to them; not to mention his own suffering if she died.

Thank heavens Hettie's condition had taken a turn for the better. As her mind cleared, would she recall the exchange between them at the cemetery, or had all recollection of that encounter dissipated like mist in the sun?

Stuart burned to know.

****

After a wash and change of linen in his chamber, Stuart returned to the parlor. He paced from the hearth to the window, sipping brandy, and peering out the wavy glass at the darkening estate. Twilight descended, and a great orange moon rose above the leafless trees.

Enough of this.

Not wanting to appear overly eager, but anxious to see how Hettie fared, he strode across the hall and rapped lightly on her chamber door. "May I enter?"

"Yes, sir. She's done with her bath and readied." Maddie, Jim's seventeen-year-old sister, opened the door. "Grandpa's with her now."

The white apron Maddie wore engulfed the girl. Her chocolate eyes reflected her pleasure at their guest's improvement. She bobbed a curtsy to Stuart and dipped her head, the white cap covering her dark curls, then stepped aside. Firelight cast a golden glow over the room, and candles shone from every available surface. The tiny flames danced in the draft. Mrs. Jenner must've given orders to make the sick room more festive.

A fragrant blend of rosemary and thyme, likely with some mullein thrown in for good measure, steamed in the iron kettle over the hearth and charged the air. These herbal vapors would sooth headache, ease breathing, whet the appetite, chase away any evil lurking about, and sharpen Hettie's memory, he hoped. She'd been terribly confused on those occasions when they'd managed to rouse her.

Maddie's dusky, gray-haired grandfather, Ezekiel, stooped from rheumatism, sat by the bedside clasping a healing tincture in his gnarled hand. The ruby-red contents were indicative of Peruvian bark. Vile tasting stuff, but miraculous, and imported. While many herbs were grown in the gardens at Thornton Hall or gathered from the surrounding field and woods, they purchased this one from the apothecary.

Looking past the old Negro, he honed in on Hettie propped up against the cushions, not prone on her back, tossing, turning, and ranting as she'd done until this morning. Quiet repose, at last. The knot in his middle eased, and his gaze explored her with pleasure rather than the coil of worry.

The azure bed curtains heightened the hue of her eyes, seeming larger than ever in her pale face. Thick black hair, brushed until it gleamed, spread down over her shoulders, fanning around her like mermaid tresses. She reminded him of a mer-creature, as unlikely a find as she was in the cemetery enveloped by haze like the mist on the sea. The ebony tumble partly hid the white shift covering an even thinner figure than when he'd borne her to Thornton Hall. Maddie had draped a blue shawl around her slender shoulders. But she was alive, thank God, and would recover, he was determined.

More than he ought.

Guilt pricked Stuart that Hettie's wellbeing mattered so dearly to him. He'd made no promise to the longsuffering Miss Smith. He also knew she trusted an unspoken understanding lay between them and anticipated a marriage proposal now that the War of Independence was finally concluded.

Certainly, Stuart esteemed the petite young woman with her unpretentious ways. She'd done much for the family in his absence and would make an excellent and industrious wife, Grandfather assured him. The elderly man, much reduced in vigor, and not entirely in his right mind, depended on the hard-working, amiable Miss Smith, and Stuart intended to wed the girl. He truly did…

Only, Hettie drew him like the tide. He couldn't take his eyes from her.

"Don't Miss Fairfax look ever so much better?" Maddie clasped her hands beneath her chin.

"Indeed." Stuart kept his voice down, his praise modest.

Hettie grimaced, and Stuart for her, as Ezekiel tipped a little of the brew into her mouth. She chased the bitterness with a swallow of red wine from the goblet she held.

"There now, Miss, not too many more doses of this here bark. I give it morning and evening for seven days."

She wiped at pale pink lips with a lace-edged handkerchief. "That leaves four, then?"

"Yes, Miss."

"Enough medicine to endure, but I'm mindful of your pains on my behalf. Truly." She set the wine glass on the bedside stand and waved a white hand at the remaining medicine bottles on the washstand. "Am I still in need of your other remedies?"

He shook his aged head. "Food and drink, warming to the stomach, and rest will speed yer recovery now." He gestured at the partially opened window. "And fresh air. Stuffy chambers will do you no good."

A vehement dislike of Ezekiel's. "You breathe in that herbal water. Fill yer lungs."

She could do little else, nor could Stuart. All who entered this chamber were assailed by the vapors. At least it was an appealing blend of fragrances, though rather pungent. Another reason to have the window ajar, and ample kindling stacked at the ready to feed the fire.

Ezekiel rose stiffly, and stepped back from the bed. "I'll leave you until the morrow, Miss, unless you take a turn fer the worse. Lord willing, you've passed out of danger."

"I pray so."

Speaking over a hunched shoulder, he turned away. "My remedy should cure you. If the fever returns, I'll repeat it. Ague sometimes makes another visit. But I think it will not, if we give it a good licking."

"I trust you will do that." Stuart had greater faith in Ezekiel than any doctor or apothecary.

"Yes, sir. M' very best."

"Your best is leaps ahead of anyone else's. Many folk yet live who should be dead without you. My grandfather, for one."

"True enough. Still, God favors a humble heart.

And death don't like being cheated." With that somber reminder, the wise healer shuffled from the room.

A subdued Maddie followed her elderly relation. "Mrs. Jenner will be along with yer supper, Miss," she said in passing.

A twinge crossed Hettie's expressive face, as if she'd been offered wriggling eels. "I shall try to summon some appetite."

"Only broth and new made cornbread. Easy on the stomach," Maddie assured her.

"Good," Hettie sighed, and fixed her eyes on Stuart. If possible, they deepened to an even more lustrous blue. Though she resembled a waif, she was a fetching waif.

Irresistibly so.

She beckoned to him. "Will you tarry awhile with me, sir?"

"Nothing I should desire more, Miss." Unnerving, how much he meant it.

Stuart refrained from sprinting to her side, and strode across the room to where she half-sat, half-lay, having slid down in the bed among the covers. "Here. Let's have you up."

He bent down, slipped his hands under her arms, and gently tugged her into place. "That's better, is it not?"

The scent of lavender water from her sponge bath titillated his nose. Even this innocent contact between them exhilarated him, though he took pains that she not realize.

Her eyes fluttered, and she nodded her appreciation. The slightest effort seemed to tire her. "I'm sorry, dear lady. I should have left you where you lay."

"Oh, no. Too long have I lain here senseless of all commencing about me. 'Tis time to bestir myself a little."

She'd definitely stirred him, and more than a little.

Her eyes returned to his. How intent was that gaze, given her weariness. She smiled faintly, enchanting him with the transformation it wrought on her wan features. What a heady rush a dazzling smile would work on his traitorous heart.

Strangely, now that she was fully conscious, he felt slightly awkward, like a shy youth. At six and twenty, and war hardened, he was anything but. Yet, for the first time since their bizarre encounter at the cemetery, they were conversing as normal folk might. And he was acutely aware of Hettie's every expression, gesture, word. *Of her.*

He stood at her bedside, uncertain whether to sit or make his excuses and bolt from the room. "I'm gratified to see you in such improved health, Miss Fairfax." His voice sounded unusually low, husky even. He inwardly chided himself.

She seemed to take no notice of his self-consciousness. "Thank you for your hospitality and exertions regarding my wellbeing, Captain Monroe. Please, sit with me. If I'm not detaining you from important business?"

This was his opportunity to hightail it out of the room and away from her intoxicating presence, but nothing in him wanted to go. Quite the opposite.

"No matter of such weight that it cannot keep." Checking his eagerness, he lowered his lanky frame onto the green upholstery of the chair recently vacated by Ezekiel.

"I'm gratified, sir."

"The pleasure is mine." Though, he trusted, not entirely.

She lifted the goblet and sipped the wine, wetting her beguiling lips. "My uncle, is he well?"

"Yes, and shall be acquainted with news of your improvement. I sent a rider bearing word. Mister Jones has been greatly concerned."

"I'm sorry to have caused him such distress. I have no memory of leaving the house that morning."

Stuart hesitated to ask but wanted to pose the question before Mrs. Jenner blew into the room. "What do you remember?"

Hettie glanced down, dark lashes sweeping across her smooth cheek, then looked up again. Her gaze pinned him. "You."

His heart drummed in his chest. "Only me?"

The ghost of a smile curved her lips. "Is that not enough?"

Heat rose to his cheeks. He was sorely in danger of blushing like a maid. "Indeed, Miss Fairfax, I am flattered to be etched so firmly in your mind. But you carried a warning. Was this borne of fever?"

Tiny creases furrowed her brow. "No. Danger hangs over you, I fear."

Stuart bent toward her. "You spoke of a man in black."

Her eyes widened. "Did I? I recall only that there were two."

"What do you fear they will do?"

She set her glass down and laid her hand on his coat sleeve. The urgency he'd sensed in her before filled her now. "Rob you. Injure you. Kill you. Beware."

An icy chill shivered through him. "I will. After years with the light dragoons, I'm accustomed to danger."

"Not this," she insisted. "They are crafty, like a fox."

"I'm also acquainted with foxes. But tell me, how do they know I have anything to steal?"

"One is acquainted with you. He's privy to your secrets. Though not all. *You are watched*," she cautioned in a whisper, as if afraid of being overheard.

Foreboding churned in Stuart's gut. The notion of a man with sinister intentions spying on him from behind trees and having him followed was unsettling. An even more disturbing thought struck him, and a pair of sly, dark eyes appeared in his mind. *No. It couldn't be whom he suspected.*

"Did you overhear the rogue's name?"

She shook her head. "Nor could I clearly see him or his companion in the haze. Only that one man was much larger than the other."

"Nothing unusual in that. However, the backstabber I have in mind is of a rather dainty build."

"Who might that be, sir?"

"A turncoat I thought we sent packing more than two years ago. I'll say no more for now." He had to be certain first.

She inclined her head, discomfort in her face.

He hadn't meant to brush her off. "Thank you for apprising me, Miss Fairfax. I shall be vigilant. Is there anything else I should be aware of?"

Candlelight revealed the earnestness in her eyes.

"Your father spoke a warning in my dream."

"Of what?"

"Danger—" She broke off, and stiffened.

Her gaze lifted from Stuart's to a place behind his chair. The fingers at his arm clamped down. She paled even more than her illness alone accounted for, and her eyes grew enormous. Biting her lips, she swallowed, but said nothing.

What on earth? Stuart covered the smaller hand at his sleeve with his larger grasp. She'd gone cold. "Pray tell me what troubles you."

"He speaks of an accursed treasure."

Stuart tilted his head, frowning. "*Speaks?*"

Again, her gaze fled over his shoulder. "He stands behind your chair."

Stuart stared at her. "Who?"

"Your father."

For a stunned moment, Stuart was baffled. Then realization came over him, and his heart sank. *Not again.*

Grandfather's reason shifted as unpredictably as the vagaries of the weather. His mother had suffered bouts of nervous hysteria until her relocation to England with Claire at the Vaughan's palatial home, which better suited her delicate mental state. And now, this captivating woman under whose spell he'd fallen was decidedly affected. Was he fated to be entwined with those whose minds were as unstable as shifting sand?

"I see." But he didn't.

Hettie implored him with those unbearably appealing eyes. "I'm not mad. Truly. I see things sometimes. People appear to me. Spirits…" she trailed off.

Good Lord. To indulge her, Stuart angled a glance over his shoulder. Nothing.

"He's gone now, anyway." Like a wilting flower, she drooped back down in the pillows.

"Poor lady. Do not distress yourself. Doubtless, fever still troubles you." But no trace of glassiness shown in her eyes, only dismay.

He couldn't resist smoothing a tendril at her forehead. "And you're worn to a thread. Likely half asleep," he added, for both their sakes.

A tear slid down her cheek. Plainly, she didn't believe his attempts at reassurance, and possibly feared for her sanity.

"Don't weep. You've been ill and are not nearly recovered."

She turned her face into the pillow. Utterly dispirited.

Whether he should or shouldn't, Stuart reached over and gathered Hettie up into his arms. Likely he held an addled woman, but she nestled against his chest as though it was the most natural thing in the world, and so it seemed. He savored her softness and the wealth of hair spilling around them. That she was alive and he held her, was almost too much to absorb. She'd nearly died.

"It will be all right," he whispered in her ear. He had no idea how, only that shielding her in his embrace was divine.

She must have overheard the two men in the cemetery speak of the treasure. There was only one left in America who had an inkling of its existence. Stuart thought him long gone. If it was the ne'er do well he suspected, by heaven, he'd thrash the traitor, or shoot him on sight and have done with it.

The reprobate must be unaware of the exact location where the wealth was buried, or he'd have dug it up by now. How much had he divulged to the second fellow?

Enough to whet his interest, without betraying his hand, Stuart wagered. Hettie might well be right that he was watched. He'd best keep his wits about him, especially when revisiting the family plot in Halifax.

For now, fierce tenderness melded with the fire coursing through him for her. *Damn it all*. He couldn't wed a mad woman, and add to the instability in the family.

As if she read his thoughts, a tremulous shudder shook her and a disconsolate sniff sounded against his waistcoat. He fished in his pocket and produced a square handkerchief, clean, thanks to Mrs. Jenner.

"There, now." He gently mopped Hettie's face and left her in possession of the linen cloth. Still, she remained in his embrace, which thrilled him far more than it should.

Searching for something, anything, to say that might ease her distress, he thought back. "Remember when you climbed the big old mulberry tree by our back pasture fence and got stuck in the high branches."

"And you climbed up to fetch me down and got hung up yourself." Her voice was shaky, but she'd replied.

"Yes. Claire laughed at us both. You always were one for getting us into predicaments," he reminded her.

"I'm gratified you remember. I hadn't realized you recalled me at all," Hettie said softly.

"How could I possibly forget you, fair lady?"

"You didn't know me at the graveyard."

Cradling her more tightly, he buried his face in her hair, scented with the essence of lavender. Maddie must've brushed a few drops of the fragrant oil through her tresses, heightening his giddiness. "That seems ages ago. And I did remember later in the coach."

"While I was senseless."

"You're conscious now." Not entirely in her right mind, but…would it be utterly insane to kiss her?

Yes. Utterly.

"I thought you spoke my name," she confided.

"I wondered if you heard." He drew back to gaze into her upturned face. "See, I didn't forget you."

Moisture glistened in the depths of her blue eyes.

Lifting his hand, he smoothed it away. "How could I?" he repeated, in the barest whisper.

Like a lunatic under the sway of the full moon, he slid his fingers beneath her chin. A wordless moment, filled with everything except speech, flowed between them.

Hurt and confusion clouded her gaze, but behind these wounded emotions he read desire. For him. And he returned her wanting tenfold.

Those eyes…that face, her mouth, her… How could he resist the force of the current sweeping him away?

Mrs. Jenner chose that moment to sail into the room. "I brought yer supper. Oh my—"

"Is something amiss?"

That query came from Abigail Smith.

Stuart slanted a gaze at the young woman standing frozen on the threshold, shock written on her plain face.

35

Chapter Four

Stuart tensed against Hettie as if someone had put a pistol to his head and cocked the trigger. The exhilarating warmth vanished from his fern-colored gaze, displaced by the discomfit of one who'd far rather not be detected in this compromising position. A frown settled on his brow beneath the sun-streaked brown hair and tightened his lips—the lips she'd been certain were about to cover hers.

She quelled a heavy sigh.

He mouthed, *Damn*.

A sentiment fully in accord with her own.

"My apologies," he whispered, though his language hadn't offended her. Uncle Ezra often swore around the house.

"I trust you are recovered from your giddiness," Stuart added in a louder tone, as if merely assisting her, not implicating either of them in a romantic involvement.

Although that was blatantly obvious, and she heartily wished he would declare it so.

Rather, he lowered her back onto the bed, straightened, and got to his feet. "I bid you good evening, Miss Fairfax, and pray you have a restful night."

With a short bow, he turned and strode across the room, pausing before the petite, young woman who stood like a statue. The top of her capped head reached well below his broad shoulders. "Miss Smith." He gave a stiff bow, which she barely acknowledged, and walked out the door.

Would he return? Ever?

He'd said nothing about seeing Hettie on the morrow. Was this the end of something precious that had only begun? She had a sinking sensation in the pit of her now churning stomach.

Once again, it seemed Hettie had lured Stuart into a predicament, if that's how he termed their current quandary. She'd hoped he would consider it a great deal more than simply an uncomfortable position. She wasn't some lowly rustic he could trifle with and depart.

No, by heaven. She was a Fairfax, one of Virginia's elite families, and her uncle the most prominent merchant in Halifax. Not that she would hold her status over a Monroe, particularly this one. But Miss Smith was nobody.

Clearly, the girl meant something to Stuart. Was he promised to her? If so, Mrs. Jenner had failed to mention the understanding between the two.

As had Stuart.

The plump housekeeper swiftly recovered herself and hastened over the floor with remarkable alacrity for one of her girth. In her hands, a tray heaped with a steaming bowl, platter of cornbread dripping molasses, and a mug of some herbal brew. Hettie craved a proper cup of tea, and only that.

Mrs. Jenner lowered her bulk onto the seat Stuart had occupied so wonderfully, his departure leaving an emptiness no one could fill. She dipped a spoon into the broth. "Let's get some of this good food in you."

After what had transpired, Hettie had no appetite. It didn't take a soothsayer to see the formidable woman would brook no argument. She resigned herself to a few swallows.

Still, Miss Smith poised in the threshold. She reminded Hettie of a Quaker with her gray striped skirts and somber jacket laced over a white shift. Atop this, she wore an apron it would never cross Hettie's mind to don. Fashionable ladies sported only non-functional aprons of sheer fabric. Miss Smith dressed more like the housekeeper.

The girl's youthful face wasn't without appeal, but muted like mist over a meadow so that nothing struck one as remarkable. Her light brown hair was tidied under the cap; only the wings showed in front. Well-set, hazel eyes were her best feature and, Hettie was sorry to see, gleamed with tears.

The distraught young woman cleared her throat. "I am gratified to find you faring better, Miss Fairfax, and leave you in Mrs. Jenner's capable hands." Her voice tremulous, she turned and fled in a flurry of petticoats, a hand clapped over her mouth.

Guilt needled Hettie as she watched her depart, and she felt like the infamous Biblical temptress, Delilah, the last thing she'd intended. "I fear I've upset her."

Mrs. Jenner clucked sympathetically. "Not you, dearie, the captain. Yer not to trouble yerself. Miss Smith has no formal engagement to him, and—just between us—shouldn't expect it. Though the old gentleman favors her."

Hettie swallowed the bland broth spooned into her mouth. So, the elder Mister Monroe liked the girl.

"She's a good body, our Miss Smith, but not on the same standing as Captain Monroe," Mrs. Jenner continued, ladling the nourishing liquid into Hettie. "No one knows who her mother is, let alone her father. Left on the parish doorstep in Williamsburg, she was, and brought up proper by a charitable family. Master Stuart—I mean Captain Monroe's—aunt took Miss Smith in when she was fourteen. She's just seen her eighteenth birthday. Still plenty of time to find herself a respectable farmer, or townsman. She don't need to go setting her cap at him. Why, his sister's wed to a future lord and lives in a grand house the size of a palace."

Mrs. Jenner looked askance at Miss Smith's lofty aspirations. Then her pale blue eyes scrutinized Hettie with a speculative gleam. "You, on the other hand, are a fittin' choice for Captain Monroe."

Was it possible Hettie had an ally?

"But we can make no plans with you lying here scarcely able to lift a spoon to yer lips," she wore on, practically. "No more strength than a sparrow."

Hettie wondered if that's what comprised the meat in the broth, but swallowed with more vigor. "I believe the late Captain Monroe approves of me."

Mrs. Jenner eyed her closely. "Doubtless, he would."

"I meant *would*." Another slip.

More kindly clucks from her good-natured companion. "Yer a bit confused still, is all. From the fever. You'll be right soon enough if you rest up and *eat*."

If only it were that simple. The wishes of the dead were a challenge to convey without being deemed addlepated, or worse. Hettie would say no more of her revelations and ease Stuart's suspicions regarding her sanity.

If only she didn't have the powerful impression that his father wished her to persuade him of the menace lying in wait. The late Captain Monroe didn't want Stuart anywhere near that treasure.

****

Damn and blast. What was he thinking?

That's the trouble, he wasn't. Not with his head, anyway. He had to stop allowing his male member to lead him.

Smacking his fist against his forehead, Stuart stormed out of the house and down the brick steps. He instinctively strode across the cobbled yard and headed for the stables.

But he couldn't put Hettie from his thoughts for a moment. She'd worked her magic on him, and he'd succumbed body and soul. Not that it was fair to blame her, poor lady. She'd only just roused from days of illness. Unquestionably, her senses were affected. Perhaps visiting spirits, and whatever else she saw, would pass as she recovered.

Who could say? Apart from their childhood escapades, he wasn't well-acquainted with Hettie, and not when she'd enjoyed good health.

Meanwhile, he must take full responsibility for his actions. The courtship he'd inadvertently begun rested with him. And now, God forgive him, he'd wounded the sweetest soul of his acquaintance, Abigail Smith. Hettie hadn't exactly appeared happy with him, either.

What a rogue he was.

He paused mid-stride and gazed up at the voluptuous moon gliding between lacy clouds. Rather than the orange hue coloring it earlier, the ethereal orb was white. The pale beauty also reminded him of Hettie. Her blue eyes held the essence of twilight, her hair, the dark sky. Stardust glittered in the spell she wove. Night's allure belonged to her. It was all he could do not to bolt back inside and share the evening with this newly awakened woman.

That would only further injure Miss Smith.

No. He must keep his distance from their enticing guest. Surely one with his training and the rigorous hardships he'd endured could discipline himself?

Nothing in him wanted to.

Torn between honoring Miss Smith and burning desire for Hettie, he gulped in the cold air. Chill breezes whipped brown lengths loose from his queue, and he was glad for his wool coat. Raking fingers through his hair, he freed the remainder to blow about his face and shoulders. Let fashion decree what it will. He was in the mood to go his own way.

The smoky tang from many hearths reminded him of supper, as did his nagging stomach. But he couldn't face the hurt in *the little Quaker's* eyes.

Not now. And he knew the truth. Realization walloped him like a fist in the gut. He didn't love her. And never had. Likely, she also knew. How could she not?

Would she wed him anyway? Should he try to sooth her hurt and propose? Perhaps he'd come to love her, in time…

What of Hettie? Her name alone shimmered through him with light, music, and divine essence, as if she were sacred.

What she likely was could be summed up in one

Scot's word, *tetched*, but that didn't stop want from searing him. He'd go up in a blaze of smoke from wanting Hettie, leaving scorched earth behind.

Dear Lord. He was in a state. And had been from the first moment he'd seen her, if he were honest with himself.

He gazed up toward her second story window. The drapes in her chamber were not yet drawn. Could he spot her?

There. He glimpsed Hettie in bed, awash in that wonderful hair. Mrs. Jenner sat beside her, a food tray in hand.

The good woman had sworn to look after her. His presence was not required. *Was not*, he sternly reiterated. No matter how badly he wished differently. Likely Hettie's uncle would snatch her away if he knew Stuart burned for his niece. Mister Jones was as possessive as a she-bear.

He couldn't lurk here staring up at her window or he'd howl at the moon. Tearing himself from the nearly unbearable sight, he dove into the stable. The earthy aroma of hay and horses greeted him as he entered the stone and timber building. Reassuring sights and scents.

All was familiar here. Safe. No shifting ground.

An oil lamp had been lit and hung from a hook, casting shadows on the walls and dusty beams overhead. Bridles, halters, and ropes dangled along one log wall. Saddles were slung over a low bench. Curry combs and other riding equipment lined a shelf. Here and there, wooden buckets to carry feed and water, pitchforks for mucking out and replacing the bedding, a barrel of oats, and mound of hay filled the crowded building. He knew each nook. Everything was right.

Jim was in one of the stalls currying Stuart's favorite bay gelding, Bryan. The faithful mount had gotten him through countless skirmishes and battles during the draw-out revolution. In a way, he missed being on campaign in the field. At least there he didn't have to deal with the delicate sensibilities of women, and he'd rather go into battle than wage war with his heart. That was one fray he had scant confidence of winning.

He stroked Bryan's velvet muzzle, but had no apple for the searching lips. "Sorry, boy. Another of my lapses."

Jim glanced around with a look of understanding. The young Negro was a daily witness to the difficulty Stuart experienced adjusting to life at Thornton Hall after so many years away and sporadic visits home. On his death, Grandfather Monroe intended to free the slave family who comprised the bulk of the help at Thornton. He'd made his wishes clear and added them to his Will. Stuart supported the old man's request and pondered what to offer in lieu of wages until the estate paid for itself and he could hire those who toiled here.

All he could think of was to allow them a bit of land and share in the horses, when he had any to spare. Jim and his older brother Joe—married and living on the estate with his wife and baby—both worked hard in the stables, and with all the livestock. The entire family labored in the house or on the grounds. Mister Ellis had rented the bulk of the cropland in Stuart's absence, but he intended to reclaim it.

If Stuart parceled off the estate and the foundation of his horses to Mister Ellis, he'd greatly weaken his assets.

There was one other potential source of income he couldn't ignore, despite Hettie's warning. Surely, that was only the ranting of one recently awakened from a dreamlike state and not true warning from his father?

Hadn't the late Captain Monroe himself been responsible for seeing to it the treasure wound up in his supposed grave in the first place?

Granted, the wealth had originally been intended as a bribe for the capture of the traitor Benedict Arnold. But that fiend escaped and was safely ensconced in England. Everyone associated with the hidden goods were gone. No one left in the country knew of it, except possibly one blackguard and his lackey. And none knew exactly where to dig, except Stuart.

And possibly, Hettie. It was devilishly difficult to assess what she truly knew. High time he clued Jim in.

Stuart motioned to the young man. "A word in your ear."

His right-hand help ought to be aware of the real reason they'd visited the cemetery, and would return again. Soon. Besides, Jim must've wondered at the shovel Stuart had in the coach. He might be a year shy of twenty, but he was the soul of discretion, and Stuart needed a confidant. When it came right down to it, he trusted this slave more than anyone else, except Brinkley.

Before Stuart uttered another word, an eerie screech tore through the still night. His hair nearly stood on end and chills shot down his spine. "What the hell?"

"Must be an owl, Captain." Dark eyes wide, Jim darted a look around. "Don't see one."

Neither did Stuart. "What else makes that kind of

cry?"

"No telling. Not sure I want to discover."

"Me either. Left my musket in the house." He hoped it wasn't a banshee keening an approaching death, much preferring something he could aim the long barrel at and halt in a gratifying explosion.

Surely, this wasn't some strange warning from his father?

It couldn't be. But he had to admit, his nerves were on edge. Thanks to Hettie, he was seeing signs everywhere.

"I'll speak to you later, Jim."

Right now, Stuart had the urge to turn on his heels, hasten back inside, and shut his chamber door. The fact that it was down the hall from Hettie wasn't lost on him, either.

"I could do with some brandy." He'd have a bath drawn, supper sent up, open a bottle, and—

Again, the goulash screech rent the evening like a soul in torment. "Damn owl."

"Reckon so, Captain. I might've seen it fly."

Or maybe Jim was only saying that for both their sakes.

Stuart hadn't seen a thing wing skyward. He'd borne a thousand fears with more courage. Something about Hettie, this strange night, and her dire warning unsettled him.

"Come on, Jim. We'll find the bottom of that bottle together."

Chapter Five

"Make haste, Maddie. Please."

Hettie perched before the dressing table in her chamber while the girl pinned up her newly cleaned hair. Maddie's nimble fingers interwove blue silk ribbons with the ebony lengths while leaving some to fall in long curls. Undergoing the hair washing had been an ordeal. Hettie spent an age by the hearth with Mrs. Jenner towel drying the wet mass and grumbling about her catching her death.

Come what may, she was determined to be fresh for Stuart. Rosewater anointed her from head to toe and she'd dabbed on the flowery perfume from England. The honey-sweet fragrance reminded her of warm summer evenings when mignonette blossoms scented the air. Before fatigue won out and Mrs. Jenner bundled her back to bed, she badly wanted to see the man who captivated her thoughts, like a pirate holding her for ransom.

Mrs. Jenner withdrew a quilted petticoat from the chest Uncle Ezra had sent round. "Don't rush the girl, Miss. You want her to do a proper job on those lustrous tresses, don't you? Never labored over such a weight of locks in m' life."

"I'll settle for tolerable." To be fair, Maddie was skillful with her hands.

"Be thankful you've still got hair fer her to arrange

after that fever. Yer fortunate we didn't have to cut it to yer chin to keep it from tangling. But we kept it free of snarls." A point Mrs. Jenner was particularly proud of.

"I'm deeply grateful. All I have are my looks, such as they are."

The bustling woman made a noise in her throat like a reproving hen. "That ain't all. You've a sweet disposition when yer not being pigheaded. Clever, too, when in yer right mind."

"Most kind of you to say." Hettie must make do with the compliments, despite the qualifications. She didn't mention her prime advantage, her inheritance, but would, if need be. Best to know how she stood first.

Mrs. Jenner flapped a length of burnished silk. "You'll have to sleep with yer head propped up on a block to keep that hair in place for Captain Monroe to admire."

"I can't wait that long. I've not received a visit from him in three days. This makes four."

Frown lines tugged at Mrs. Jenner's mouth, and double chins wobbled as she shook her head. "He's distracted. That's all. Time enough fer visiting when yer up and about."

"What time do you fancy I have? Uncle Ezra will require me at home when I'm deemed fit. Opportunities for seeing Captain Monroe will be dismal indeed then, unless he's invited regularly to dine."

"Doubtful," Mrs. Jenner grunted. "Yer uncle and the Monroes don't have much liking fer each other."

"Not a lot."

Whispers of Uncle Ezra's Loyalist leanings during the war hadn't endeared him to the rebellious Monroe clan, or the town. But he'd hung on. His sympathies with the Crown never went past speculation on folks' part, and his obliging son, Jonas, had donated generous provisions to the cause, soothing disgruntled Patriot breasts.

Wagging tongues grew still, but the muted accusations were true. Furthermore, Hettie shared them. Did Stuart suspect she'd been a Loyalist at heart?

"Thankfully, the war's over," Mrs. Jenner muttered.

"Indeed." Hettie cocked an eye at the astute woman. "If I elicit a proposal from Captain Monroe, my uncle will give his approval."

"Old Mister Monroe may object."

"I pray not. I've enough to contend with."

"Aye. You do."

Hettie shifted her gaze at the sun sinking low above the murky trees. Hope and patience were wearing thin. Mrs. Jenner had insisted she remain in bed with brief turns around the room, but she'd had her fill of confinement.

"'Tis time to act. I am descending the stairs for supper this evening, even if I'm bundled to the ears."

"You will be, Miss," the housekeeper thrust back. "And yer to stay in the house after that panther the captain shot."

Hettie sat up straighter. "What—when?"

"Yesterday morning. In the back pasture." Mrs. Jenner smoothed the silk with work-worn fingers. "Didn't I say?"

"Not a word." And the gossipy woman normally held forth.

"Thought Maddie would've told you." Mrs. Jenner flapped a second petticoat, as if to obscure being caught in a slip.

The girl's eyes were wide. "You recall the captain didn't want to frighten Miss Fairfax? Her being poorly and all."

Mrs. Jenner's florid complexion flushed a deeper shade of red. "Best she knows. Forewarned is forearmed. Thank the good Lord the devil cat only got a lamb. Could've been that new foal the captain dotes on."

Hettie cringed at the thought.

"Or a child," Mrs. Jenner added ghoulishly. "And now we hear tell a wolf's been sighted. Not just any wolf, a black one, Jim says. Thought I left these wild beasts behind in Backcountry."

Hettie pursed her lips, then opened them. "He's certain it wasn't a hound?"

Mrs. Jenner raised both arms heavenward, her sleeves sliding back to reveal dimpled arms. She should've been an actress with her flair for the theatrical. "Hellhound, if it was. Eyes like red coals. Beast took off before Jim got a closer look, but he kin tell the difference between 'em."

"Weren't no dog, Miss," Maddie inserted in the steady flow coming from Mrs. Jenner. "We're all afeared. Haven't had wolves in these parts in years."

Hettie laid a hand on her arm. "Don't fear so. The captain will protect you."

"If he gets off a shot before the demon attacks and carries off something or *someone*," Mrs. Jenner added, with morbid satisfaction.

Maddie appeared ready to hide under the bed. "He says no one's to stray about the grounds alone 'specially, after sunset. He's been out hunting it, Miss."

"I've no intention of wandering in the night wind. Do as the captain advises. I'm sure all will be well."

Mrs. Jenner shook her head. "Peculiar goings-on at Thornton these days, Miss. Mighty peculiar."

A rogue wolf on top of the panther was highly unusual. Were these creatures portents of the future? Odd warnings from the late Captain Monroe?

No. He couldn't summon wild animals...

These must simply be strange occurrences, weirdly coinciding with her arrival, and his visitation. At least, sighting the beasts had kept Stuart at Thornton and away from the cemetery. For now.

Part of Hettie was relieved to learn he'd been preoccupied riding the grounds and securing the livestock against attack. As long as that was the extent of his doings, and wooing the wounded Miss Smith didn't rank among them. She pitied the girl, but not enough to make a present of him to her rival.

Mrs. Jenner shuddered with dramatic emphasis. "We'll all be tucked in close by the hearth this night. I'm stopping up the keyholes, too."

"Why? What on earth do you fear will come through them?"

Her head whipped around, and Mrs. Jenner eyed Hettie as though she'd missed the obvious. "A witch can change herself into a snake and slither in."

"I thought he was hunting a wolf not a witch?"

"Might be one and the same," Mrs. Jenner said darkly.

"And God help us if it's a warlock," Maddie whispered, as if hardly daring to speak the name aloud.

"Aye. They're the worst. Witches are a plaguy nuisance in comparison." Mrs. Jenner spoke like one with experience. "But don't you fret, Miss. I put mountain ash twigs with them red berries over the doorways, tied 'em with red thread. too."

"And elderberry. Don't forget them boughs," Maddie interjected.

Mrs. Jenner nodded. "And elder. Sacred trees, both."

Hettie gaped at her.

Waving a scarlet ribbon, Mrs. Jenner explained. "Fer wearing around yer neck. Witches stay clear of red. And I ain't stopping there. I've got Minnie sprinkling angelica water in every corner of the house and Jim seeing to the stable. Got some betony and sticklewort out there, too. Holy herbs ought to hinder 'em. Whatever they be."

Hettie hadn't considered witchcraft as the source of the strange happenings and wondered at Mrs. Jenner's superstitions. Still, who was she to say for certain black magic wasn't at work? She knew little of such ways.

With sinister men lying in wait, fearsome animals on the prowl, the plight of poor Miss Smith, and now the possible threat of witches, stealing a moment alone with Stuart seemed an even greater challenge. And that was assuming he returned to Thornton for supper and didn't spend all night out hunting.

Surely, he'd stop to eat and warm himself. Either way, Hettie was escaping her chamber, and praying she encountered him downstairs.

Chapter Six

Gathering dusk cloaked the trees. The scent of humus on the breeze, Stuart shifted in the saddle and peered through the branches, bare except where a few dry leaves still clung. A rustling sounded alongside the liquid spill of water. Here and there, an evergreen rose amid the barrenness of late autumn.

Normally, he didn't give a second thought to being on his own in the darkening woods, or anywhere else. Now…it was eerie.

Was he truly alone?

Every shadow seemed to conceal a black wolf. Rare coloring. He hadn't spotted any gray wolves since riding through Backcountry to fight in the bloody Battle of Guilford Courthouse over two years ago. And he'd mostly heard them.

Wolves were clever at evasion. Clever at everything. He'd found signs of this one among the trees bordering the back pasture, tracks in the damp earth, and on the green moss along the small stream. A bent branch, bit of fur in the thicket, all spoke of the unseen creature.

There. His gaze fell on the prostrate doe lying amid fern browned by frost.

He trotted Bryan over to the partially eaten carcass. The horse lowered his head, sniffing the remains. He snorted at the killer's lingering scent, his breath white in the cold air. Throwing his head up, he backed away.

Stuart glanced around uneasily.

Nothing. Heaven only knows where the predator had gotten to. He'd searched much of the day.

Granted, the countryside around Halifax had been tamed in recent years, and wolf sightings were rare. But only yesterday, he'd shot a panther. It would take a mighty big dog to leave those paw prints and take down that deer. And there were plenty of spots to hide.

All the while he sought the wolf, he had the sense of being watched. Whether by man or beast, he didn't know, but it made the hair on the back of his neck stand on end. As long as it was something, or someone, he could shoot.

No ghouls. Those prints and the dead deer were real enough.

Banishing tales of phantom hounds from his mind, he fingered the pistol at his side. The polished wood and metal hardware were reassuring to the touch. He'd carried the sidearm, once belonging to his grandfather, and his musket throughout the war. And he was a crack shot.

A twig snapped.

Stuart swiveled his head. Were his eyes deceiving him or had he glimpsed the furry outline of an animal before it vanished?

Yes. No. Maybe.

Impossible to tell.

"Let's go, boy."

More unnerved than he cared to admit, he turned his mount in the direction of the house and nudged him into a canter. Bryan sped over the trail through trees smudged in inky shadows. He found himself wishing for a torch to illuminate the path and brandish at the beast—or any attacker. The wolf wasn't the only threat.

His thoughts flew like the leaves scattering beneath the gelding's hooves. Everything seemed foreboding these days, ever since he'd discovered Hettie at the cemetery. Despite this, he chafed under his self-imposed exile from her.

He'd had plenty to occupy himself, but images of Hettie flowed through his mind, an ever-present, fevered stream. The light in her eyes when she gazed at him, the hint of a smile at her pale pink lips, snatches of the conversation and humor they'd shared. Above all, Hettie in his arms.

Those brief moments with her were branded on him. He couldn't forget anything for an instant. Nor did he want to. She'd surely drive him to distraction.

Avoiding Abigail Smith was far easier than evading his own mind. When their paths did cross, he couldn't sidestep the pain she attempted to conceal in those greenish-gray eyes, like haze over a secluded stream.

"You'll have her, will you not, sir?" Grandfather had demanded this morning, his blue eyes flashing, cheeks flushed. Irksome to the extreme.

Stuart had stopped in to find the old gentleman sitting up in bed eating his breakfast. "I feel duty bound to comply, sir. But Miss Smith is not my choice," he'd said in response to the imperious request.

"Yer not thinking on that sickly Miss Fairfax, are you?" Grandfather ladled on disapproval like the molasses dripping from his corncakes.

"Frankly, yes. And little else."

Stuart's admission further vexed him. Grandfather

even muttered about changing his Will and leaving Thornton to Stuart's younger brother, William. Hardly practical.

The unruly fourteen-year-old had been roped in and was attending school in England, thanks to Claire's wealthy husband and his indulgent family. With the high-spirited lad and their emotionally fragile mother well provided for, Stuart could better focus on the estate.

"Have I no say in my own affairs? No right to happiness?" he'd demanded in turn.

Grandfather's hand shook as he lifted his teacup. "Open your eyes, sir. Miss Smith is as good a woman as you'll find."

"There's more to love than goodness alone."

"Love doesn't come into it! We're discussing marriage. You don't want to go wedding that flighty young thing, John," he warned, confusing Stuart with his late father.

Unarguably, Hettie was a bit *tetched*. But she'd been ill. Given half a chance, Stuart would let his fears of possible madness go and embrace her with a glad cry.

Grandfather thrashed among the pillows, sloshing his tea. "You'll rue the day, John. Mark my words."

Once again, he was lost in the past and grew increasingly agitated. Not that the present would totally relieve his troubled mind.

Stuart had summoned Ezekiel to soothe the excitable old man with a tincture of valerian and a few drops of laudanum. There was little else to be done. He'd left Grandfather dozing, then rode out to track the wolf.

Now evening was on him. He had nothing to show for his hours in the saddle except hunger and fatigue. Returning without proof of the creature's demise wouldn't allay anyone's fears.

The thin howl trailing behind him on the strengthening breeze gave him more to ponder. He had the distinct impression the wolf was following him. Keeping just out of sight.

Was the hunter, the hunted?

He swiveled again. *Nothing.* But he'd swear it was there.

Damn. Where was the blasted animal?

A thought occurred. Did he really want to discover the creature, alone, with twilight descending? The light was fading fast. Soon, it would be pitch black.

If he happened upon the wolf, all he'd see were glowing red eyes—before it went for the horse's throat. Or his.

And didn't wolves normally hunt in packs? Waiting for the others to gather held scant appeal. The swift gelding required no prodding to gallop at breakneck speed back toward the security of Thornton Hall.

Candles and firelight shone in the windows of the stately home. The scent of wood smoke from many hearths tinged the gathering dusk. Hettie's chamber was brightly lit.

Perhaps she was out of bed, even dressing. Mrs. Jenner and Ezekiel kept him apprised of her steady recovery. He tried not to appear too keen, while hanging onto their every word.

Would Hettie venture downstairs this evening?

If she did, could he find some means to converse

with her apart from Miss Smith and his grandfather, if the elderly gentleman also descended from his chamber?

Stuart could hardly suggest a stroll about the chilly grounds with a recovering invalid and a wolf on the prowl. Any moonlit walks he'd dreamt of, floated away.

The scheming Mrs. Jenner might be of some help, after she'd shielded the house with every sacred herb in her arsenal. An enlightened man, Stuart normally balked at the housekeeper's superstitions, but in this event, he didn't object. Let her hang boughs and anoint corners.

What could it hurt?

She'd even slipped an amulet of ash wood twigs tied with red thread into his pocket. And had him throw a pinch of salt over his left shoulder to keep the devil and all evil at bay, and salt was in short supply since the war. And he'd had a dunk in her holy herbal water.

All this he'd allowed, but he counted on Mrs. Jenner for some reasoned assistance with Hettie. After all, she had a soft spot for the young lady, and he needed all the support he could muster.

Yes. Mrs. Jenner was just the one to aid him.

His chest hammered as the darkened path flew by, and not only from the hair-raising howls at his back.

Chapter Seven

Wafting the spicy, floral fragrance from the scent bottle in her chamber, Hettie descended the stairs with Mrs. Jenner's assistance. Stuart's arm would've been far, far better, but at least she was out of her sickroom, and back among the living.

Barely. She tottered at the housekeeper's side.

The steaming cup of tea Minnie had brought her earlier should have bolstered her energy. If anything, she felt drained since sipping it.

"I could be walking a wee kitten for all yer strength, and you'll get chilled," Mrs. Jenner chided.

The stiff breeze chased clouds across the starry sky beyond the panes of glass under assault. Over her embroidered, skirted jacket, Hettie wore a lavender stole made of finest wool. Like a prize lamb, she was well-swaddled.

"Do not fret, Mrs. Jenner. This shawl is wonderfully warm."

The housekeeper didn't appear convinced. "Wind's from the north this evening. Sets the windows to rattling like witches giving 'em a fearsome shake."

Witchcraft again. If Mrs. Jenner knew what Hettie sometimes saw, would she consider her a witch, too?

"I'll keep the dark forces at bay, never you fear," her companion assured her. "You got that scarlet ribbon on you?"

"In my pocket with the amulet of mountain ash twigs."

A grunt from Mrs. Jenner. "Druther it were around yer neck, but that'll do. What of the pinch of salt?"

"Also in my pocket."

"Wish we didn't have to be so miserly with the stuff," the superstitious woman grumbled.

If salt were more readily available, Hettie suspected Mrs. Jenner would pour a line of the tiny crystals across every threshold.

"Mighty nice of yer uncle to send the shawl," she allowed, after being satisfied as to her other concerns.

"Oh, Uncle Ezra's unfailingly generous. Though I long to be allowed my own way upon occasion, and told him so."

"Did you, now? What did he say to that, my bold Miss?"

Despite the ache forming behind her eyes, Hettie answered in her best imitation. "Very well, Niece. Find an honorable man of good family, and I'll not have to seek one for you. 'Tis a simple enough quest for a young lady of your persuasion."

"Aye," Mrs. Jenner agreed.

Hettie shook her carefully coiffed head. "But it isn't."

"Keep yer spirits up, lass. You've been too ill to fret over gaining a husband. What would you do with one if you did?"

"If the man were Captain Monroe, I should fast regain my strength."

A rare, dimpled smile from Mrs. Jenner. She nodded at the yellow silk fluttering at Hettie's waist. "Mighty fetching apron."

"Another remembrance from my uncle." *To cheer you, dear girl*, he'd written on the accompanying note. She loved color and keeping her hands busy with useful and creative tasks, but hadn't had the energy to sew in days.

She touched the pearls dangling at her ears in an iridescent cluster. "A present from Uncle Ezra on my last birthday. I'm rather like a magpie adding bright trinkets to my nest. He knows my weakness. If he didn't already possess my undying affection, he'd purchase it."

"He thinks a lot of you, my girl. Suppose with a son as bland as porridge and as likely to wed as the fencepost, old Ezra kicked up his heels at having you in his home."

Hettie wrinkled her nose. "And to think, Jonas will inherit everything."

"Yer uncle is as hale as a horse for a man of his years. Won't be leaving nothing to nobody for some time."

"I hope so. For all his quirks, I adore him."

"Course you do. He's yer blood."

From portraits on the wall, the eyes of Monroe ancestors followed their descent. These folk were gone, reminders of the fleeting nature of life. There was no guarantee Uncle Ezra would still be here in the New Year, that anyone would. Only hope and prayer to see her through.

Hettie glanced down at her skirts brushing the wooden steps. The gilded silk against the blue taffeta evoked the pleasing hues of sun and sky. Beneath that ensemble she wore three petticoats, one quilted, over ivory stockings and matching brocade shoes with shiny buckles. The frothy muslin scarf tucked above her bodice lent added warmth and modesty.

No bosoms on display, was Uncle Ezra's decree.

He didn't give a fig if low décolletage was in vogue. Not that Hettie was dressed in the absolute height of fashion—no one expected a recovering invalid to be—but she fancied she was presentable.

More importantly, how would Stuart react?

A squeak, like a startled mouse, escaped Miss Smith when she encountered them at the bottom of the stairs.

The shrill exhalation ratcheted through Hettie. Anymore outbursts like that and she'd need the smelling salts, as peculiar as she felt. "Goodness. Whatever's the matter?"

Miss Smith clasped a hand to her bodice. "Forgive me. You gave me a start is all, Miss Fairfax. I didn't see you there."

Mrs. Jenner snorted. "Yer mind must be miles away, my girl. You can't miss her in all this finery. Like royalty among us is Miss Fairfax. We spent an age on that hair."

Hazel eyes roved over Hettie. Lines of uncertainty creased the young woman's face, then she dipped her head in a polite nod. "Indeed. How elegant you look."

Hettie curtsied. "Most kind of you to say." Particularly as the compliment seemed forced, and Miss Smith was garbed like a drab gray mare. Was she truly a Quaker?

The young woman smiled faintly. "The effect is quite appealing. I'm glad you were able to manage the stairs."

"Only just. Miss Fairfax oughtn't to have left her

chamber yet," Mrs. Jenner scolded.

Hettie was keenly aware of the cost to her limited endurance. Even more than she'd expected.

Unexpected sympathy warmed Miss Smith's gaze. "Allow me to assist you to a chair before the hearth in the west parlor. 'Tis cozy and you can take your supper there."

Hettie offered a wan smile. "Sounds lovely."

"I'll see to yer supper while you get settled. Then it's back to bed fer you, Miss. I shouldn't like to answer to Ezra Jones if you take a turn. Or Captain Monroe, for that matter." Mrs. Jenner scurried off in a whirl of petticoats, leaving Hettie with Miss Smith.

"Will you join me?" Hettie invited. "I should enjoy some company." Days in that chamber had been dull indeed.

A change seemed to come over Miss Smith, and she fluttered her eyes as if seeking an excuse. "Thank you. I fear I must decline. I'm required elsewhere. I read to Mister Monroe most evenings."

Abigail Smith was a martyr to her duties.

Hettie had never learned to read properly. Words did strange things on the page. But she didn't voice these tidings aloud. "How good of you to lessen the tedium of his hours, though I should have thought him to be asleep by now." She only hung on by a thread, and Mister Monroe was little more than an invalid.

Her reluctant companion glanced away. "He dozes and wakes. But depends so upon me."

A point Miss Smith seemed determined to make. The reverse, of course, being that Hettie was useless in this household and forever would be. Particularly if she were expected to read aloud.

She replied coolly. "In that case, please tend to your business. I shall make my way to the parlor."

Though how she'd manage in her deteriorating state, she didn't know. She longed for the walking stick she'd left in her chamber, its silver head knotted with lavender ribbons. At least, the cane would support her.

"As Miss Smith is otherwise occupied, I should be happy to accompany you and be your supper companion, if you like."

Stuart! Hettie's heart leapt, and it already beat erratically.

"Captain." Miss Smith's eyes dimmed.

They both turned to find him striding toward them in gleaming mahogany boots. These must be his best, and the other pair for every day.

The surge of excitement coursing through Hettie at his arrival, struck her anew. What a contrast to the dreariness his absence had left. He appeared more inviting than ever, and she hadn't thought that possible.

After a long day in the saddle, he'd bathed and wore a fawn coat and green waistcoat that complemented his eyes, sandy-brown brows, and neatly pulled back hair. The proportions of his features were perfect. If she drew a line down the center of his face, his forehead, eyes, nose, cheeks, and mouth equally matched the other.

Not lost on her artistic eye.

As for the rest of him, leather breeches fit his long, well-muscled legs and met his boots. He looked both fashionable and pure male. No fop, was he. Exuding masculine energy, he breathed fresh life into what promised to be an otherwise dull evening. If she mustered the endurance to enjoy his presence.

Would Miss Smith stammer a reason to linger?

If the situation were reversed, Hettie would. But she'd never abandon one staying in the home to the cheerlessness of supper alone, after days of confinement, as Miss Smith had proposed to do. Consideration for a guest should also rank among her duties. Perhaps the saint wasn't quite as irreproachable as everyone deemed her.

Stuart drew up in front of them and offered a short bow. "Good evening, ladies. Miss Fairfax, what a pleasure to see you downstairs. Shall we adjourn to the parlor?"

Hettie curtsied and took the arm he extended. "Good evening, Captain Monroe. Yes, please. I should be delighted with your company, sir."

"I'm gratified to be found acceptable." Humor heightened the magnetism in his gaze.

He angled his head at Miss Smith. "Please tell Mrs. Jenner to bring supper for two." He spoke mildly to the woman who stood goggling at him, but grit edged his tone.

Hettie noted he didn't press her to join them.

He grew brisk. "Now Miss Fairfax, let's get you out of this draft and off your feet—seated," he amended.

To Hettie's surprise and delight, he flicked her a wink, then hastened her down the hall away from their onlooker.

Her legs refused to support her properly, and she staggered. "Forgive me, Captain."

He paused. "The fault is mine, dear lady. I forgot myself. You are not yet recovered for such a pace."

"With you to bear me along, sir, I might manage."

"Then please accept my support." Slipping his arm from hers, he encircled it around her waist.

Delicious tingles ran through her. "Gladly."

The remaining steps to the parlor pulsed with elation. Perhaps too much. She was lightheaded, and scarcely managed to put one foot before the other.

She definitely could've done without the apparition of Captain John Monroe seated in an armchair, wearing his blue and red regimentals, but decided not to mention him to Stuart and spoil the moment. And Lord only knows what Mrs. Jenner would say because Hettie had no intention of enlightening her.

Likely it was a fleeting vision, anyway. The room revolved. She was giddy with fatigue, or whatever ailed her, and the thrill of being close to Stuart.

Afraid he might fade any moment, like the dream she feared him to be, she clasped his arm. "Help me."

Stuart held her close to his solid warmth. "I'll not let you slump to the floor." But he couldn't prevent her from sagging in his grasp.

She breathed in his masculine scent mingled with soap. More than merely appealing, it was like finding her other half with the most primal instinct she possessed. If the notion of soul mates were true, she'd know no greater joy than to be joined with him.

Her eyes closed, his handsome face etched in her mind. Very like a younger version of his father who looked on with sympathy and concern. The senior Monroe tucked upstairs mightn't have any use for Hettie, but the late captain seemed to. What, exactly, did he want, and was he truly there?

Her head grew muzzy.

"I've got you, Hettie. You'll be all right." The

voice was Stuart's. The sentiment also suited his father.

Her last thought—he'd called her *Hettie*, like before, in the coach. She treasured the sound, as blackness swirled.

"Poor lady." Stuart swept Hettie up into his arms and bore her across the parlor to settle her before the hearth.

She roused slightly and opened her lips. "Not the armchair."

There were two floral covered seats before the hearth. She didn't specify which one. Puzzled, but perfectly willing to comply, he carried her to the couch. Gently, as if she were made of crystal, he lowered her onto the gold upholstery.

She loosed a small sigh, and stretched the length of the sofa. "Your father's in the chair." Her voice a murmur.

Had he heard her aright?

Her forehead creased like one puzzling through a dream. "Not certain why he's here."

Neither was Stuart. "You do realize John Monroe is dead?"

"Makes no difference," she whispered.

God help him. Why was he fated to love a mad woman?

Retrieving one of the walnut, splat-back chairs clustered along the gray-blue paneled wall, he sat beside her. Surely, she was simply confused from swooning. And worn out. Judging by her sumptuous attire, she'd labored over her toilette. Too much, too soon, for one so recently ill.

He slid his gaze over her. How exquisite she was, blue ribbons wound in that mass of hair, lengths of curls tumbled down over her jacket, embroidered with a field of flowers. Some seamstress had spent hours plying her needle, or Hettie had. He guessed the latter, and tucked the wool shawl more securely about her.

Bending near, he gazed at her face. The smudges under her eyes had faded, and black lashes swept over smooth cheeks. Her alluring lips had gained more color, and not from a pot of makeup. She must've succumbed to exhaustion brought on by overtiring herself.

Still, he wondered. Something was amiss. And this was the third time she'd referred to the late captain as if he were visible to her.

Paintings done by his father covered the walls. Certainly, this less formal parlor had been a favorite sitting room. If the late Captain Monroe were to haunt a chamber, this would be it.

Why now? Was his father speaking through Hettie for some reason?

She'd mentioned the treasure, but why that should be denied to Stuart when his father was intimately tied to it, he couldn't fathom. And he needed the hidden wealth. Soon.

Another anomaly nagged at Stuart. Did any of this have to do with that blasted wolf? His appearance was inexplicable.

Perhaps Hettie was more attuned to the other world while in this peculiar state, like drifting in that place between wake and sleep. It was strangely easier to converse with her now, as if they were both wrapped in a spell. One Stuart could in no way break.

Curling his fingers at her shoulder, he shook her lightly. "Hettie, a wolf follows me."

"He's your spirit guide," she said softly.

"My *what*?"

"He has come to lead you…and maybe me…"

Stuart weighed her startling disclosure while studying her more closely. Hettie's exotic beauty, the wavy black hair coupled with clear blue eyes, those high cheekbones, and strong white teeth, lips colored like the wild rose. The rumors must be true. Her Fairfax ancestor had wed a Cherokee woman, and Hettie was their sole remaining descendent.

The Mulatto woman in the Fairfax ancestry was fairly common knowledge, but the Indian bride had been kept a secret. This explained a lot. Some Indians were reputed to have 'the sight' and they held beliefs in animals that went far beyond Stuart's understanding. Perhaps, intuitively, Hettie had tapped into her heritage, and acted as a sort of conduit.

Was she even aware of her roots?

He doubted anyone ever told her. With the ongoing warfare in the frontier between settlers and Indians, the family had likely concealed any connection with the tribe.

Not that Hettie's mixed lineage troubled him. He found it intriguing. Grandfather might object, as might others in Halifax, if they discerned what he had about her.

As for Stuart, he only knew Hettie was infinitely dear and vulnerable. Ezekiel's herbal tinctures ministered to her body, but her spirit needed nurturing. She wilted before him like an uprooted flower. An exceedingly rare one he didn't intend to lose. But how on earth could he keep her?

He smoothed a tendril at her forehead. "What am I to do about the wolf?"

"Watch for him. He watches you."

"You don't want me to kill the creature?"

"Let no one do him harm. This is your father's wish."

Again, she spoke of the late captain as though he were present. "Is my father still here?"

Her eyes fluttered and opened. She turned her head and surveyed the room. "He remains at hand until it is finished."

"What is?"

She lifted her gaze to Stuart's. "The threat lying over this house."

Goosebumps scattered down his spine and traveled his arms. She blinked owlishly at him, like one struggling to stay awake. Her pupils were dilated. She shivered, and a flush reddened her cheeks that he'd swear hadn't been there moments before.

Fear churned in his gut, worse than any he'd known. "I'm not the only one in danger, am I?"

"Some force pulls me down." Her breathing was labored.

"You're strong."

"Not stronger than this, Stuart."

How naturally his given name fell from her lips. As if they were children again.

So many had perished in the recent war from violence and disease. This exquisite woman would not swell their ranks. She was barely conscious.

"Hettie, I must summon Ezekiel."

"Don't leave me."

"Propriety be damned." Getting to his feet, he bent low and slid his arms under her. Lifting his precious burden, he cradled her tightly. "Draw strength from

69

me."

She circled her arms around his neck and clung to him. It seemed to take all her energy to raise her lips near his ear. "Stuart—the tea. Tell Ezekiel." Her head lolled back, and his heart nearly stopped.

Chapter Eight

"Belladonna poisoning? In this house!" Stuart wanted to rip into the culprit but didn't know their identity. And he couldn't tear himself away from the parlor and Hettie.

"She's not as bad as may be, Captain. Miss Fairfax didn't drain the cup." Ezekiel spoke in low tones.

Stuart felt anything but soothed. Minnie had carried the tea upstairs to Hettie's bedchamber. He trusted the scatterbrained girl not to harm her intentionally, but anyone could've added a few drops of the lethal tincture to the cup beforehand.

Had they dipped into Ezekiel's stock? He mightn't miss a minute portion. And that's all it took.

Wild to discover who was at fault, and desperate over Hettie's plight, he paced back and forth, raking his hand through his hair. "Is there something you can give her to fight the effects?"

"There is." Ezekiel had taken Stuart's spot in the walnut chair beside the couch. Maddie stood at the ready, clutching his large leather pouch filled with dried herbs, roots, salves, and tinctures.

"This." The old healer dipped brown fingers into the worn bag his granddaughter extended and withdrew a ram's horn.

Stuart halted in mid-stride. "Gun powder?"

"Nae. Charcoal. 'Twill bind to the poison and flush

it out." He uncorked the horn with his teeth and tipped the blackish gray powder into a spoon, then stirred the mixture into the cup of tea Mrs. Jenner held steady.

"Dandelion and peppermint with honey for the bitterness," she said, in answer to Stuart's unspoken question.

"But tea is what poisoned her in the first place."

Ezekiel recorked the horn. "Not my tea. Brewed it myself. This'll do her good."

Reassured the poisoner couldn't be at work, Stuart fixed his gaze on what he could see of Hettie while Mrs. Jenner and Ezekiel labored over the figure prone on the couch. With their encouragement, she swallowed every last drop.

Poor, sweet lady.

"Now what?" Stuart asked.

"We wait and see. Mrs. Jenner, the wet cloth." Ezekiel remained hunched where he was, the horn in hand, while Mrs. Jenner applied a cool compress to Hettie's forehead.

Maddie waited with the pouch, and a subdued Minnie held the basin of herbal scented water. "Also bathe her throat and chest. A rash may form. I've added plantain and calendula to the water. Soothing to the skin," Ezekiel explained.

Intent on her task, Mrs. Jenner gave a nod. Hettie had come to mean a lot to the outspoken housekeeper, Stuart knew. But no one could possibly overflow with the depth of emotion welling up in him.

Like the wolf Hettie declared protected him, he wanted to growl everyone away, spring though the gathering around her, and clutch her to his heart. It would be unseemly to do so with Mrs. Jenner stripping off the scarf tucked into her bodice to sponge her chest. He'd viewed more of women than this at dinner parties, though not more of Hettie.

Despising his helplessness, he kept his distance but could not keep from looking on. When he found the culprit, he'd snap their neck. Who could do such a despicable act?

Shivers ran through Hettie under Mrs. Jenner's ministrations, but she made no protest. Maddie was sent to fetch fresh linen and Minnie for ale. Still, they waited, while Stuart paced, straining to see and hear.

Ezekiel spoke quietly to Hettie. Now and then she murmured in reply. Other times, she drifted seemingly without awareness, until a firm nudge summoned her back.

He slanted sage eyes at Stuart. "We got to keep her awake, Captain."

Nearly mad with rage and worry, he waved his assent. The suspense was unbearable. If Hettie died, he wouldn't be fit to live with ever again. He'd become the wolf—a crazed one.

He drained a mug of ale and wiped his lips, glancing around as the parlor door opened. *Who dared intrude?*

Miss Smith fluttered in, took one look at the scene, and stopped. She clapped a hand to her mouth, then released it. "What on earth has befallen Miss Fairfax?"

A terrible suspicion filled Stuart's mind. Was she truly unaware? The eyes he turned on the seemingly unsuspecting woman made her flinch.

Ezekiel spoke first. "Poisoned."

"How? With what?"

"Deadly nightshade. Devil's cherries."

Just the name of the herb toned a death knell. Stuart weighed Abigail's white face and stark eyes. Was she really unaware? Perhaps she was a consummate actress.

Ezekiel shifted his gaze from the gaping newcomer to Stuart. "Captain, thought you should know Minnie says goods were sent round from the Jones' place for Miss Fairfax this afternoon while you were out."

"Tea?"

"No. That shawl she's wearing for one. But the driver and one other fellow stayed for refreshment in the kitchen."

"Ah." Giving them access to the tea as it was prepared.

Who would wish to harm Hettie in that household? Her uncle adored her. Cousin Jonas might resent his father's lavish affection. Still, to go so far as to poison her?

Highly unlikely. Jonas seemed absolutely benign. But his complicity in this affair couldn't be ruled out until Stuart further investigated.

He returned his scrutiny to Miss Smith. Whoever the guilty party was would down a cup of the same brew. He'd force it past their lips with his own hand. Even if it was her.

The flustered young woman skirted around him to Mrs. Jenner. "How is she faring?"

"A bit better, I think." The anxious housekeeper eyed Ezekiel questioningly.

"Yes, Ma'am. Breathing more easily now. Keep freshening the cloths and I'll give her another cup of tea with the charcoal after a bit."

Mrs. Jenner clucked sympathetically. "This was all

the poor dear needed on top of her illness. And she was getting better, too."

Precisely why the assailant chose this time to strike.

Stuart could no longer trust the Jones' home or his own. He must double his efforts to keep Hettie safe.

At least knowledge of belladonna reassured him in regard to her visions of his father. The herb caused hallucinations, among other symptoms. The visions were said to be vivid.

Mrs. Jenner swiped at a tear with trembling fingers. "Peculiar thing about that tea. The cup fell on the floor before Miss Fairfax drank half of it. Didn't it, Maddie?"

The shaken girl nodded mutely.

"That's a mercy," Miss Smith allowed. Without nearly enough emphasis, Stuart thought.

"But none of us touched the cup," Mrs. Jenner continued.

"Could it not have fallen on its own?" Miss Smith's query was more of a demand than a question.

The larger woman shrugged ample shoulders. "The dressing table might have gotten jostled. Or an unseen hand gave the cup a toss," she added, significantly. "What say you to that, Maddie?"

Her brown eyes widened. "Yes'm. It surely could have done."

Miss Smith blanched. "You mean a ghost?" The word escaped her with tremulous reluctance.

"I do." Mrs. Jenner thrived on drama. Miss Smith's hesitancy, coupled with Minnie and Maddie hanging onto her every word, emboldened her. "I tell you there's strange happenings at Thornton. Good thing I took precautions. Might be the very thing helping the poor lady right this instant."

Before she embarked on a diatribe about witchcraft, ghosts, and her remedies, Stuart strode to the hearth and turned to face them. He'd delivered endless instructions to soldiers serving beneath him during the war. Even stirring speeches to rally the troops. This seemed more of a challenge.

"Be that as it may, Mrs. Jenner, from now on, you, Minnie, or Maddie are to remain with Miss Fairfax at all times. And nothing—not a morsel or a swallow—is to pass her lips not intended for everyone in this house. Only Ezekiel's medicines administered by his own hand."

Miss Smith spoke out. "I am fully willing to take a turn sitting with her, Captain."

"That will *not* be necessary." Her name still headed his list of suspects.

If he hadn't arrived when he had, Hettie would've been alone when the poison took effect after Miss Smith brushed her off, or left her unattended on purpose. He cared not a whit for the flush reddening her face, or the tears in her eyes.

As for Jonas Jones, Stuart must shield Hettie from him as well while he determined who was responsible for this outrage. It was one thing to accept his own life being in danger, an entirely different matter to risk hers. But how and why the shadow had fallen over them both, he didn't know.

Who could better guard her than Stuart?

****

Like a ship adrift on a foggy sea, Hettie floated in an uncharted realm. The colors in the room were unnaturally garish. Shadows darkened the corners where the firelight didn't penetrate, and all the candles had been extinguished at Ezekiel's prompting. He'd warned of her sensitivity to light.

Still, she squinted as if gazing into the glaring sun and the ceiling revolved. Even with her eyes shut, gaudy splotches shone behind her closed lids. And oh, how her head throbbed.

She had a vague awareness of the gentle healer and the sweetened musky swallows he tipped down her dry throat. A peculiar brew, but her stomach churned less. His low voice droned in her ear. Sometimes, his firmed tone required an answer.

She fought an unaccountable urge to laugh manically. Totally unlike her. And there was nothing to chortle about.

Rather than cackle, she murmured assurances. "Yes. I hear you. I'm awake."

Sort of. Reality and dreams were indistinguishable.

Mrs. Jenner's presence was a comfort in this uncertain place. Tremors ran through Hettie, and she shook but welcomed the cool moisture the woman pressed against her hot skin. The motherly woman peeled away layers of Hettie's clothing to lay damp cloths over more of her body.

Did she lie only in her shift?

Apparently so, and she'd taken such pains with her toilette. She couldn't remember why. Something to do with Stuart.

Winking against the light, she sought him. His eyes were wrung with pain. Anger smoldered behind the fear.

Why was he so furious?

Someone tried to kill you.

The reply to her unvoiced question came from Stuart's father, keeping watch from his floral seat before the hearth. The blue and red of his regimentals were blinding.

Kill me? The horrible accusation echoed in her mind.

Yes. He was insistent.

She remembered now. The tea, the poison. Who would do this?

You know who. Again, he spoke in her head.

No, she didn't. She had no idea who wanted her dead.

Tell them what you do know.

Images swirled through the haze muffling her thoughts. The foggy cemetery. Figures hidden behind trees and gravestones watching for Stuart.

They were also there for you.

Her? *No.*

Yes. Speak out.

For a dead man, the late captain was extremely persistent.

Tell them now.

He'd never relent until she did as he bid. "There were two men in the cemetery. *Two*," she emphasized, struggling to force the words past her tight throat. From the corner of her eye, she detected approval in the gaze colored the same shade as Stuart's.

Mrs. Jenner sponged her heated cheeks. "Rambling again, poor thing."

When? Hettie didn't recall rambling before.

"No. She spoke of them earlier when I first found her," Stuart reasoned. "There may be truth in this."

He was listening, and Hettie loved him for it.

"But she was ill," Mrs. Jenner countered.

"That doesn't mean she didn't overhear something she recalls."

"I don't think you can credit anything she blathers this evening."

"Even so." Stuart stepped around Mrs. Jenner's bulk and bent over Hettie. She blinked up at him. "Why talk about these men now?" he asked.

"Your father."

Stuart grimaced. "Still here, is he?"

"Never left." She even saw him with her eyes closed.

"Looking after you, is he?"

It pained her to nod.

"Very well. Tell me. What did he say?"

"They threaten danger to us both." Each word was an effort.

Stuart narrowed his eyes. "They may not be the only ones," he muttered.

Hettie was too lightheaded to clearly follow the focus of his sharp scrutiny, but it slanted toward Abigail Smith.

What of his father? She slid her gaze back at the late captain, but he no longer sat in his seat. He'd risen and assumed a position directly behind the uneasy young woman who'd also fallen under his study. And she didn't even realize she was the subject of close regard from both father and son.

Hettie failed to suppress a groan. Why had Miss Smith gotten so wide? And pink. She should be slender and gray.

Closing her eyes, she left the Monroe males to contend with this strange phenomenon. She still hadn't fathomed the identities of the two men in the graveyard. And that struck her as important.

Tomorrow. She'd ponder this tomorrow. If she survived the night. Somehow, she didn't think Stuart or his father would allow her to die. Ezekiel certainly wouldn't.

Footfalls scattered on the floorboards.

She glanced around through pain-blurred eyes to see Miss Smith fleeing the room. Stuart went in pursuit, and not as a suitor.

Chapter Nine

Stuart charged after Abigail Smith's vanishing figure. She couldn't seem to make her escape from the parlor fast enough, jerked up her petticoats, and hightailed it away. Whatever spooked her went beyond his stern demeanor.

Who or what that was, he neither knew nor cared. She owed him an answer. First, he must overtake her. She scurried down the hall without a backward glance.

Calling a halt to her flight was undignified, assuming she'd even heed him. A shout might disturb his grandfather. He lengthened his stride and caught her up before she mounted the stairs to her, formerly his mother's, bedchamber—unless she thought to seek sanctuary with Grandfather and cower in his chamber.

Backed against the tall walnut clock, she trembled like the cornered mouse she resembled. A pang of guilt struck Stuart as the moon-faced sentinel chimed nine. If he were mistaken and she'd played no part in the poisoning, he was unjustly censoring her and causing undue alarm. But his gut was seldom wrong. Instinct was how he'd survived the war. And he suspected she'd had a hand in the unthinkable act.

He barred her exit. "Why such haste to depart?"

Reproach heated her reluctant gaze. "'Tis plain you do not want me near Miss Fairfax."

"For good reason."

"I am not at fault for the mishap that befell her."

"Mrs. Jenner says you were remarkably startled to see Miss Fairfax descend the stairs, and offered your assistance to help her gain the parlor. She left her in your care, yet I heard you decline further aid when clearly Miss Fairfax was in want of support. Had I not arrived, she would have been alone in her hour of need."

The accused darted her eyes everywhere except at Stuart. "An oversight on my part, I owe, yet nothing more. For that, I apologize. I must attend to Mister Monroe."

"Grandfather is senseless by this hour."

"He sometimes wakes and may need me." She attempted to duck past Stuart and shoot around him.

"Not yet." He snagged her elbow, whipped her back toward him, and clamped both hands around her slight shoulders.

He probed her evasive eyes. "You have rendered faithful service to this family of which I am mindful, else I would toss you out the door and alert my aunt to your behavior."

The look Miss Smith cast him held so much venom he scarcely knew her as the meek, wounded creature of his acquaintance. He almost dropped his hands, so startled was he at the transformation from mouse to demon.

She stuck out her lower lip. "Mrs. Peyton adores me."

"Mrs. Peyton will heed my word above yours, and you've been replaced in that household. Tell me the truth, what are you concealing?"

"Nothing." She stamped her foot. "Why do you

care so deeply for Miss Fairfax? I've observed your feeble attempts to hide your ardor."

Truly, jealously wore an ugly face, and it twisted hers into an unrecognizable mask.

Stuart held firm. "My regard for that lady is none of your affair."

"Is it not? We have an understanding."

"Not formally."

She sucked in her breath. "Informally then, and of longstanding. Will you supplant me with her? Hasn't your family enough madness among the ranks without joining yourself to that troubled soul?"

If she'd slapped him, Stuart couldn't have been more taken aback. How he'd ever felt obligated to wed this disagreeable creature, he couldn't imagine. Had he always been the prize, the reason, she'd seemed so good-natured?

"The state of Miss Fairfax's mind is not for you to assess."

"She belongs in an asylum."

He tightened his grip on her upper arms. "If that charge ever escapes your mouth again, you shall rue the day. Would you also send my grandfather to that dreadful place?"

Regret rushed into her eyes. "Never the old gentleman. I swear."

"Then keep silent on the matter," he growled. "And hear me well. Any perceived understanding between us is at an end. No matter the wishes of Mister Monroe. Do you understand, Miss Smith?"

"Perfectly, sir," she hissed.

"I must insist you release me, Captain Monroe. My shoulders ache from your ungentlemanly grasp, and I am in need of respite."

He didn't relent. "Miss Fairfax suffers far greater distress. You may depart after you confide whatever it is you are secreting."

Her lips crimped in a stubborn line.

Wind whistled beyond the walls. Candles flickered atop their stands and the passage was chill. She shivered in the draft and from the distasteful confrontation with him, no doubt. Still, she said not a word.

"Do you think to outlast me? If need be, I will remain here all night on these cold floorboards. Or, I could escort you back to the parlor and the sight you found so disturbing."

At that threat, she opened her mouth. "'Tisn't what I saw so much, as *felt*. The breath of the departed on the back of my neck, I tell you."

Not his father again. "Did you also imbibe the tea, or have you joined the ranks of the addled?"

A shudder ran through her. "Weren't natural, whatever it was."

Stuart pivoted her toward the parlor. "Let's go discover. Perhaps he will loosen your tongue."

Fear crossed her eyes, and her resistance crumbled. "No. Wait—I had no notion it was belladonna."

He stared at her. "What are you saying?"

"One of the men who came this afternoon from the Jones' house with goods for Miss Fairfax gave me a vial. He said I should add a few drops to her tea, that it would strengthen her, like a tonic."

Stuart weighed the blurted confession in amazement. His younger brother, William, had greater sense. "I don't know which is more outrageous, the man who convinced you to take part in this murderous scheme, or that you believed him. Assuming, you truly were in ignorance of the vial's contents."

Panic furrowed the girl's brow and shone back at him in pleading eyes. "I swear by all that's sacred, by the Almighty himself, I did not know. Miss Fairfax's uncle wouldn't do her harm. Why should I suspect ill intent?"

"You should be wary of anyone who behaves in such a suspicious manner. Particularly where the wealthy are concerned and there are gains to be made."

Her jaw dropped. "Mister Jones wouldn't kill his niece to get at her inheritance. Has Miss Fairfax a large one?"

She really did seem in ignorance of what was owed to Hettie. "Miss Fairfax is the last of her line. I assume it's substantial."

"Or frittered away," Miss Smith thrust back.

"Whether it is, or isn't, I have no suspicion regarding Ezra Jones. I doubt he has the faintest idea what transpired here today."

"Who, then? His son?"

"I cannot make that conjecture. Nor should you. Who came to Thornton from the Jones' residence? Exactly, mind."

"The driver, old Daniel."

The elderly Negro was a trusted slave in the Jones' household. "Who else? Old Daniel couldn't unload more than a loaf of bread alone."

"I didn't recognize the second man. White, though. He appeared to work for the Jones' family. Perhaps in their merchant trade. Said his name was Mister Davis."

"What did he look like? Large, small? Short,

lanky?"

"He was of large build, wore a gray wig under his black tricorn, and a black suit with brass buttons—"

"Wait—black?" Stuart pounced.

She startled. Once again the mouse. "Entirely. Apart from the gold trim on the hat, and a dark, green waistcoat. He unloaded a small trunk with gifts for Miss Fairfax and bore it indoors. The two men lingered to warm themselves by the kitchen hearth and take some refreshment."

"That was when this Mister Davis slipped you the vial?"

She squirmed in Stuart's hold. "Not exactly."

"What, then?" He was fast losing the little patience he possessed.

"Mister Davis asked for me by name. Minnie was sent to fetch me."

This item of news, coupled with the black suit, struck Stuart as the most useful pieces of information yet. "Someone has made a study of this household. They are acquainted with your regard for me, and your resentment toward Miss Fairfax."

She ducked her face, rosy now from mortification. Unless she was a better actress than he assumed her to be.

"The crux of the matter is not yet established. Did you truly think the contents of the vial would aid Miss Fairfax, or did you hope for her undoing?"

"I vow I thought to see her improved."

"Yet she was not."

Indignation flooded the eyes lifting to his. "Was the lady not fashionably attired and her hair done to perfection? Did she not descend the stairs to take supper below? Was I to remain and observe how much fairer she is than I?"

Spoken like a female in the throes of envy, not one with murderous intent. Stuart almost pitied her, then remembered how she'd abandoned Hettie and cooperated with an unknown assailant to sneak a deadly potion into her tea.

Abigail Smith must bear the full weight of her transgression, and he couldn't resist referencing his father. "I know not what the late Captain Monroe would say, were we to ask him, but I am deeply disappointed in your stealthy behavior and lapse in judgment. You nearly killed Miss Fairfax. If it weren't for the tea only partly consumed and Ezekiel's skills, you might well stand trial for murder."

A quaver escaped her, and she slumped in his grasp. "Dear God, no. What of Mister Davis?"

"If that is indeed his name. I shall track down the black-hearted scoundrel. Though I expect he will deny any involvement and pin all on you. Nor was he acting alone."

She jerked up her head. "Whom do you suspect?"

"I'll not say for now. From this moment forward, you are to report to me, immediately, if you ever observe that cunning assassin on these premises again. Or any other dubious activity. Someone, possibly more than one man, desires nothing more than Miss Fairfax's and my demise."

She appeared dumbstruck. "You?"

"Oh, yes. Mine above all. You are to confine your services to Mister Monroe until I determine if Miss Fairfax is safe in your presence. Now go."

Red-faced, her eyes streaming tears, she turned and

bolted upstairs. Stuart stayed where he was pondering the baffling disclosure of this strange man's connection to the Jones' household, and how much he should divulge to Ezra Jones.

Was the older man also in danger, or only his niece? And what of his son, Jonas? Innocent on this count, or rotten to the core? Accusation without proof was dangerous.

Chapter Ten

Pungent, piney, with a hint of roses, herbs scented Hettie's bedchamber. A special blend of fragrances emanated from her. Slathered in a salve made of Ezekiel's sovereign remedy for the skin, she lay propped against the pillows wearing a clean shift edged with ribbons and lace. He hunched near her bed in the green armchair. Maddie hovered at his shoulder, ready to be of assistance.

Hettie spoke in a husky whisper. "Once again, you snatched me back from the grave. I'm unspeakably grateful."

Ezekiel inclined a head the color of sheep's wool. "Be warned. The effects from devil's cherries kin last fer days."

"Which ones?"

"Any of 'em, Miss."

"So I may continue to be visited by the late captain?"

The corners of his lined eyes crinkled. "You may. But, I believe Captain John was visible to you afore you drank the tea." He made this observation in a low voice.

"Might that have been from the fever?" Hettie desperately wanted to be normal.

"It might. Only…" An aura of mystery imbued Ezekiel, and he seemed to see beyond her.

"What?"

His brow puckered more than the crisscross of wrinkles accounted for. "I sometimes fancy I glimpse Captain John here in the house. The sleeve of his uniform, the side of his face, maybe a shadow slanting across the floor when no one's there."

Relief washed through Hettie; she wasn't the only one. "Did the sightings begin at his death?"

"Not right off. Since Captain Stuart come home from the war. 'Specially with yer coming."

Chills prickled down her neck. "Why me?"

The old healer turned his inscrutable regard on Hettie, like the farsighted gaze of a cat. For a contemplative moment, he said nothing. "You been near the divide, Miss."

She plucked at the lace on her sleeve. "I've sometimes seen the departed before I was truly ill."

He pointed a dusky finger at her. "Yer a seer."

"Of sorts, I suppose. I don't know what I am. But I'm no witch. I swear. Please tell Mrs. Jenner."

"Great God Almighty, Miss." Ezekiel silenced her with a wave of his bent hand. "No one said you was, and we ain't telling nobody nothing. Don't be speaking them words out loud."

"Can't be too careful," Maddie whispered. "Yer a proper lady, but folk kin still make trouble."

Hettie nodded mutely.

"What you got don't come from spells." Ezekiel leaned back in the chair, his leathered face creased like ancient parchment, eyes distant. "I tell you true, I thought a lot of Captain John. A good, God-fearing man. If he's got a message to get through, it's important. I only see a little of those who've crossed over to the other side. Don't hear so good neither. I'll wager you hear him speaking too, don't you?"

"Sometimes. In my head."

"That's a gift." Ezekiel gestured at Maddie. "She don't see Captain John, do you, girl?"

"No one does, except you, Miss. And Grandpa a little."

Hettie fingered the silky edge of her coverlet. "Folk think me odd. Or worse."

Ezekiel snorted. "They turn them beady eyes on anyone who's different. Like a pack of crows. Me, I'm just a slave."

"But people listen to you. They respect your wisdom," Hettie reasoned.

"The Monroes do. And Mrs. Jenner. Others, only heed me by the hardest. Keep yer eyes and ears open, Miss, and mind what you say. You'll be all right."

"And someday you will be free."

He shook his head. "Naw. I don't reckon to live that long. I'm content if Maddie and the others see that day."

The calm assertion of his passing struck Hettie like a fist in the gut. Her eyes blurred. "Surely, you won't die before Mister Monroe? What on earth would we do without you, Ezekiel?"

"I'm right touched you care, Miss. Not many would shed tears over a slave. Take heart. Maddie's at my elbow learning. And I ain't dying tomorrow."

Hettie didn't dare ask when. She prayed he'd postpone his passing as long as possible.

He shifted in his chair. "I got to go look in on Mister Monroe now. I'll be back to see how you fare later." With his granddaughter's help, he got heavily to his feet. Clutching his worn leather pouch filled with herbal potions, he shuffled from the room.

There was no denying he grew feebler daily. Despite his wisdom, he couldn't heal himself or ward off death forever.

A heavy sigh escaped Maddie. "His heart's slowly giving out, Miss. How can I ever know all he does? He's like Moses."

"Indeed he is. But you're a clever girl," Hettie encouraged, wondering exactly the same thing.

Maddie grew quiet, then jerked as if stung. "Lord help us, Miss. You reckon he's seeing Captain John cause he's nearer the divide?"

"Could be. Best learn fast."

Her demeanor subdued, Maddie nodded. "I'll do my best."

Hettie didn't attempt to suggest anyone other than Ezekiel might be of help to the girl. There was no one better equipped to instruct her in healing.

"God be with me," Maddie murmured.

"With us both. I sense much is also required of me, in a different way."

Maddie was solemn. "Likely so, given yer gift."

"If that's what it is. Sometimes feels more like a curse."

"Take heart, Miss."

"And you see to it your grandfather gets as much rest as possible."

Eyes somber, she bobbed her head.

Hettie's spirits lifted as Stuart rounded the doorway to her chamber. He must have grabbed a few hours of sleep after sitting up with her most of the night, or so she'd been told. She didn't remember him carrying her to bed. He was freshly shaven, and unbearably handsome in a clean linen shirt, olive waistcoat and jacket that brought out the green in his eyes. His long legs were sleek in formfitting leather breeches and he wore riding boots.

A surge of energy swept through her like a new wind.

If she were a bit stronger, she'd leap from bed and rush at him. How surprised he'd be by her immodest behavior. But, she suspected, not disapproving.

He nodded at Maddie. An arm on either side of his waist, he bowed to Hettie. "I'm delighted to find you much improved this morning, Miss Fairfax."

"As am I to be found among the living, Captain Monroe."

He strode toward her bed. "What did Ezekiel have to say?"

Nothing Hettie cared to share. She waved aside his query. "No matter."

"If you insist, but I'm not convinced. Ezekiel always has something of consequence to impart. Even if it's only a few words." Arching a quizzical brow, he swiveled his head toward Maddie. "Have you anything to add to this?"

"No, sir."

Clearly, Maddie felt equally unable to convey the recent exchange with her grandfather.

Stuart smiled and gestured her toward the door. "You may go. I'll summon you to stay with Miss Fairfax when I depart."

"She ought to spend more time in Ezekiel's company," Hettie interjected.

He eyed her questioningly but gave a shrug. "Very well. We'll send Minnie up, then."

"I'll alert her, sir. Thank you." Maddie curtsied and darted from the chamber.

"In rather a hurry, isn't she?" he observed.

"I sense we are all running short of time."

Fixing his concerned gaze on Hettie, he lowered himself into the bedside chair. "You are better, are you not? You aren't concealing something from me?"

"No. No. A little weak from the ordeal, but nothing like last evening. The worst is passed. I'll soon mend."

He exhaled in relief. "Welcome tidings, indeed. Are you still keeping company with my father?"

"Not at present."

"Downstairs, is he?"

She lowered her gaze. "Perhaps."

Stuart reached out and clasped her smaller hand in his. "Pray do not trouble yourself about it."

A sweet thrill ran through Hettie at the natural way he touched her. She lifted her eyes to the warmth in his.

"Converse with my father all you like. Say hello for me. I miss him."

"He knows," she said softly.

Stuart was pensive. "After the belladonna fades, you may no longer see him."

"And if I do? Folk think me strange enough as it is."

He squeezed her hand reassuringly. "First of all, who can say how long it may take for the effects of the herb to wear off? And second, no one will be informed of any unusual occurrences on your part by me or anyone else in this household. Miss Smith is under particularly strict instructions not to come near you or to leave this house."

His tenderness soothed her like a balm. "Thank

you. But you mustn't blame her for what happened. She was a pawn."

"To whom? That's the question. And don't be too forgiving until all is revealed." He slid his fingers beneath Hettie's chin. "There's more. I may have found your man in black."

Chills crawled down her spine. "Where?"

"In your uncle's employ."

She eyed him in disbelief. "Never. Uncle Ezra is absolutely devoted to me. I would wager my life on it."

"And have. Yet, I agree, he worships you." Stuart entwined his fingers with hers. "This so called Mister Davis may be in another's employ while supposedly working for your uncle. But I cannot rule out your cousin, Jonas Jones."

"Dear Lord, Stuart. Nor can we rule him in. Jonas may be a useless lump, but a murderer? Pray God you are mistaken."

"I have no wish to be correct in this matter, which is why I must pay your relations a visit."

"To what end? Accuse them of plotting my demise?"

"Not outright. I must get to the bottom of this mystery. And find Mister Davis. Despite your confusion over events, I suspect the answers lie with you."

She'd heard that before. "Your father said the same thing last evening."

Stuart smiled faintly. "Very talkative for a deceased man, isn't he?"

"That's what I told him."

Emotion welled up in his eyes. "Oh, Hettie. My dear, strange, beloved girl."

Had he actually called her *beloved*? Strange, she'd expected.

"You will get better, my dearest."

"What if I don't, and I continue to converse with the dead?"

"Perhaps, if you know how ardently I esteem you, the need to attach yourself to the departed will ease."

"Perhaps." If they'd stop appearing to her. But with Stuart professing such wondrous sentiments, she wasn't about to jeopardize his fervent rush.

He lifted his hand and cupped her cheek. "There's an unearthly quality about you, dear lady, as if you're not entirely of this realm, which I trust will fade as you grow stronger."

She gazed at him through sparkling tears. "I also trust but can make no promise."

Yearning shone back at her. "I long for you to fully resume your life and share it with me."

She could scarcely believe his ardent profession. "I would love nothing better. But will you still feel this way if I have visitations from the departed?"

"Whatever the cause, whether from illness, a vivid imagination, or that you do, indeed, have *the sight*, it is all a part of this unique being who is fast becoming unspeakably precious to me."

Cupping the hand at her face, she exhaled slowly. "Not all will share your view."

He firmed his chin. "I will protect you from them."

"That must be a familiar urge."

"Granted, I have family not entirely of sound mind."

"Will they, or anyone, object if you add yet another?"

"Even if they do, I don't care, dearest girl. I've nearly lost you twice, and refuse to risk losing you again." Sliding his hand from her cheek, he reached out both arms and gently enfolded her against him.

She nestled in his warm strength, savoring the wonder of her place in his arms. "But I cannot ask you to risk your reputation, your standing in society, for me. You are a respected member of this community, with much ahead of—"

Any further attempts to argue were silenced as he tilted her face and tenderly covered her lips with his.

He'd planted a bold peck on her cheek when they were childhood playmates that summer long ago, but never anything remotely like this. To some, it was only a kiss. To Hettie, it was the promise of far more. She knew Stuart hadn't meant to trifle with her earlier, and he wasn't trifling now.

She ought to pull away, dissuade him from pursuing courtship with a potentially unstable woman who might undermine his position in Halifax. But no part of her wanted to retreat. Everything in her urged her forward.

Time lost meaning cradled in his arms, caught up in the sublime summons on her mouth. Whether moments or minutes spent in cherished wonder, she didn't know. All was *now*.

Even so, she should forewarn him. So much was at stake. His reputation, sacred honor, very life. She was an ill wind.

Searing and sacred. Rapturous desire scorched Stuart while a heavenly choir throbbed in his very being. Hettie was *The One*. A celestial being here on earth.

Making heroic efforts not to press her for more than she could give in her weakened state, he reveled in every second his mouth sealed her protest, and the quivering wonder of Hettie in his embrace. So soft, so fragrant. The bouquet of scents titillated his nose.

Whether she was or wasn't the proper choice for him, according to his grandfather and the wider community, mattered not a jot. He wanted her more than any woman of his acquaintance, more than anything in his entire life. Now, and always. Her lips answered his invitation, and he ached to his marrow for her, even if she might be addled.

No. She couldn't be. Not truly.

The afflicted didn't coherently discuss the possibility of their insanity. His grandfather was unaware of his failings and faltered in his confusion. He didn't recall the brilliant man who once held sway. Only for fleeting minutes, at best, hours, was he rational. Then the veil returned, and he was again lost to Stuart—to everyone. Ezekiel had tried herbal treatments. There was no lasting cure. If Hettie fell into shadow, there could be none for her.

Confound it all. It was her very uniqueness that drew him. Everything about Hettie intrigued him, a mysterious bequest sent by Providence. How many women could convey what his deceased father had said the evening before?

Granted, none should. But she'd been given belladonna. Who knows, maybe she'd had small amounts of the herb snuck into her tea before. Jonas could've had a hand, or this mystery man.

Even if no one had tampered with her, Hettie couldn't be more than a wee bit *tetched*. She'd always danced to her own melody. Her mixed ancestry coupled with her eccentricity was bound to set her apart. That was to Stuart's advantage, though. If not for these oddities, she might already be married. And he wouldn't be relishing the most glorious moment of his life.

Lengths of her wonderful hair spilled over them both. Despite her thin frame, feminine curves tempted him beneath her linen shift. God help him, if he were tumbling in love with a mad woman, she possessed a most intoxicating form of insanity. Like a well once drunk from, there could be no other source to quench his thirst. And Stuart was parched.

She whispered against his lips. "There's something you must know. I was a king's man, at heart."

Was she trying to put him off this courtship, to protect him from himself? "Hettie, you aren't a man."

"I mean, I was a Loyalist, at heart."

"I know."

She caught her breath and pulled away. "You do?"

"Yes. As was your uncle. Yet, here I am." He buried his lips in the sweet curve of her neck, eliciting quivers in response. "Your heart lies with me now."

"But I'm so very odd."

"You are the only one for me."

"You say that now—"

There really was only one way to silence her. Stuart recaptured her mouth, yearning for the day she was strong enough for him to dare far more. He might be making the greatest mistake of his life, but oh, how intoxicating were her lips.

Chapter Eleven

Gusts of wind whirled dry leaves along the rutted dirt street and tossed bare branches as Stuart rode into Halifax. After an early dinner of chicken pot pie, General Washington's favorite dish, he'd cantered off on Bryan. Now, the sun hung low above the trees and dark clouds sailed across the sky.

Good thing he'd worn his heavy coat, with the high turned up collar and capes. The stiff breeze had that raw cold feel with moisture in its teeth. He'd be riding back in black windswept rain, unless the storm blew itself out.

Only a few folk scuttled past him, bundled to the ears, their heads covered. He wasn't even certain who they were. No one did more than throw up a hand in greeting, except Mister Ellis. There were no vendors along King Street, or on the commons. They'd packed up their wares. Market Square was an empty green swathe. Whatever the elderly man's reason for coming to town, he was headed home.

The bay gelding stood quietly, his black mane and tail tossing, as Stuart reached down and shook Mister Ellis's gloved fingers. "Good afternoon, sir."

"Not much good about it, Captain. Getting to be quite a bluster. 'Twill be evening soon. Best conduct your business in haste, or stay the night."

"I've endured worse."

A frown deepened the creases furrowing Mister Ellis's forehead beneath the black tricorn. "No doubt. Suit yourself, then. You generally do." He turned to his driver who assisted him into the waiting coach. The older Negro was outfitted in a great coat with the collar well up around his ears, and a scarf tied beneath the wide brimmed hat on his head. No one could say Mister Ellis didn't care for his slaves. But his short reply annoyed Stuart.

He had no intention of lodging at the *Sign of the Thistle* or *Dudley's Tavern,* no matter what his disapproving neighbor advised. Bryan would bear up for the journey home, and Stuart burned to be with Hettie. First, he had a mission to accomplish, not of a particularly savory nature.

Head bent against the wind, he trotted Bryan past the cemetery he must soon visit some dark night. Hooves resounded on the cobbles as he rode into the yard. The Jones' house arched several stories above him. Though the white wooden home, with its stone foundation, vaulted no higher than Thornton Hall, it was more opulent.

The wealth accumulated by Ezra Jones made no difference to his mission, Stuart chided himself, refusing to be intimidated by the power money could wield.

He reined in Bryan, dismounted, and tethered him to a hitching post. "You there!" He summoned a stable boy to tend to the gelding. Bryan's welfare was paramount. "See my mount is watered and well rubbed down. We leave in an hour." His instruction was nearly lost in the cacophony, as were the clip clop of hooves as the youth led Bryan toward the stable.

Satisfied his horse would be properly seen to, Stuart slapped gloved hands against his sides to warm them, then gulped several reviving swallows of brandy from the flask in his coat pocket. No one apart from the stable boy had noted his arrival and come to greet him. The buffeting wind must've driven them all indoors.

There was nothing for it other than to stride up the brick walkway to the front entrance. Two bulldog statues crouched on either side of the stoop at the top of the steps as if guarding the house. Not terribly welcoming.

Stuart pounded on the wood echoing under his fist, the brass knob polished to a gloss. This stout door could keep out the gale, but it wasn't preventing him from gaining entry. He was having a word with Ezra and Jonas, and a look around the premises. Maybe he'd spot the villain he sought.

He didn't intend to attack anyone, but was prepared for potential threats in town or along the way to and from Halifax. His officer's pistol rode in the side of his right boot. He'd tucked a sheathed dagger in the left one. The tall boots hid both weapons. A short blade hung from the leather belt buckled at his waist, concealed beneath his brown coat. The ram's horn he, his father, and grandfather, had used for hunting, so translucent from use the black powder inside it was visible, along with spare shot, and cloth patches for reloading, were in the pouch suspended around his shoulder by a strap.

The cartridge box he'd worn during the revolution was rather obvious. The only thing he hadn't brought was that and his musket. He mustn't appear as if he'd come to take the Jones' residence by force, like a one man company. But if the infamous man in black were within, there was no telling what he might do.

More hammering and the door finally opened. A young Negro footman attired in red and black livery ushered him into the foyer. The best Thornton Hall could muster for receiving visitors was Mrs. Jenner. As often as not, new arrivals were greeted by Minnie. Her prattling wasn't the most impressive introduction, and if shyness struck, she spoke not a word.

"I'm come to see Mister Jones," Stuart explained.

"Which one, sir?"

"Either or both." He grew impatient.

"If you'll wait here, I'll go and tell Mister Ezra and Mister Jonas."

With that, the footman left him standing on the cheerless flagstone floor inside the door and vanished down the long, and quite wide, hallway, lit by candles. Dances were held here, and the passage kept spotless. Even the foyer was clean apart from his boot marks. Thornton wasn't as immaculate, but Stuart didn't have nearly as many slaves as Ezra Jones—in fact, he had none. His grandfather did. It was awkward trying to manage an estate he didn't yet own, and climb out from under a mountain of debt. In some ways, the war had been easier.

He glowered at the tall clock in the foyer, its moon face keeping watch over him, and everything else. 5:00. He wanted to be back in the saddle by 6:00 at the latest, unless a worthy delay arose. This should give Bryan ample respite; it didn't matter about Stuart. He was prepared for a bracing ride home.

The high-back wooden settle positioned against one blue wall awaited his hat and coat, if he cared to deposit them. He left the brown tricorn, but retained his heavy outer garment. He needed the coat for more than just warmth, also as a means to conceal his weapons.

Tapping one boot on the flagstones, he ran his gaze over the elaborately worked cornices and motifs embellishing the ceiling. The ornate chandelier high overhead wasn't lit. Rather, the stand beside the settle held an iron candelabra that wavered in the draft. Farther ahead, a stand with a three-tiered candlestick flickered at the base of the curved staircase leading to the second story.

"Captain Monroe. Welcome." A portly figure, swaddled in a lavender coat, crimson vest, and lengths of red wool wrapped around his neck, hobbled toward Stuart, leaning on a brass-headed cane. Jonas hadn't changed out of his slippers and must have been settled before the hearth warming his toes.

"Good afternoon, sir." Stuart offered a short bow and strode to where Jonas had paused at the hall entrance.

Ezra's only surviving offspring had been born with one leg notably shorter than the other, or one considerably longer, depending on how you regarded his affliction, and a clawed left hand. This, he concealed with white gloves and mostly used his right hand. A sickly infant, he wasn't expected to long survive his birth. Remarkably, he'd gained strength, adjusted to his infirmities, and outlived his two brothers. His deformities had spared him fighting in the war.

A widowed aunt and her brood remained to inherit after Jonas, unless he wed and produced an heir. Doubtful. In his late thirties, he seemed content with his bachelor state. Possibly the thought of sharing his wealth with anyone was abhorrent. He was clever and of a scholarly bent, but could do with more charity in his heart. Miserly came to mind.

A head shorter than Stuart, Jonas tilted his round, dimpled face to scrutinize him from beneath the brown wig. Spectacles aided his weak vision, his close set eyes reminding Stuart of a bird intent on a worm. They were fixed on him now.

"What brings you out in this ill weather, Captain Monroe?"

Was Jonas merely curious, or trying to ascertain Stuart's mission without betraying any previous knowledge? He appeared in ignorance. Difficult to be certain.

Stuart weighed every flicker in those seemingly guileless blue eyes. "I am here on an urgent matter."

Jonas arched reddish brows. "Does this concern my cousin's health?"

"It does."

A pained expression crossed his visage. "God help us." Jonas dropped his voice. "I loathe bearing bad tidings to Father. He's suffered a relapse of his respiratory complaints. A shock might worsen his state. I fear for him. I do."

Stuart laid a solicitous hand on the rounded shoulder. "Miss Fairfax lives," he assured her cousin, trying to judge if Jonas's concern was solely for the elder Mister Jones, or if he spared any true sentiment for Hettie.

Jonas breathed out in evident relief. "That's a mercy. Come with me to the parlor, Captain, and warm yourself. Father bids you to speak with him there. You may acquaint us both with the details of Miss Fairfax's condition. I pray you be as gentle as possible with the senior Mister Jones."

"As you wish."

Stuart slowed his pace to match his host's halting gait. Jonas was odd, but nothing about him struck a note of wariness. Jonas seemed as he always did. Dull, but harmless.

They passed ancestral portraits lining the hall. Eerie, those eyes following them in the winking light. Porcelain statuettes and books covered a long table against the wall, illuminated by the candles in a holder. Jonas read avidly and absently, leaving books about the house, according to Hettie.

No crime in that. Although losing himself in a book, particularly one of Jonas's selection, held scant appeal for Stuart. He'd far rather be about the bustle of life. His grandfather, father, and Claire, were the readers in the family. Or had been.

Carved chairs, with cushioned gold seats, also lined portions of the wall, and a second laden table. Jonas gestured at the collection of birds' eggs on its surface, directing Stuart's attention to a large white egg with brown mottling.

"I've acquired a great auk," he said proudly.

Stuart gave a polite nod. Jonas was a strange little man.

Beyond the parlors leading off either side of the hall were the formal dining room, the office where Jonas worked, and a small bedchamber at the back. More bedchambers and a sitting room were upstairs. Despite its size, the Jones' house was stuffed full of furniture and whatever caught their eye. Being merchants, they imported goods from all over.

"After you, sir." Jonas gestured Stuart ahead to the cracked door on the right. He strode into the less formal of the parlors. The room was every bit as grand, or more so, than the fancier parlor at Thornton Hall.

Stuart wasn't envious. He preferred his home as it was. Not shabby, but comfortable, like a broken-in pair of boots.

He surveyed the red and pink flowered wallpaper that matched the ornate square of plush carpet on the floor. A glass front cabinet overflowed with china dishes jostling for space among statuettes of dogs, shepherdesses, their swains, and frolicking dancers. In one corner, a blue porcelain pitcher and bowl for rinsing dusty hands waited in the center of a washstand, the towel rack above it hung with fresh linen. Gruff he might be, but Ezra had an eye for beauty.

Against one back wall stood a crimson couch, occasional tables and chairs scattered on either side. These were not in use. The footman gestured to the gold armchair he placed alongside Ezra's before the crackling fireplace. A third padded chair was intended for Jonas. The end table beside it held a book of sermons, in Latin, Stuart noted. Perhaps these would inspire Jonas to greater generosity. It was unlikely reading matter if he were complicit in a murder attempt.

His father hunched in the upholstered seat as near to the hearth as possible, wrapped in a woolen blanket draped to his slippered toes. A large towel covered his gray head, currently bent over a low stool with a steaming basin of herbal scented water. This accounted for the added pungency in the room. If all that weren't protection enough, a decorative screen guarded Ezra from any draft escaping the windows.

He lifted his head, overhung with the towel. Watery eyes surveyed Stuart as he dabbed the dew beaded on the end of his bulbous red nose with a wad of linen. Unlike Jonas, his features were sharper, except the nose. A real honker. Hettie didn't gain her looks from this side of the family.

Ezra sniffed. "Forgive me, Captain Monroe. My indisposition prevents me from extending the usual courtesy. I trust you bring us good tidings."

As if Stuart dared do otherwise.

"Sit you down, man. Jonas, you too, sir. Otis, bring us some mulled cider," Ezra directed in a gravelly voice. "And close that door. The draft is swirling about my ankles. No wonder the captain retains his coat."

"Yes, sir." The footman trod over the flowered carpet and departed the room, shutting the door behind him.

Stuart sat in the chair Otis indicated was intended for him, and Jonas settled on his usual seat.

Ezra turned inquiring eyes on Stuart. "What brings you out in this dreary weather?"

It was plain neither of Hettie's relations had any idea what had happened to her the past evening. If Stuart enlightened them, both men, especially Ezra, would grow exceedingly alarmed. Ezra wasn't well. Neither was he as near to death as Jonas would have Stuart believe. It was evident he had a head cold. Miserable, but not generally fatal.

After blowing noisily into his handkerchief, Ezra spoke again. "You must pardon me, sir. Please extend my apologies to dear Hettie for neglecting to visit her of late."

Stuart nodded. "I shall. You mustn't venture forth in this lamentable state. She will understand."

Her uncle appeared mollified.

"I'm certain business detains Jonas from favoring his cousin with a visit," Stuart added.

"Indeed," Jonas hastened to assure him, a faint blush coloring his plump face. He hadn't once darkened her door.

"Did she like the gifts I sent round?" Ezra hacked into his handkerchief and bent back over the steam.

Stuart chose his words with care. "Vastly. There was one item, however, that caused some unexpected trouble."

Ezra jerked his draped head around. Comical, if Stuart hadn't come on such a grievous matter.

"How so, Captain? I selected every gift with care."

"You did not intend this for her, Mister Jones, but it accompanied your presents."

He eyed Stuart from beneath the towel. "What was it?"

Stuart shifted his gaze between father and son. "A vial of belladonna."

For a shocked moment, neither man spoke. Then Ezra flushed the shade of his nose. "What in blazes?"

"First let me assure you, Miss Fairfax is faring far better today than last evening. However, the man who delivered the vial, a Mister Davis, proclaimed it a tonic to our Miss Smith and instructed her to pour some into your niece's tea."

No recognition of the name hinted in Ezra's enraged glare. "The hell you say! But—but—" he stammered snuffily. "How do you know Miss Smith didn't undertake this evil deed herself? Anyone can see the girl's set her cap at you."

Stuart anticipated this charge. "I questioned Miss Smith and am satisfied her intent was not malicious. Fortunately, Miss Fairfax drank little of the tea and is in Ezekiel's excellent care. But it could have turned out dreadfully otherwise had Mister Davis succeeded in his murderous aim."

Rather than coloring like the stormy patriarch, Jonas blanched white. "I sent Mister Davis to Thornton Hall with the chest of goods Father requested. The shawl, petticoat, gloves, and bracelet. I checked the contents myself. No vial of belladonna or any other herb was included in the offerings."

His father erupted. "I should bloody well hope not! I've made damn sure Ezekiel has all the medicine she needs. Where did this Davis fellow come from?"

Jonas sucked in air as if stricken by consumption. "He arrived requesting employment last week with a letter of introduction from a merchant in New York. I set him to work overseeing the unloading of shipments. He seemed quite able."

Ezra snorted. "Where is this *Mister Davis* now?"

Jonas pressed a trembling hand against his forehead. "I can't speak to his whereabouts. I didn't visit the dock or warehouse today. I was here, in the office."

Stuart broke in. "He must be found and questioned. By me."

"Why you?" Ezra snapped.

"You lack the health, sir, and Jonas the disposition for such a task."

Ezra waved him off testily. "Yes, yes. I see your point. Make inquiries amongst the workers, Jonas.

Summon them to your office this evening. Perhaps Mister Vaughan can be of assistance when he returns."

Stuart clamped his fingers on the arms of the chair. "Mister *Thomas* Vaughan?"

Both men swiveled their heads at him. "The same," Ezra grunted.

"Why do you ask?" This uneducated query from the already badly rattled Jonas.

Circumstances were about to get a great deal more disagreeable. "Why is that turncoat back in Halifax?"

Ezra narrowed rheumy eyes at him. "Mister Vaughan claims he was falsely accused by his cousin, *your brother-in-law*, Major Vaughan, and forced to leave Halifax with Cornwallis's army. After two years in New York, he has returned to reclaim his business in Halifax."

"The hell he has. I'll shoot the traitor on sight."

"Then you, sir, will hang. Need I remind you of your less than laudable relations? Your sister, mother, and younger brother all reside in England with Major Vaughan, formerly of the infamous British Legion."

Stuart refrained from reminding Ezra of his suspected Loyalist ties. "Major Vaughan's affiliation during the war is in the past. He manages the family estates in Devon and Wales, and shall someday be Lord Vaughan."

"God grant we were all so fortunate."

Ezra's acid tone belied his own wealth. Stuart forbore to mention it, for Hettie's sake, and gritted his teeth.

Her uncle wore on. "Thomas Vaughan's path has been less blessed than his fortuitous cousin, but folk have rallied to his aid. He's a respectable citizen now, and will carry assorted teas, coffee, and chocolate for us in his shop. He is also staying here as our guest until repairs are completed on his house. The property stood vacant and was vandalized. You shall behave civilly toward him, Captain, or answer for it. Mister Ellis also proposes doing business with the fellow."

Damn. That upright Puritan had fallen prey to Thomas Vaughan's wiles. He'd bet that's why Ellis had been in town, and in such haste to leave, no matter the weather. He knew Stuart's feelings on the subject and couldn't get away fast enough. Well, his neighbor must face him, sooner or later.

And what would Brinkley say when he finally arrived? He knew the whole sordid tale from Stuart, but would be expected to side with his uncle. Brinkley would do as he would do. Stuart was ready to explode.

Jonas cleared the frog in his throat and shakily pushed back the spectacles that had slid down his squat nose. "I assure you, Mister Vaughan has behaved in the most exemplary manner since his return."

Stuart bent toward Jonas until he quaked in his chair. "Apart from the attempted poisoning of your cousin, which I wager he was behind."

"Nonsense, man!" Ezra barked, choking on his protest.

Stuart didn't relent. "Furthermore, I'll wager he's in league with Mister Davis, whom we will likely not see again, unless he's lying in ambush for me."

Jonas trembled like a frightened hare, while Ezra quivered with indignation. "Enough of this libelous speech. It will land you in court with a lawsuit which you can ill afford. If you're bent on ruin, I must insist you return my niece to me the instant she is able to travel."

Stuart shook his head. "I cannot allow her to return here. Her life is in danger."

"Don't be absurd, Captain. We shall take every care of her. This is her home."

"Your home is befouled, Mister Jones."

He wiped vigorously at his nose. "How dare you, sir!"

"I dare because Miss Fairfax and I are betrothed."

Jonas looked on blankly.

"Since when?" Ezra clutched the crumpled linen.

"This morning." Stuart hadn't proposed, exactly, but he'd made his commitment clear to Hettie. What else did she expect would come of his proclamation?

Ezra's complexion mottled purple and red. "How is it you are proposing while my niece is prostrate from poisoning?"

"Ezekiel snatched her back from the brink, again. It was miraculous. As I said, she was much improved before I left. Well enough for me to gently suggest she consider wedding me, when she's recovered, of course." Stuart wasn't a dolt.

Ezra thrust out a pointed jaw. "I suppose her dowry has whetted your interest?"

"She never mentioned it to me."

"No?" His watery eyes widened.

"Not a word."

"You must know she has a large inheritance coming to her on her twenty-second birthday?"

"Enlighten me."

"Ah ha!" Ezra pounced. "Thought you'd take notice."

"Only in that this money will be of aid to her."

His sputtering jaw dropped. "You'll not take it to pay your debts?"

Stuart crossed both arms over his chest. "I prefer to make my own way, Mister Jones."

Ezra studied him with a watery eye. "That's rather a different matter, then, sir. Considering the sum you owe."

Stuart bristled. "I hadn't realized my affairs were common knowledge."

"Nor are they. I had a word with Mister Ellis."

"Who should keep my confidence to himself, sir."

"Indeed, Captain," Ezra allowed. "We are entering into business together, so your name arose."

"He likely cautioned you not to extend me any credit."

Neither of the Jones' made a denial.

If any doubt existed, Stuart knew his credit was nil all over town. "I assure you, I will find a way to clear my debt."

"More easily said than done." Ezra sank back in his chair, hugging the blanket around him and hacking. "Yet a way must be found."

Stuart didn't mention grave robbing.

The senior Mister Jones blew into his handkerchief, and blotted his nose. "Are you game for a horse race? I'm sponsoring one next week with a generous purse. You have a first rate mare, I believe."

Ellis must've told him. "Yes. La Belle. But she hasn't been sufficiently conditioned since foaling last year."

"Think on getting that mare in shape, and ride her. I'll cover your entrance fee myself."

"Most generous, sir."

He waved aside Stuart's thanks. "Enter the race. Ride whatever you like. Your gelding is swift, is he not?"

Before Stuart replied, Otis, the footman, appeared with mugs of mulled cider. No one spoke while he passed the welcome refreshment around. Stuart reined himself in and allowed Ezra to slurp noisily. He and Jonas sipped in silence. Otis collected the empty vessels and removed them from the parlor.

Ezra had another go with his hankie, then spoke gruffly. "If you and my niece are in earnest regarding your intent to wed, we must discuss the situation."

"I assure you of my devotion to Miss Fairfax."

"She has yet to assure me of hers," Ezra countered.

"She shall." Stuart would persuade Hettie to overcome her fear of ruining his reputation and burdening him with the care of another potentially troubled soul.

"Likely, this is so," Ezra sniffed. "Our Hettie always had a soft spot for you."

Jonas appeared relieved. "Yes, she has. I am not opposed to the match, if Father agrees."

Stuart could well imagine Jonas would be only too pleased to shift her onto another. The scholarly man shuddered at the expense women entailed with their wardrobes, hair, perfume, jewelry…and God forbid they should demand excessive dinner parties and dances. No, Jonas would happily surrender Hettie to Stuart and lose himself in his books and bird eggs.

Ezra wasn't as easily appeased. "Certain conditions must first be met. Clear your debts without her funds. Use these for your life together. *And* refrain from shooting Mister Vaughan, or otherwise maiming him, when next you meet. I do not desire to attend your trial rather than her wedding."

Stuart grunted his acquiescence.

"In return, I shall hold a ball for the pair of you as soon as dearest Hettie regains her health. You will enter society with my blessing. Perhaps, even wed at Yuletide."

"A Christmas wedding. How jolly." Jonas attempted a short laugh. It fell flat at Ezra's scowl.

"There are provisos to be met first."

Stuart shouldered back in the chair. "Indeed." Including his apprehending Thomas and Davis while not appearing to provoke an assault. He'd no doubt Thomas was behind the poisoning of Hettie, and had sent Davis to follow him.

Why? Because Thomas wanted to destroy Stuart for his ties to Major Vaughan. He hated his British cousin, the heir to the title, and Claire for wedding him rather than Thomas. Stuart had helped make all that possible and was partly responsible for driving Thomas out of town. He'd made it difficult for him to smoothly reenter society. Hell, he even shot Thomas's former accomplice in the Battle of the Hook and saved Major Vaughan's life.

Thomas must've learned Stuart pulled the trigger. And he was the one remaining person, apart from Hettie, with knowledge of the treasure. He just didn't know its exact site.

Stuart must keep it that way. "I won't disappoint you, sir," he offered to Ezra. "You can count me in for the race."

"Good man." He snuffled approvingly.

Even if Stuart won, he'd still need the treasure to

have enough funds to clear his debt. Unless he sold—
Damn and blast. Thomas Vaughan. He tensed as the
dainty and despised figure entered the room.

Ever the dandy, Thomas was attired in a lavender
coat and floral waistcoat, a lacy cravat and fluted
sleeves showing at the neck and cuffs. Plum breeches
and purple shoes with ridiculously large gilt buckles
completed the wardrobe, likely furnished by Ezra.
Jonas would never tolerate such frivolous expenditure
at the tailor's.

Twirling a beribboned walking stick, Thomas
swept all present an exaggerated bow. Did he fancy
himself gentry? That ship had sailed, bearing his cousin
and Claire to England and a future title. And leaving
them this deplorable fop.

"Speak of the devil," Stuart said under his breath.

Ezra shot him a meaning look.

Jonas appeared as though he'd rather be most
anywhere else, probably in his chamber absorbed in
Latin verse. He leapt to his feet in a far sprightlier
manner than Stuart had ever witnessed, and offered a
short bow to the new arrival.

"Mister Vaughan, pray excuse me. I'll attend to the
matter we discussed, Father. Good evening, Captain."
Jonas nodded to the seated men and bolted from the
room as swiftly as his infirmity allowed. Astonishing
how fast he could move.

That Jonas didn't first approach Thomas for
assistance with *the matter under discussion* led Stuart to
believe he wasn't entirely persuaded of his innocence
where Mister Davis was involved. Though he'd never
defy his father. Not the Jonas Stuart knew. From what
he could tell, this was the Jonas still in control of

himself. Such as he was.

Stuart rose like an affronted dog. If he'd had hackles they would rise too. It was all he could do not to bare his teeth at the *guest* in the home.

Thomas feigned ignorance of the obvious. He didn't go so far as to extend a white hand which would've been refused, but a smirk flitted over the face many had declared exquisite. The beauty his short-lived French mother possessed had been bestowed on her son. He should've been a girl. What an evil witch that would combine to make.

Humor hinted in black eyes as he bent his dark head in an exaggerated bow. "What a pleasure to see you again, Captain."

"Not the greeting I would convey, but as we are in Mister Jones' home, I will forbear to utter it."

A violent sneeze and more mopping commenced before their host could manage a coherent syllable. "Captain Monroe, the war is behind us. Let us deport ourselves as gentlemen."

Stuart thought he'd done exceedingly well not to punch Thomas in the nose, and he hadn't grasped any of his weapons. What more did Ezra require?

An ingratiating smile, and Thomas leaned jauntily on his walking stick. "Tell me, sir, how fares my dear cousin and his lovely wife?"

"Quite well, last I heard. Claire gave birth to a healthy boy and is expecting again in the New Year." No inheritance for Thomas if she continued to supply the noble family line.

He didn't entirely mask his annoyance. "How fortunate for my uncle, Lord Vaughan, to have his title assured."

"Not that you would object to claiming it," Stuart thrust back.

"It would seem that will not be necessary." Thomas fluttered a perfumed handkerchief under his nostrils as though Stuart's presence offended his delicate sensibilities. "Pray do not let me keep you, Captain Monroe. The weather deteriorates. Unless, forgive me, you are staying the night?"

As if Stuart would consider lingering under this roof with such loathsome company. "I am leaving, Mister Vaughan. Do not trouble to rise, Mister Jones. I shall convey your warmest regards to Miss Fairfax." He turned and strode to the door.

"Pray extend my best wishes for her speedy recovery!" Thomas called after him.

Stuart swung around. "How did you know she's in need of such wishes, Mister Vaughan?"

The sneer in his gaze changed to caution. "All are aware she's recovering from remittent fever at Thornton Hall."

With his toweled head bent back over the herbal water steaming by the fireside, Ezra missed what Stuart caught.

He barely refrained from hurling Thomas against the wall. "Until we meet again, sir." On that low growl, he strode from the chamber.

Chapter Twelve

When was Stuart ever coming home? Had he been struck down? Did he lie wounded and bleeding along the road?

Like an ominous refrain, these unsettling questions repeated inside Hettie. She dozed fitfully. The hall clock chimed midnight. She'd heard every hour strike since he'd left at midday. Initially, tedium accompanied the tolling, then a pall surrounded each chime. A nameless, gnawing dread.

Unable to endure the wait any longer, she rose and gathered the coverlet about her. She slid her chilled feet into slippers. The room had gone cold, like a tomb devoid of sunlight.

Minnie slumbered on a roll of blankets before the hearth. Her duties were to keep the fire going and Hettie company. She'd failed at both. The fire burned low, and Hettie was driven to distraction with worry.

Rousing Minnie wouldn't ease her fears. She let the weary girl sleep. Though God knows, she was unspeakably fatigued herself. Her stomach in knots, she crept to the window and peered through the streaked glass. Not much was visible below in the murky yard. Still, if Stuart rode in, she'd detect him.

She strained for the sound of hooves. *God let him come.*

What a wretched night to be out. Sleety drizzle fell

from the misty sky. At least, the wind had died down; she'd had visions of him blowing away.

"He'll catch his death," she murmured.

No. Stuart is strong.

She recognized that low voice. Without turning to look, she knew who stood behind her. Whether from the lingering effects of belladonna, or because this sixth sense was her lot in life, Captain John was still with her.

"Even the strong fall. You did," she countered in a whisper.

I was shot.

"So could Stuart be. Is he safe?" she whispered.

For now.

Oddly, she believed her ghostly companion. Even though he might only be a hallucination. She pressed her forehead against the icy pane in relief.

The dark man follows him.

Reassurance fled. She jerked upright. "The man in black?"

Yes.

Her knees shook from weakness and alarm. "Will he overtake Stuart?"

Yes. Though not to harm him.

Again, she sagged against the window. "Thank God."

He comes for you.

Her heart nearly stopped, then a wild hammering set in. Without Stuart, she was defenseless. They all were.

The household was unarmed. Slaves weren't allowed to bear weapons, and the elder Mister Monroe scarcely left his chamber. Any fight in him was gone.

Their closest neighbor, Mister Ellis, was miles away. That left a handful of women, and she wasn't sure Miss Smith would take her side.

She gripped the window sill. "That man tried to poison me. Why does he come now?"

The treasure.

"But I don't know its exact location."

Stuart does. He'd do anything for you.

So that was his game. She'd be a pawn, used to force Stuart to reveal the site. And when he did—

"No! God help us!" Head reeling, she stumbled back.

Unseen arms caught her as she collapsed, nearly senseless.

"Miss!" Minnie tugged Hettie onto the bed. "What you doing up? You kin barely stand. You take a turn?"

She truly must have. Was she dreaming or awake?

Foreboding gripped her. That much was real. "Get help."

"Lie quiet. I'll run fetch Mrs. Jenner." A flustered Minnie whirled away.

Minutes passed in quaking terror. Only the faint glow from the fireplace lent any illumination to the dark room. If Hettie could get to the poker, that was something. But her legs were like water.

Don't be afraid. I'm with you.

Dear Lord. She was losing her mind, relying on a ghost. She didn't see him, only heard his voice in her head. Even he was fading. "Captain, if you're really here. Show me."

A feathery hand smoothed her forehead, so that she couldn't be sure of the touch. And yet—

"Send the wolf," she pleaded.

"What you want with that wild beast? Rambling again, I shouldn't wonder, poor lady. Is yer fever back?" Mrs. Jenner's presence filled the room. She laid her palm on Hettie's brow. "Chilled through, more like."

The boisterous housekeeper withdrew her hand and gestured at Minnie. "Stir up the fire and toss on some kindling. You never should have let it die down. Her teeth are chattering."

The clunk of wood feeding the dwindling flames accompanied the housekeeper's bustle. Cloth flapped and she spread another blanket over Hettie, tucking it around her. "Poor thing. Shaking like a leaf."

Minnie tossed another stick into the fire. "Should I fetch Grandpa to tend Miss Fairfax? She's been acting peculiar."

"No. Let him rest his old bones. Maddie can cope. Tell her to brew a cup of chamomile and add a few drops of valerian tincture. I must've lost my good sense to leave you in charge of her. I can see I'll have to stay myself."

Hettie pushed up shakily on one elbow. The reviving flames crackled and cast weird shadows in the chamber. "Wait, Minnie. Arm yourself with something, Mrs. Jenner. *He's* coming."

She paused in her flurry. "Who is?"

"The man in black." Mrs. Jenner could wield the poker and anything else that came to hand. But only if she believed her.

"The one here yesterday?"

"Yes. Mister Davis. He's coming back."

Concern in her eyes, she bent over Hettie. "How do you know that?"

"Captain John warned me."

Her brow creased under the white cap. "You oughtn't to be talking to ghosts."

"He's talking to me."

"It's them devil's cherries muddling your mind, Miss."

"Maybe so. And maybe not." Hettie was desperate to be heard by one single living soul on this side of the divide. She blurted her ultimate threat. "You feared a warlock, Mrs. Jenner. The man in black is one."

Minnie sucked in her breath. "Great God Almighty. You hear that?"

"Hettie's talking gibberish, girl."

But fear edged Mrs. Jenner's voice, and she'd called her Hettie.

The whites showed in Minnie's wide eyes. "What if she knows? What if Captain John did come back to warn her? Just the sort of thing he might do."

A frown pulled at Mrs. Jenner's mouth, and she swept an all-encompassing hand around her. "Didn't we take precautions only yesterday? Didn't you sprinkle angelica water in every corner of this house? Ain't we got sticklewort, betony, and mountain ash boughs up over the doors and out in the stable? Blessed herbs everywhere. Ain't I plugged up the keyholes?"

"Yes, Ma'am. But this is a warlock." Minnie whispered the fearsome name.

Mrs. Jenner faltered. "We'll lay brooms in front of the doors. No witch will step over a broom to enter a house. Must go for a warlock too."

"What if it don't?" Minnie argued. "We kin sing hymns. Holy verse might scare him away."

A sense of urgency roared in Hettie like the

pounding surf. "For God's sake, singing will only attract him. Don't you understand? We've got to be silent and conceal ourselves."

They swiveled their heads at her. "What—now?" Mrs. Jenner asked.

Hettie struggled to sit. "We haven't a moment to lose. Get me to my feet and out of this room. It's the first place he'll look."

Mrs. Jenner's mouth opened in protest, but Hettie was having none of it. "I don't care if you think I'm stark raving mad, or poisoned out of my mind. Grab the poker. Let's go. I'm the one he wants, but he may fell any of you to get to me."

"Best do as she bids, Ma'am." Minnie looked ready to run for the hills.

For once, Mrs. Jenner didn't argue. Apparently, she wasn't taking any chances. "Come on, then. Give me a hand, Minnie. Right or wrong, it never hurts to be on our guard."

"Exactly so. We haven't been through a war for nothing," Hettie whispered. "Think of him as the enemy coming. Because he is."

They helped Hettie to her feet, clutching the blanket around her for warmth. She still wore the slippers and made her way across the chamber with their assistance. Action gave her a much needed rush of energy and fortitude.

She paused in the doorway. "I'm feeling a bit stronger. Leave me now, Minnie. Slip through the house and warn the others to conceal themselves."

"Alone?" Her voice squeaked.

"Get Maddie to help you."

"What of the old master?"

"Better let Mister Monroe sleep. He might shout out and worsen matters. Alert those in outbuildings. Tell your mama and Aunt Beulah to barricade the kitchen and hide above stairs with the little ones. Tell Jim to head to the stable. Stay in the back with him. Now go."

"At once, Miss." Minnie fled down the hall.

"Pray Captain Stuart reaches Thornton before this menace," Hettie whispered to Mrs. Jenner.

Her onion-laced breath tickled Hettie's ear. "Has Captain Stuart got power over the man in black?"

"Yes. But the captain may need help. As may we, if it comes to a fight."

"You think it will?"

Hettie battled to think. She mustn't let fear dictate her actions. "We cannot remain out of sight forever. If Mister Davis lights a lantern or torch, he can search room by room."

"There's the cellar."

"He may discover it. And us. We don't want to be trapped down there." She shuddered at the thought.

"A hidden door leads out into the yard," Mrs. Jenner confided.

"We'd have to scramble mighty fast if we're seen, or he'll be on us before we can escape. Even give chase into the yard. Some of us can't move that fast."

Mrs. Jenner hesitated before offering further disclosure. "It's a family secret, but a passage runs through Thornton. Miss Claire and Captain Stuart played there as young'uns."

"Do you know an entrance?"

"One opening's hid in the west parlor. I've never done more than peek in. Hung with cobwebs and pitch black, it is. Only them as knows the way can find it. Like a maze, and tight. You gotta bend low. Mightn't accommodate my girth."

"Or Ezekiel's rheumatism," Hettie reminded her. "We can't all scatter inside the walls like squirrels. We need something to stop him from entering the house."

"Like a spell? I recited an incantation for protection when we put the herbs around."

"I was thinking of a weapon."

Mrs. Jenner leaned in. "The captain left his musket and cartridge box behind, if a warlock can be shot."

Hettie lacked the strength to even lift a musket to her shoulder, let alone take aim, but Mrs. Jenner's stout arms could do the job. "Can you load and fire?"

"My late husband taught me. God rest him."

"Good. Get them, and stand guard downstairs. Secret yourself near the front door. Listen for hooves in the yard, then footfall. Don't fire unless you're certain it's not Captain Stuart. And not until he's too close to miss."

"What if he gets back up? Takes a bit to reload."

"Get me down the steps and I'll strike him with the poker. He'll not rise again."

"You?" Mrs. Jenner was slack jawed.

Hettie supposed it was time to tell her. "I'm part Cherokee. Uncle Ezra doesn't think I know. No one does. But I do. Deep down, I've always known. I'm also part Mulatto. Strong women, Mrs. Jenner. Not just ladies. And I've got the sight. The belladonna only made it more powerful. I'll hide in the shadows and keep watch with you."

She glimpsed the blur of blue and red regimentals in the firelight. "Captain John will help us, too."

****

Finally, the sleety rain ceased. Clouds sailed across a brilliant moon and stars shone in the gaps between them. Stuart could see a little distance ahead. Keeping Bryan on the road was all he'd managed before.

Nearly wet through despite his heavy coat, he was long past ready to be home by the fireside. An added misery, his stomach had growled for hours. If the kind cook at the Jones' residence hadn't been partial to Hettie and aware of her fondness for him, he'd be even hungrier. She'd skirted out to the yard as he'd prepared to mount, and thrust a hunk of bread smeared with butter and molasses, and a mug of ale into his hand. He'd fed half to Bryan, including the brew.

The faithful horse trudged on. But trudged was the word. After such a long day, he couldn't ask more of Bryan, and the thin crust of ice scattered on the rutted road made riding at any speed dangerous.

At this rate, he'd not see Thornton Hall until the wee hours. That shouldn't matter so much. He was accustomed to hardship, having endured plenty during the war. Something more than longing for comfort and a return to Hettie drove him on.

Uneasiness nagged at him. Was he followed? He'd seen no one, apart from the lights in isolated farmsteads, since riding beyond the outskirts of town. He'd heard nothing to indicate another presence. The wind could've drowned out anyone in pursuit, until recently. He didn't need to hear for that unnerving sensation of being watched to ripple the hair at his nape.

Did the wolf trail him on silent paws? If so, was that a good or bad thing? If not for the notion Hettie had planted in his mind of an animal guide, he'd never even entertain the possibility of a wolf as a positive addition.

Then he detected it—the drum of approaching hooves. Coming up behind him faster now. The rider must've waited for the moon to break through. He chanced his mount slipping on the icy crust, but didn't seem to care.

It mightn't be sinister, Stuart reasoned with himself; it wasn't out of the question that this was an innocuous rider going about his business. But at this hour, on such a wretched night? Too late for a social call, and town was the other way. He might stop at *Person's Ordinary*, Stuart supposed.

Stronger and stronger, the impression grew in him that this was the infamous Mister Davis. His heart raced as the horse and rider neared. They were almost upon him.

Should he turn and fire? Vision was limited. If he was mistaken, he didn't want to fell a harmless soul.

Too late to turn. Without a greeting or apology, the horseman thundered past, bumping Bryan's flank, forcing them off the road. Again, Stuart was glad for the gelding's steady temperament. Another horse might have spooked or reared. Black coat flapping, the mysterious rider galloped on as if Stuart and his horse were invisible.

Stuart didn't know if he was more enraged or alarmed. He'd expected a challenge, the glint of moonlight on a pistol barrel, or the blade of a sword, and he'd been left untouched.

The truth came to him with horrifying clarity— Mister Davis was headed for Thornton Hall and Hettie. Dear God. They didn't stand a chance.

Stuart cast caution to the wind and urged Bryan into action. "Come on, boy! Run as if Hettie's life depends on it." Most likely, it did.

The gelding seemed to sense the dire need. Years of training during arduous battle campaigns had given Bryan the endurance to race after the disappearing rider.

Mister Davis had the benefit of a fresh horse that hadn't already made this journey once today. And by the looks of it, his mount was fast. But for all his advantage, Davis lacked one vital piece of knowledge that Stuart possessed. He was in ignorance of the shortcut to Thornton Hall, which was used only in emergencies to guard its existence, and then, only by the Monroe family.

Now was the time. And Bryan knew the way.

Chapter Thirteen

A musket report shattered the night. Stuart's chest hammered like an anvil striking sparks. Praying Hettie wasn't on the receiving end of that blast, he leaned over Bryan's neck, whispering encouragement in his ear. The gelding found a last burst of energy and flattened out in a dead run on the final length of the lane at Thornton Hall.

They clattered into the yard. The horse lost his footing on the icy cobbles and careened sideways, nearly going down. Stuart hung on as Bryan scrambled, finally recovering his balance. Bryan's sides heaved, and even in the cold, a thin sheen of sweat glazed his coat. The froth around the bit sent a pang through Stuart. The horse needed care, but first—

Where was Hettie? Darkness made it difficult to discern shapes. Faint light from the open door of the house and the bright moon above shed some clarity.

What in the world?

The man in the black cloak reeled in the yard, clutching his shoulder. Apparently, shot by Mrs. Jenner who'd been thrown against the door frame from the force of firing what had to be Stuart's musket. She still grasped the smoking gun.

The wounded man—it must be Mister Davis—lurched onto the crusted stones and went down on one knee. Groans comingled with snarls. "Damn you, woman! You fire on all visitors?"

Her reply was gibberish, like some sort of incantation.

More astonishing than Mrs. Jenner's rant, the sight of Hettie rushing at Davis with a poker. She lifted tremulous arms and brought the improvised weapon down onto his howling head. Stuart hadn't thought she possessed the strength or the nerve. Throwing himself from the saddle, he pulled the pistol from his boot, and tore at Davis.

Not swiftly enough.

The perpetrator of evil wasn't as disabled as he'd hoped by the shot or the blow. Snaking out his good arm, Davis seized Hettie by the ankles. She swung at him with the poker, but he snagged the weapon and threw it aside. Nothing remained for her defense when he pulled a knife from beneath his cloak with the injured limb. In a flash he was on his feet, Hettie in his grasp, and the knife at her throat. Her cry pierced Stuart through the heart.

"Come any nearer and I'll cut her!" Davis dragged Hettie back.

Stuart froze.

Mrs. Jenner reloaded, drawing the man's ire.

"Drop that musket, woman!"

She reluctantly laid it down and shook a broom at him menacingly. Why it was lying on the doorstep, Stuart couldn't surmise. Again, the gibberish flowed from the housekeeper.

"I don't know what in hell you're railing about, you crazed bitch, but shut your mouth!"

While Davis cursed Mrs. Jenner, Stuart concealed the pistol beneath his coat. He couldn't shoot the devil, though, without the risk of hitting Hettie.

"Let her go or it'll be the worse for you, Davis!" he shouted, clueing him in that he knew his name.

Blood running down his arm and hand, Davis waved the knife. "Fancy you're clever, do you, Captain Monroe?"

"Clever enough not to be bleeding to death—shot by the housekeeper!" Stuart flung back.

"Ain't dead yet!"

"Soon enough, if you don't stop the spill." But not as fast as Stuart needed.

Hettie wore only her shift and slippers. Her blanket had slid to the cobbles, and she shivered violently. Apart from the threat to her life from the wicked blade, immediate warmth was imperative.

Stuart was forced to bargain. "What do you want, Davis?"

"You know damn well! Tell me where it's buried or I slit her throat!"

"You're in no shape to dig. Wouldn't you rather warm yourself by the fire, let us tend that wound. You can go at first light with all the information you require."

"Think I'm thick in the head? Stop your nonsense!" Davis pricked Hettie with the point of the blade so she cried out. "The next cut will count!"

Stuart furiously weighed whether the scoundrel's head was high enough above hers to risk the shot—he was a superior marksman—but got no farther. A black form sprang snarling from the shadows. He never saw the wolf coming until the animal slammed into Davis. Neither did he. Caught off guard, Davis hurled Hettie aside to fight for his life. She fell to the cobbles.

"Bloody hell!" His formerly uninjured arm in the beast's jaws, he writhed bellowing on the ground. Only his coat sleeve and glove stood between him and those gnashing teeth.

He slashed wildly with the knife. The infuriated beast tore the blade from his hand. It clinked on the stones.

Stuart left Davis to the wolf and raced to Hettie. She tried shakily to rise. He stuck the pistol back into his boot and bent over her.

"I've got you, sweetheart." Scooping her up, he wrapped the blanket around her. It was damp from the icy rain. Better than nothing, though.

He swept her into the house. Blood trickled down her neck from the nick at her throat, though some of the stains covering her originated with Davis. She was bruised, scraped, chilled to the bone, and exhausted from her ordeal on top of the recent poisoning, but otherwise unharmed.

Once more, Mrs. Jenner grasped the musket. "I'll shoot that murderous beast, Captain. You deal with the warlock."

"Wait." Stuart set Hettie in a chair out of harm's way and spun around. He threw out an arm to block Mrs. Jenner's aim as she fired at their defender. "The creature's protecting us! Let it be."

Her shot burst harmlessly overhead. The wolf turned on its heels and vanished into the night as swiftly as it had come. Davis clambered to his feet. He staggered to his waiting mount and heaved himself up into the saddle. Before Stuart got off a volley, the horse galloped away.

"Damn. He's gone."

"Sorry, Captain," Mrs. Jenner offered.

Too late now. Stuart waved her aside. He bent back to Hettie, where he'd ungentlemanly deposited her.

Sliding his arms beneath her, he lifted his precious burden and cradled her against him. "Thank God, you're safe."

"And your father. Thank him too," she added, between chattering lips.

Mrs. Jenner propped the musket against the wall. "Claims she sees him. Says he speaks to her."

"I know." Stuart couldn't not love Hettie because she was strange. And if any woman needed him, it was Hettie.

Brushing down her skirts, Mrs. Jenner continued. "She says Captain John told her that demon was on his way here."

"Fortuitous, indeed. But let's keep this between ourselves. We don't want Miss Fairfax to become the talk of the town."

The housekeeper nodded and tucked stray auburn tendrils beneath her cap. "Course not. I'll tell Minnie to watch her mouth. Forgive my actions regarding the wolf, Captain. I didn't know you was partial to the creature."

"Neither did I, until that moment. He seems to have taken a fancy to us."

"Like a dog, you mean?"

"I suppose." Stuart glanced past Mrs. Jenner and swiveled his head. Not a soul in sight. He'd expected a huddled gathering. "Where is everyone?"

"Hiding. Miss Fairfax's idea, what with the warlock coming."

He eyed her in bemusement. "Wise. Tell them they

may venture forth now. Bring hot water, brandy, and help me tend to her. Likely Jim is already seeing to Bryan."

"Yes, sir. He was hid back in the stable. I'll fetch what you need for Miss Fairfax." She ducked her head and scurried off, skirts flying.

Stuart carried Hettie down the hall toward the staircase. The floor echoed under his boots. "Poor lady. I'll bear you to your chamber."

"I could walk, if you lend me your arm."

"I prefer you in them. Tell me, what's all this about a warlock? And what was Mrs. Jenner jabbering?"

Her lips curved in a faint smile. "Spells—to keep him out of the house."

"So, Davis is the warlock?"

"I might have led her to believe that to enlist her aid."

"Ah." Stuart was relieved Hettie didn't seem to hold this belief. She was strange enough. "What of you?"

Her eyes wore a hunted look. "After being attacked by him, twice now, I'm convinced he's evil. And he'll be back."

Stuart paused, tightening his hold on her. "I swear to double my efforts in your defense. There's something you ought to know. Davis is a former employee of your Cousin Jonas."

She tensed in his grasp. "*Former*?"

"Your relations knew nothing of his vile intentions."

Breath escaped her in a rush, and she relaxed visibly.

He continued. "Another thing that may mean

nothing to you, but is crucial. Thomas Vaughan is back in business and residing with your uncle. I believe Davis is in his hire."

She studied Stuart knowingly. "The second man."

"What?"

"There were two men in the graveyard. Two," she repeated, as she had the previous evening. "One much larger than the other."

"Right. I suspected that snake, Thomas Vaughan."

A wounded look touched her eyes. "You never said."

"I had to be certain first. Davis may no longer be employed by your family, but Mister Vaughan still pulls his strings. And your uncle's. Has him under his thumb."

"Not for long. We'll bring Mister Vaughan down," she said faintly.

Hettie didn't appear strong enough to lift a cup of tea. "After you're up and about, we'll contrive a plan together."

Her eyes fluttered and drifted shut. "Your father will help."

Would she ever cease to count on him? Stuart was right here; it was bizarre to resent her reliance on his ghostly father, even if he was only a hallucination.

It was true, though, Stuart had arrived late on the scene. If Hettie hadn't been forewarned, if the wolf hadn't come, matters might have been otherwise. Still, he wanted to be the one she sought for protection, not his father's spirit. There must be some way to elevate himself in her eyes. He intended to find it.

"Hettie?" He gently nudged her.

She blinked sleepily at him.

"Thought you ought to know. We're betrothed."

"Wait—what?"

If he'd announced their nuptials were to take place first thing after breakfast, she could hardly have appeared more shocked. And dazed. She couldn't absorb another thing in her present state.

Stuart smiled. "I'll explain tomorrow. You're all in."

He would walk the hero's path, and she would see there were two Captain Monroes...and the second one still lived and adored her.

Chapter Fourteen

Only invalids and the indolent slumbered the day away. Hettie was resolved to be neither, and badly wanted to visit with Stuart—it seemed to her that they had some important matter to discuss—but heaviness weighed her like the heated stone tucked at her feet near the end of the bed.

Hettie. His summons had the softness of snow, the strength of steel.

She stirred groggily. Was it Captain John, or did some other call her? Who else would glide into her chamber?

Wake up.

I'm trying, she protested.

Try harder.

Mrs. Jenner had dosed her with brandy. and God only knows what else, a sleeping potion, maybe. She'd left Hettie to slumber in a fresh shift, her body cleansed of blood stains, hers and that fiend's, Mister Davis. Which Hettie appreciated, but she remembered nothing after that, and not a great deal before, except the threat from Davis, Stuart's arrival, and the black wolf springing from the shadows.

You sent the wolf, Captain John?

Yes. Wake now. Danger lurks.

Didn't it always? She floundered, as though in a bog, beneath the thick blankets Mrs. Jenner had generously layered over her. Too many. A smothering heap.

Why was it so difficult to rouse herself?

You sleep too heavily. Open your eyes.

You are damnably pushy for a ghost.

Ladies do not swear.

And lecturing, she shot back.

You are like a daughter to me, like my Claire.

Touched by the tribute, Hettie struggled to do as he bid.

Mist greeted the drowsy gaze she slanted through slitted eyes at the chamber window. Impossible to gauge the hour by the sun when there was none. But the day must be far advanced. Mrs. Jenner may have returned to see if her heart still beat. If it didn't, the fault was that woman's.

She shifted her head to the side. Captain John sat in the armchair by her bed. His greenish gaze held hers, steady, unblinking. Like a cat's.

I must show you something.

Was she still dreaming, had the belladonna exerted itself again, or was he actually here? Reality had become terribly convoluted. She would indeed be fortunate if Stuart didn't shut her away in an insane asylum, given the apparitions she heard and saw.

Captain John didn't answer or comment. Rather, he beckoned. *Look.*

Mist followed on the heels of his directive. White cloudiness pervaded the room, as though the windows were wide open and sea fog rolled in, only they were not on the coast. Thicker and thicker the shroud grew, until she could scarcely see him, or the trees.

Why are trees in my chamber?

Remember the cemetery, he prompted.

Back her thoughts swirled with the fog, and she was there again in the graveyard, waiting for Stuart. Before the two men arrived with their threats.

A figure appeared in the veil, Captain John gesturing her to follow. He turned. The blue and red of his uniform, the only color in the smokiness cloaking the cemetery.

She slipped noiselessly after him. All was silent, muffled. *Where are you going?*

No answer. He glided ahead, his boots leaving no tracks. She hastened behind.

He stopped beside the Monroe family plot outlined by an iron fence. Then he was inside the private enclosure, standing beside a grave. His grave. He waved her closer, his face white in the mist.

See what's buried here.

The thought of unearthing anything or anyone in this sacred site, made her recoil. Nor did she wish to view whatever he wanted her to see.

No. Shaking her head, she backed away, or tried. But couldn't put distance between herself and the grave.

Wait. It wasn't a suggestion on his part.

Rooted in place, she had no choice other than to look on.

A breeze sprang up from nowhere. Dry leaves spun away in the whirlwind. The tempest left her untouched, her hair unruffled. She felt no chill. Nothing, except wonder and trepidation.

With a slicing motion of his gloved hand above the grave, Captain John parted the mound of earth beside the headstone, like an invisible blade cutting cake. Like magic. He needed no shovel. Deeper and deeper, the fissure in the ground widened until a wooden coffin was exposed six feet below.

She especially didn't want to view the remains inside.

Her companion paid her no heed. With no apparent effort on his part, the lid slowly lifted as if by invisible ropes.

Despite her revulsion, she couldn't keep her eyes from exploring what lay inside the spine-chilling box. Silver bowls, pitchers, plates, vessels, spoons, knifes, arm bands, and ornate boxes for holding whatever the owner desired of the appropriate size, gold rings and necklaces greeted her inspection. Other jewels dangled from ribbons to be worn around the neck or clustered in teardrops for earrings. All were collected in and cushioned by a large coverlet. Gilded embroidery covered the sumptuous cloth.

The treasure she'd heard of was truly here and must be worth a fortune. She lifted her gaze to Captain John's. *Why show it to me?*

There. He motioned further down in the coffin.

She peered closely, gasping when she spied the hand. A human hand. Mostly bone, now. Chills ran through her. A body was buried beneath the valuables.

She lifted her horrified gaze. *Is that you?*

No. My remains rest in Bruton Parish.

Who, then? What unfortunate soul is this?

Regret touched his eyes. *A Tory who refused to give way.*

Did you kill him?

No. One in our party ran him through. Now, all in our party are dead.

She shuddered and glanced back down at the gleaming accumulation. An image of the fallen man appeared in her mind. *Did you know he lay here?*

Not while I clung to life.

Are these his belongings?

Some. Not all. Yet he claims all.

Her horror doubled, and she returned her gaze to the captain's. *His spirit is still present, isn't it?*

It is. This wealth, this man, must remain undisturbed.

Afraid to glance down again, she kept her eyes on Captain John. *He guards this trove?*

And cursed it. He is powerful.

She inhaled. *Dear God.*

Yes.

She was compelled to know his identity. *Please tell me his name.*

Manley Collins. Captain John spoke in the barest whisper. *Have care when you utter it. Do not waken the curse.*

I will—I mean won't waken it—him. She blathered in fear.

Now wake up, Hettie!

His brusque command jerked her from the foggy graveyard.

She opened her eyes to find herself in bed and Abigail Smith bent over her—the young woman's face twisted in a murderous mask. The slender arms raised above Hettie clutched a heavy vase she was about to bring down on her skull.

"No!" Shrieking, she threw her hands up to shield her head.

"Hettie! It's all right. I'm here." A firm grasp on

her shoulders accompanied Stuart's voice.

His face took shape, concern creasing his eyes. He sat on the edge of her bed. No Abigail. No mist. Late day sunlight streamed past the window. "What's happening?"

"You were dreaming, sweetheart."

But it was so much more than that. *Wasn't it?*

She looked around wildly for the culprit. "I saw her in here, Stuart."

"Who?"

"Miss Smith. Trying to kill me."

"Poor lady. I'm not surprised you fear that after all you've endured. But Miss Smith has been with Grandfather, or assisting in the kitchen today." He gestured at Minnie, who approached Hettie timidly. "Minnie or Maddie stayed with you. Mrs. Jenner tells me she trotted in and out."

Tears blurred Hettie's vision. "Am I losing my mind?"

"No, dearest. Mrs. Jenner confessed to giving you laudanum with brandy in the night, thinking to soothe you after your fright. The dose made you sleep like the dead. I've scolded her sternly. She's heartily penitent."

The regret in Stuart's greenish gaze was like his father's, who'd warned Hettie she slept too deeply. "We've all tried to waken you."

Was that who she'd heard? She'd swear it was Captain John. "How long have you been with me?"

"For the past hour."

"Was it misty earlier?"

"No. Sunny all day." Stuart leaned in, and smoothed her cheek. "I'm sorry you're so confused. You've had entirely too much of many things lately.

Except reassurance. I fear I have failed you again, Hettie."

She lifted her hand to his face and lightly traced his clean shaven chin. "The fault is not yours."

"But I should have been by your side today, instead of out riding all hours."

"Not still seeking the wolf, are you?"

He shook his head. "The creature comes in his own way, and means us no harm, it would seem. With Jim's help, I've thrown myself into training La Belle for the big race your uncle's sponsoring next week."

She regarded him for a long moment. "Likely, that is when Davis will strike next."

"Perhaps." A cunning expression displaced the remorse in Stuart's eyes. "And perhaps, I'll strike first. I mean to be ready and win that purse."

His confidence was contagious. A flicker of newfound courage took flame in her. "You just might prevail on both counts, sir."

"I have triumphed over worse, Miss." He flashed her a dazzling smile, and swept his hand at the fireplace. "If you are inclined to dine together, I should be delighted to have supper with you before the hearth, whenever you have completed your toilette and are ready for the evening."

"Nothing would please me more."

"Excellent. Then I shall leave you to your preparations and see you anon."

Chest fluttering, she smiled in anticipation. "As soon as may be."

He rose to his feet and bowed with a flourish worthy of a duke. "Until then."

Minnie nodded her capped head and ushered him

from the chamber. "Shall I fetch hot water, Miss?"

"Yes, do. And send Maddie to arrange my hair." Hettie was determined to enjoy the evening she'd been robbed of before.

Tales of the treasure and its ghostly guardian must wait. Stuart wouldn't believe her, anyway, and Hettie couldn't blame him after all the potions she'd been given. She didn't know what to believe herself. Only that a dark presence hovered over that grave.

She couldn't shake the name Manley Collins from her mind. Then she remembered. Some members of the Collins family had associations with witchcraft.

Mayhap this was the warlock Mrs. Jenner had unwittingly gone on about. The real one, assuming Hettie believed in such beings. Whether she did or didn't, she was doing her utmost to keep Stuart away from the cemetery and that grave.

The whole business filled her with foreboding. No good could come of it. Only death.

Hadn't Captain John said as much?

Even if he spoke to her through dreams and hallucinations, she was persuaded his message rang true. Warnings from beyond were rare and of the utmost importance.

Heed it, they must. To disregard such a portentous caution spelled doom.

Chapter Fifteen

At last, the gods smiled on Stuart, and he smiled at the vision seated across the table from him before the cheery crackle of flames. Firelight played over Hettie's face and the responsive curve at her mouth. She'd pinkened her cheeks with a little rouge. Her lips needed none, but she'd reddened them. The effect was pleasing, and he approved the dusting of powder on her neck and bosom, smelling divinely of violets.

"How enchanting you are this evening, Miss Fairfax."

She inclined her head with the innate elegance she possessed. "Most kind. You are exceedingly handsome, sir."

"I'm not a patch on your looks."

"*Au contraire*, Captain."

He chuckled. "This hardened soldier shall not make comparisons of beauty with the exquisite creature before him."

"If you insist."

"Heartily." He wanted to kiss those fair lips by way of reply. Instead, he gloried in the sight that was Hettie.

The glow from the hearth shone on the lustrous black hair piled on her head, and burnished the greenish-gold taffeta gracing her slender figure. The gown, a gift from her doting uncle, was delivered by coach this afternoon. Even Jonas, who abhorred costly display, had sent the apricot silk stole draped over her shoulders. His way of apologizing for inadvertently hiring the man who'd tried to poison her and held a blade to her throat.

Stuart gestured at the costly shawl, well beyond his own meager means to give her. "Most generous of Jonas. A boon to know he isn't devoid of sentiment for his cousin."

She grimaced good-naturedly. "He's an odd duck, but not without all awareness of his relations. He might need us at some point."

"Or you, him. Though I pray that day never comes." His somber reflection an unintentional addition to the evening.

Her eyes mirrored his gravity. "As do I."

Stuart was resolved to be the one to care for her. That he already cherished her was undeniable. He raised a glass. "Enough solemnity. A toast to your good health, dear lady."

She lifted a goblet of amber fluid. "And yours, sir."

"Such joy to have the pleasure of your company." He breathed her name. "Hettie."

The smile she rewarded him with was wealth beyond measure. Nothing in this world could purchase that radiance.

Mrs. Jenner blew into the room bearing a tray of small seed cakes, dusted with cinnamon. She added this rich dessert to the burgeoning spread laid out on the small table, then hovered like a mother anxious for the welfare of her offspring.

"Everything to yer liking, Captain, Miss Fairfax?"

He raised a glass. "Excellent."

"'Tis appetizing in sight and scent, Mrs. Jenner."

Hettie articulated what the housekeeper wanted to hear.

Mrs. Jenner beamed at the praise and opportunity to atone for her error in overdosing the poor lady. "I'll pass on yer compliments to Sally and the girls." Drying her hands on her apron, she stood ready to attend to their every whim.

What Stuart truly wanted was no one in attendance. What bliss to have Hettie to himself for the span of several hours.

The floral fragrance wafting from her blended with the delectable aroma of steaming chicken baked in pastry, spicy currant pudding, and sweetened, stewed persimmons gathered from the woods. The frothy pitcher of ale, bottles of brandy, assorted wines, and cider could quench the thirst of half a dozen stout men, let alone one couple bent on romance. Mrs. Jenner had raided the cellar.

She brought her plump hands together in a resounding clap. "Time for celebration."

"Indeed." Stuart could scarcely believe his good fortune. After all Hettie had endured, she was still with him.

Folk often died from maladies and injury, particularly during the war. Many of his friends were gone, and his father. Though, in regards to the late captain, dead and gone weren't necessarily the same thing. He hoped as Hettie recovered, they might put his father to rest.

More—he wished nothing, not even the table, stood between them, that they lounged together on her bed in their night attire, or less, supping from plates. But proper etiquette must be observed. It was enough they dined together in such an intimate site as her chamber. Still, he couldn't resist hinting at his deeper desire, and winked at her.

Soft rose suffused her face, in addition to the rouge. She hadn't completely masked the bruise on one cheek, but she appeared far better than he'd seen her in days. She dropped her eyes demurely, dark lashes sweeping her cheek, then raised them to meet his bold gaze.

Fire shot through him at the invitation in her long glance. He quelled the urge to catch her in his arms. Just.

Exerting all his willpower, he bore with Mrs. Jenner as she served them, glad to see Hettie's appetite whetted. She ate most of what the enthusiastic housekeeper ladled onto her plate, and sipped willingly from the crystal glass.

Perhaps the enforced rest from laudanum had done her some good after all, or she was gaining strength. Truth be told, she appeared restored enough to dine downstairs, but he coveted an evening apart from the others and had ordered no intrusions, barring an emergency. Or attack.

At times like this, he wished he had soldiers to post on guard. Brinkley would be a boon. Stuart felt like a one man army. No surprise, given the assault he and this household had come under. That scoundrel, Davis, and Thomas Vaughan had much to answer for. And he was determined that they would.

Unaware of his internal tirade, Hettie blotted her lips on snowy linen. "A welcome repast, Mrs. Jenner."

The housekeeper smiled broadly and passed round the seed cakes. Hettie nibbled daintily. Clearly, she'd had sufficient. Before the evening fled and she tired,

Stuart badly wanted to be with her, unfettered by watchful eyes.

"Mrs. Jenner, if you will allow us a moment, I should like to discuss our upcoming nuptials with my intended."

The housekeeper's jaw dropped and she stared from him to the equally astonished Hettie. Neither woman spoke a word.

He smiled. "Both of you are struck mute. What an extraordinary state of affairs."

Mrs. Jenner ducked her head. "Gracious, Captain. Ain't you the dark horse? Will you let a body know when the wedding's to be?"

"Certainly. Sometime following the ball Ezra Jones is holding in our honor."

Hettie gaped at him. "My uncle is hosting a ball for us?"

Stuart fingered his chin. "Yes. We should return the favor with a dinner party. Nothing large, Mister Ezra and Jonas Jones, and a few other guests. Mrs. Jenner, take note."

She bobbed her head, hanging on his every word. "Yes, sir."

"Assuming I gain Ezra's blessing to proceed with the wedding as planned," he added, with forced nonchalance.

Mrs. Jenner leaned in closer. "How you gonna do that?"

"Win the horse race, and reduce my debt. I'm not to rely on Miss Fairfax's inheritance to cover my obligations."

Hettie stiffened. "I didn't realize you were aware of that."

"Nor was I, until your uncle accused me of plotting to wed you for your bequest."

"He would, too, old Ezra," Mrs. Jenner assented.

Stuart waved her aside. "You shall learn all you need directly. Now, off with you."

She sidled, crabwise, toward the door, lest she miss another juicy tidbit. "And shut it behind you," he directed. It clicked with her reluctant parting.

"At last." His gaze on Hettie, he stood and stretched. She eyed him uncertainly. "Will you allow me to pull my chair alongside yours, sweetheart?"

"Certainly. 'Tis your home, sir."

"Soon to be yours, too, I hope."

He shifted the armchair around the table, pushed the furnishing and supper leftovers back toward the wall, and lowered himself into the upholstered depths. "Now, we are more comfortably settled."

Hettie frowned at him. "Will you speak plainly? Tell me when we became engaged to marry?"

"I've scarcely had the opportunity to discuss the matter with you, but had every intention."

"That's a mercy, else I might find myself reciting my vows on the morrow."

He smiled sheepishly. "Not quite that soon. When I informed your uncle of the attempted poisoning, he insisted I return you as soon as possible. I was loathe to relinquish your presence. What would Thornton Hall be without you?"

The tension he'd sensed in Hettie lessened. She pursed lips still tinged crimson, then parted them. "I allow, I have no wish to leave Thornton. So, you announced your intention then?"

"I did. Also your acceptance, which you have not

yet granted."

"You, sir, have not yet made a formal request."

"Which I shall promptly amend." Reaching down, he clasped her smaller hand, fisted in her lap, and entwined his fingers with hers. "Dearest Hettie, it is my fervent wish that you will accept my proposal to be my wife. My heart is yours. I vow to do all within my power to protect and provide for you."

Her eyes glistened in the orange glow from the hearth. "You have no notion how I have longed to hear those words."

His heart thudded. "Then you accept?"

"How can I refuse? And yet, I fear I ought."

Baffled, he bent toward her. "Why so?"

"As I said before, to spare you from being paired with one who may be regarded as peculiar by the community."

"I care nothing for that."

"I may be a noose around your neck," she warned.

"Nae. Your kind heart and beauty will win over all but the hardest hearts. These cold souls are not worthy to breathe the same air as you, my dearest."

An unladylike sniff escaped her. Regaining her hand, she drew a handkerchief from her bodice and blotted her eyes and nose. "You are tenderness itself. I always knew you would be a worthy husband because of your kindness to Claire when she wed a British dragoon officer. Many Patriots would have cast her aside. Not you. And your devotion to your poor mother and addled grandfather shows your true character."

Her emotional tribute touched Stuart more than he could say. His own eyes misted. "It hasn't been easy."

She wadded the linen in her hand. "No. But you are

faithful. The question is, will you still bear the devotion you avow for me now, after I'm your wife?"

"I swear it by all that's sacred."

"What of the spirits?"

He raised a hand to halt the inevitable protest, and ran his fingers along the tresses cascading from the mound on her head. "If you have visitations from the departed, then so be it. Though I pray you will not have the need."

"Best pray they haven't the need for me. I do not seek them out. 'Tis quite the reverse."

"However it is, I shall bear with you." Mindful of her bruise, he cupped her face in his hands. "Give me the chance to prove myself."

Hesitancy crossed her gaze.

"What still troubles you?"

"You said winning the race would decrease your debt, not clear it. How can you fulfill all your obligations?"

"There is only one other way I know of, and that is to dig for the treasure my father left behind."

She paled. "Dear God, Stuart. 'Tis cursed, I tell you, by the damned."

"How can you know?"

"I saw this very day. Your father showed me."

"While you slumbered in an unnatural sleep, in a laudanum induced dream?"

"It was as real as you are now." Her voice quavered.

"Dreams can seem so," he soothed. "And you may still suffer the effects of belladonna. Didn't Ezekiel say these could last for days?"

She made no denial. Neither did she appear

persuaded.

"Dear lady, I have no desire to dig among the dead. And know I'm watched. I am aware of the danger from Davis, likely Thomas Vaughan as well."

"And the curse," she murmured.

"I have more concern for what the living may do, than spirits. Trust me to have every care, if I do approach that cemetery again."

"I beg you to forego this expedition."

He tempered exasperation with patience, a hard-won virtue from contending with difficult family members. And realized he would need an abundance of it with Hettie. "If another opportunity presents itself, I will act. Our neighbor, Mister Ellis, has offered to purchase much of our crop land and my best horses, leaving the house and a few acres."

She inhaled sharply. "You mustn't sell your birthright."

"I have refused him, but the offer stands. My debts must be cleared, and not only to gratify your uncle."

Reaching a hand to his shoulder, she pleaded. "Surpass all contenders in the race. Some unforeseen boon may follow."

"If La Belle wins, she and her filly gain in value. But I'm averse to selling either and forfeiting their line."

She shook her head. "I should hate you to part with them and lose all future foals. Still, promise me you will wait and consider what may be done before undertaking the dig."

"I shall wait as long as may be. But December is on us. Can snow be far behind? Harsh weather will impede a dig, when it must be done in haste and stealth.

Those at Thornton Hall will find winter difficult to endure with dwindling supplies. Merchants refuse to extend my credit to purchase provisions."

The corners of her mouth pulled down. "'Tis mean of them, after all you sacrificed for your country."

"No use gnashing my teeth over it. And contemplating next year's harvest does nothing to compensate us now."

Her eyes implored him. "Even so, I urge caution in venturing back to that cemetery. I've seen what you have not."

"In dreams, sweetheart. Have you no faith in me?"

"Yes. Also much apprehension regarding others. Any word of Davis?"

"Your uncle has ordered a manhunt for him. I suspect that fox is holed up while he mends."

She narrowed her gaze. "Uncle Ezra will not abandon the search. Davis may yet be dragged from his den. Then we shall see how arrogant he is with the noose dangled before him, the black-hearted devil."

Stuart gave a low whistle. "That's the spirit. Fight back as you did last night, Hettie. Don't allow fear to rule you."

"Brave words, sir. The deed is far harder."

"I know. Have I not faced innumerable battles?"

"As have I of late," she reminded him.

"To my utter regret. I swear to make every effort toward your protection."

She firmed her chin. "You cannot defend me from all. I must also do battle in my own way."

"A point I am forced to concede." He took her hand in his. "Dearest Hettie, will you agree to face what lies before us together, as man and wife?"

Eyes brimming, she nodded. "I will, so help me God."

"May God help us both." So exultant he could crow, he enfolded her in his arms. "We have an accord. And a Yuletide wedding in little more than three weeks' time."

"So soon. Will Uncle Ezra allow you to post the banns?"

"Whether he will or he won't, I shall. And fulfill my side of the bargain. Let him plan his ball, I will be ready."

Any protest she might make as to the manner of resolving his debt was muffled when he sealed their agreement with a kiss. The crackle and hiss of kindling displaced speech as he covered her soft lips, savoring every moment his heated mouth pressed hers. She tasted of wine and seed cakes, her honeyed lips inviting beyond human resistance.

With herculean effort, he drew back. "Thank you for granting my deepest wish and saying yes."

"I pray you do not regret your choice."

"Cease talk of regret. Sweetheart, I adore you. Let us rejoice, not lament."

Doubt warred with the love sparkling in Hettie's eyes. If he couldn't articulate his ardor so she believed him, maybe he could show her. Every sinew of his being yearned to try.

Reclaiming her mouth, he rose, lifting her with him as he did. Clasping her in his arms, he paused in the center of the room, and poured his soul into that kiss. She circled her arms around his neck, kissing him back between sighs.

Such sweet exhalations. He could never give

enough, and savored everything she gave in turn.

The war had been long, and women few; the flame they lit in him soon quenched. Hettie sent fire rushing through him like wind in dry grass. Heat seared him in wanting waves. He mustn't press her for more than she could give, so soon after her stirrings of strength, but he was famished.

Panting for breath, he buried his face in her neck, and carried her to the bed. He laid her gently on the coverlet and stretched beside her, as he'd longed to do. "Soon, my dearest, we shall sleep together lawfully as man and wife."

She nestled against him with her head in the crook of his elbow. "Stuart, stay with me tonight."

He lurched, so violent was his desire. And caught himself before he crushed her to him. Staying his hand, he lightly stroked her hair.

"I would love nothing more in this world, but cannot tarnish your name, sweet lady. Or endanger your health. You have not yet fully recovered. I should not even be alone with you now."

"My qualms are not of you, dearest, but *for you*. Of what marriage to me may mean, of what may happen if you come to harm gaining my uncle's approval. When I reach two and twenty, the inheritance is mine to use as I choose. Not his. I choose to help you with your debt, to restore Thornton Hall."

"Your declaration stirs me more than I can say, sweetheart. And I love you all the more for it. I will allow you to help restore Thornton, but must clear my debt myself. Else, I forfeit my honor."

She raised up on one elbow, curling her hand at his cheek. "Damn your honor, if it risks your life."

He arched an eyebrow at her in mock censure. "Strong speech, my darling."

"Forgive me. Uncle Ezra swears continually. His curses echo in my mind."

Stuart smiled. "I admire your pluck. Fan the flames, Hettie. You are stronger than you know. Most would lie dead from what you've endured, yet here you are in my arms."

"And here I shall remain."

"Not tonight, my love." With the greatest reluctance, he extricated himself.

To his surprise, she clasped his shoulder and pulled him back down beside her. "Stay yet awhile. It can do no harm to taste my lips once more."

"No? Mrs. Jenner may have her ear at the keyhole."

"She plugged them up to keep out the witches."

Laughing, Stuart drew Hettie back into his embrace. "If you think our being together in here is a secret from the household, you are as naïve as Claire when she stayed the night in Vaughan's chamber. She thought me too fuddled with drink to know what transpired between them."

Hettie explored him with widened eyes. "What did you do?"

"More important, is what I did *not* do. Thrash him, and reprimand her severely."

"Quite forbearing of you."

He shrugged. "Vaughan had me under house arrest at the time, so rather challenging to carry out my threats. Besides, Claire loved him and he gave us every assurance of his intention to wed her. Which he did at his first opportunity."

"You must miss your sister terribly. You were so close."

"I do, but she's sublimely happy with Vaughan in England. And I confess, their assistance with my mother and younger brother is most welcome."

"And now you wish to take on another miscreant." A teasing light warmed Hettie's eyes.

"I would hardly term you a mischief-maker. Well, perhaps a little, as you tempt me so." Rolling over with her in his arms, he covered her smiling lips with his. "One more moment, and then I must depart," he whispered against her mouth.

"Before you bid me goodnight, sir, consider this. If you revisit the cemetery, I shall be by your side."

Her defiant whisper stunned him. "No, Ma'am, you are not accompanying me to the graveyard if and when I go."

Chapter Sixteen

At long last! Freedom! Hettie exploded out the front door.

Jerking up her skirts, she ran down the steps of Thornton Hall. How glorious to be free from the confines of her chamber, from the house. She was so exhilarated she could fly.

After weeks of illness—months, since she'd first contracted the fever—Ezekiel had declared her fit enough to resume her life, within reason. But she was finished with caution. Renewed health brought determination and desire to live with a vengeance.

Not only did she intend to be by Stuart's side if he ventured to the graveyard despite her, and Captain John's, warning, she was set on riding with him too. He'd find her a force to reckon with. Most assuredly, a mischief-maker.

Cobbles under her boots, she strode toward the stable in the fringed green riding habit and black tricorn delivered by the near daily coach runs from Uncle Ezra. The peerless blue sky vaulted to the heavens and cool breezes lifted her hair, but her tailored outfit was of finest wool and she wore two petticoats beneath the skirt. A green scarf secured the hat to her head and offered an added buffer from the chill. In her gloved hand, she grasped the crop.

A few more steps and she walked through the

double doors into the stable. Dust motes floated in the rays of sunshine slanting inside and on the beams overhead. She swept her gaze over bridles, halters, and ropes dangling along one log wall; saddles hung over a low bench. Riding equipment lined a shelf. Wooden buckets for feed and water, a barrel of oats, and a mound of hay occupied part of the crowded space.

She spotted Jim tossing hay to hungry mouths with a pitchfork. He paused in his labor and raised a hand. Thumbing toward the back, he indicated Stuart's whereabouts.

With a nod to the young Negro, she headed for the stall where Stuart was bent currying the striking chestnut mare. She stole in behind him, admiring both man and horse. Both were stunning.

La Belle's coat gleamed and her mane and tail flowed without a tangle. Her head was well-proportioned, ears nicely set, with a slight arch to her long, muscular neck and slope to her strong shoulders. She must stand fifteen and one-half hands tall. Her powerful back, loins, and flawless legs could bear a general. How could Stuart lose with such perfection?

Still, races were unpredictable.

"I know you're there." He spoke in teasing tones over his shoulder.

"How? Eyes in the back of your head? I was silent."

"Years of watchfulness. La Belle noted you first."

"The twitch in her ears gave me away?"

"And your divine perfume."

"Oh. I guess you can smell violets over the horsiness in here."

"Horsiness? An apt term, I suppose." He laid the

brush on the side of the stall and turned.

No riding habit for him. He wore his thick brown coat, matching tricorn, and leather breeches. Black boots reached well up his muscular legs. A dusting of whiskers grazed his chin, and lengths of brown hair had worked loose from where he'd pulled his hair back at his neck. Gazing at him made her heart drum like pounding hooves.

He eyed her quizzically. "Where to, Duchess?"

"A title you know full well I'll never own."

"You resemble one."

She waved a hand at her attire. "In this? You're easily impressed."

"Not so easily."

The heat in his gaze sent a ribbon of fire scorching through her. It was all she could do to remember her quest. "If it isn't blatantly apparent, I've come to ride with you."

A dubious look crossed his eyes. "You do realize I'm training for a race."

"I've ridden to hounds."

"At a breakneck gallop, or a more sedate pace?"

She drew herself up. "I'm perfectly able to keep you in sight, if you provide me with a capable mount. Like Bryan."

"Bryan's not accustomed to ladies."

"Claire rode him."

Stuart arched sandy-brown eye brows at her. "How do you know that?"

"Word travels when a lady rides across country in the company of a British dragoon officer."

"So it would seem." He loosed a sigh. "I'll have Bryan bridled and fitted with a side saddle. You can accompany me for an hour or so. I'll ride circles around you, if need be."

"The very notion. You are not as well acquainted with me as you suppose, sir."

His lips twitched. "Is that so, Miss?"

"Set me atop Bryan and see."

"Challenge accepted. But you must stay in view. I don't want you on your own in the event Davis reappears."

"I'm prepared for that, too."

He cocked his head at her. "How? Dare I ask?"

Lifting her coat, she revealed the modest sized pistol slung in the leather belt fashioned for her waist.

He shook his head as if to clear it, in the event he was asleep. "Do you even know how to fire that?"

"Thanks to Mrs. Jenner." Hettie patted the leather pouch hanging over one shoulder. Unlike Stuart's, it was new and styled for a woman. "Cartridges for reloading are in here."

"Where did you get all of this?"

"Uncle Ezra. Even Jonas agreed these are exceptional circumstances. I mustn't be caught unawares if you're away."

"So, if you see Mister Davis—"

"I'll shoot him."

Stuart pressed the tips of his gloved fingers to his forehead. "There's more involved than simply firing. You have to perfect your aim."

"I'm perfectly willing to practice."

"Away from people and livestock, I trust."

"I hoped you might help me."

Again, the rush of air escaped him. "Most ladies would be choosing bridal clothes, preparing a guest list, and the dishes to serve after the wedding. Not riding and shooting."

"I can do both."

Admiration mixed with the exasperation in his gaze. "I dare say you can."

"So, you will help me?"

"I suppose—"

The rumble of a wagon and team of draft horses trotting into the yard drowned his reply. "Who in the world?"

Feigning ignorance, Hettie followed him out the stable door. The wagon stopped. The team of four bay horses blew from the load.

Mounds of goods were stacked in barrels and chests in the wagon bed. She recognized the large Negro driver in his blue coat and hat with black trim, reins around his thick hand, and the second, wiry man perched on the seat beside him. Both worked for her uncle.

Good heavens. Uncle Ezra had outdone himself.

"Where you want the stuff, Captain?" the driver boomed.

Stuart stared from him to Hettie. She squirmed at the censure in his eyes. "What do you know of this delivery?"

"I might have hinted in a note to Uncle Ezra that I craved a few provisions."

His mouth tightened in a hard line, then parted. "I see." He lifted his gaze to the driver. "Unload into the pantry and cellar. I'll get some men to lend a hand."

He pivoted and strode back toward the stable. Hettie trotted at his heels. Even his back bespoke disapproval and an aura of tension cloaked him.

Awkward addressing his rear, but she attempted to explain. "You know how Uncle Ezra is. He can't bear to think of me going without in the slightest way."

Stuart swiveled. "Are you deprived?"

"No—"

He waved at the yard. "There's enough out there to last weeks, even if we feast like lords from sunup to sundown."

"We're in no real want. I only thought to help add to your supplies."

"Your way of filling the larder?"

"You said winter would be a challenge for all at Thornton Hall."

He studied her with an expression between sorrow and indignation. "Did you consider what light this casts on me? Your relations, and Lord only knows who else looking on as the delivery passed by, will assume I'm unable to provide for you."

"Would you rather stand on pride or have plenty?"

"I'd rather have respect." With that, he swung around.

"Men and their almighty pride!" she flung after him.

He turned, flushed with annoyance. "Hettie Louise—"

She stopped. "You remember my whole name?"

He halted in mid scold. "Of course."

"I can't remember the last time I heard it. Probably from Mama."

Eyeing her in bemusement, he shook his head. "I suspect you'll be hearing it a great deal from me, the way you're carrying on."

Before he uttered another word, she hurled herself

at him. Whether he caught her in his arms before she threw hers around his neck or vice versa, she wasn't sure. Heedless of who looked on, she pressed her lips to his startled, but undeniable welcoming mouth.

He kissed her harder than he ever had before, breaths escaping them both in pants. "That damn pistol of yours had better not discharge in my middle," he managed between inhalations.

She giggled. "It's not loaded."

"You said Mrs. Jenner—"

"I only looked on when she loaded. I haven't quite mastered the rudiments, and need you to teach me everything about shooting," she admitted.

He chuckled. "You truly are a miscreant, you realize that. What am I to do with you?" Sweeping her up, he circled around with her in his arms, both of them laughing.

"Jim!" Stuart called. "Go unload that wagon, and round up whatever help you need." He nuzzled Hettie's neck. "I have a lovely lunatic to tend to."

"What about riding and shooting?" she whispered.

He groaned. "We better get the horses saddled. You'll be the death of me yet, Miss."

Alarm twinged in her like a bell tolling his demise. "I pray not."

"I meant from wanting you."

Relief melded with the heat rippling through her. "Oh. Well, that makes two of us."

But the shade of dread still shadowed the day.

Chapter Seventeen

Exhilarating! The bracing day was perfect for a bloody good gallop, far preferable than a sultry summer morning with heat clinging like molasses.

Stuart bent forward in the saddle beneath the piercing blue sky. The earthy scent of the pasture mixed with the familiar aroma of leather and horses. Turf nipped by frost flew up under La Belle's hooves, and her breath snorted white in the frigid air.

The supreme and unexpected addition to his training session—Hettie. He shot glances over his shoulder at her pounding behind him on Bryan. She sat the gelding well and kept apace with him and La Belle far better than he'd anticipated.

Hettie must've done quite a bit of riding before illness laid her low. He had to admit she was a skilled equestrian. The smile at her lips told him she was aware of his heightened impression, as did the cocky wave of her crop.

Tempted to shake his head at her, he smiled back. He ought to shout a caution to slow down, but doubted his reproof would have the desired effect. Claire never heeded such warnings, and Hettie possessed equal tenacity.

How vibrantly altered she was from the pale, feverish woman who'd come alarmingly near to death in the days since he'd discovered her in the cemetery.

Actually, she'd discovered him there. Anticipated his coming.

Enough thoughts of that haunting site for now! He wished he never had to set foot in that forbidding place again. His debts were such, though, he feared he would.

Grandfather's gambling before mental confusion caused Claire and Mrs. Jenner to confine him at Thornton Hall had contributed to the weight. Stuart had kept the older man's indiscretion as private as possible, though this was difficult in a closely woven community. His addled grandparent was subject to enough gossip without word of his gambling spreading far and wide.

As Robert Monroe's oldest living male relative, in line to inherit Thornton Hall, Stuart must also cover these debts. A gentleman fulfilled his obligations. That was what he meant to do.

"Come on!" Waving at Hettie to follow, he circled La Belle around and galloped the mare at the split rail fence bordering the wide field.

If Hettie was accustomed to tearing across the countryside fox hunting with a pack of baying hounds, she must've learned how to jump stones walls and fences. Both horses could leap high enough to nick the moon and race like a strong south wind. Could she stay on?

La Belle easily scaled the fence and landed smoothly on the other side. Angling his head, Stuart glanced back to see how Hettie fared. Admittedly, he was slightly apprehensive. Not for Bryan, but for her. She'd be indignant if she knew.

Bryan's long legs reached out and he sprang across the rails, touching down with his rider elegantly seated.

And on a side saddle. Imagine what she could accomplish if she rode astride.

"Bravo, milady!" Stuart reined in and applauded her.

Black tendrils whipping around her, she drew in beside him. Her face creased with pleasure. "High praise coming from such a one as you, Captain."

"And not lightly awarded. Come, let's make for the Ordinary. Several miles from here."

She eyed him wonderingly, as though surprised he was taking her out in public. "And then what?"

"Have a drink before racing home. Did you think I would leave you sitting in the yard on Bryan while I go inside?"

Her rosy cheeks grew rosier. "If you wish to escort me into *Person's Ordinary*, sir, I'm most willing."

"I should be delighted, Miss." He reached out and clasped her gloved hand, circled around the reins. "Hettie, we are soon to be wed. I am honored to escort you anywhere."

A tremulous smile, and she parted her fetching lips. "Even if that fiend, Davis, is foolish enough to appear and I fire at him?"

"Even then, but I prefer you allow me the first shot."

****

Stuart cantered into the tree-lined yard at *Person's Ordinary*. Hettie, on Bryan, rode closely behind him. He waved his crop at her.

A leafy grove at the rear of the property spread into the countryside. Leafless branches tossed and evergreen boughs waved in the heightened breeze. Smoke curled from the stone chimney in the main building and the hearth in the log and stone kitchen behind it. The tang of meat roasting over a hickory fire tinged the cold air.

Male voices carried from inside the sturdy walls. Judging by the volume and the number of horses in the yard and stable, the tavern was doing a brisk business today. Several coaches were also evident. Stable boys rushed around tending to their charges.

Swinging a leg over the saddle, Stuart sprang to the ground. La Belle waited quietly while he turned and reached up for Hettie. "Let's have you down."

Uncertainty crinkled her eyes. Her cheeks were flushed from cantering much of the way and she possessed the same vitality, but the boldness he'd witnessed in her earlier had dimmed. She cast a wary look over the premises.

What had become of the woman he'd ridden with?

"Have you a premonition I should be aware of?" She might be a bit odd, but sometimes perceived things that were lost on him, and everyone else. Her insights could be valuable.

She bent toward his upstretched arms. "I sense a dark presence."

"Someone unsavory?"

"Not necessarily of this world."

Puzzled and not persuaded, he helped her dismount, savoring the slide of feminine softness into his arms. "One of your spirits, you mean?"

She frowned. "None of them belong to me."

"Of course. Forgive my flippancy."

He held Hettie to him a moment longer than necessary then stood her on the cobbles, her skirts blowing around her ankles. "If you see my father, or any other of the departed, please confide their presence and intention to me alone. Not the room at large."

She eyed him as though he'd missed the obvious. "You are fortunate I confide in you. 'Tis a rare disclosure. Not all are privy to the secrets of the dead."

"Again, forgive me. I didn't realize." He also fervently hoped she wouldn't create a scene inside.

As if she sensed his concern, she pursed her lips. He wanted to kiss and hush her in one.

"I will behave with decorum, sir. And if you caution me again, I shan't tell you a damn thing."

"Fair enough." He stifled a smile at her indignation. Leaving their mounts to the care of an able youth, he took her arm. "Shall we proceed?"

Head held high, she gave a nod. "As you wish. Or I can remain in the stable with the horses."

He'd vexed her and no mistake. What a strange, wonderful, maddening woman. He desired her more than ever, though at the moment, she didn't appear particularly pleased with him.

"I want you by my side, sweetheart," he assured her, dismissing her remark about the stable.

Hettie caught up her skirts with one hand, so as not to trip over the cloth, and they mounted the steps side by side. Together, they walked inside the inn. A small chamber serving as a foyer buffered them from the gathering in the central room.

He paused with her before the archway to the larger room to survey the predominantly masculine assembly. Here and there sat a woman in a cloak and bonnet. Some of far better quality than others.

Tables surrounded by chairs were occupied by folk vying for the limited floor space. The oak sideboard along one wall held a steaming soup tureen and foamy jugs of ale. The boisterous assembly spilled over into the back room. Bed chambers were upstairs. Not enough for this swell. Many would break their journey for a short while and continue after shoveling meaty stew into their mouths and swigging ale.

Stuart scanned the room. At the far end of the chamber, a fire crackled in the hearth, its simple blue mantel framed by white plaster walls.

Damn it all.

By the light of the flames, he spotted that conniving fox, Thomas Vaughan. He'd tucked into a corner. If Thomas fancied himself out of view, he was much mistaken.

His back was to them, but the thick dark hair smoothed in a queue and tied with a black ribbon, the ruffled lace at his throat, and stylish figure in a finely tailored plum coat was unmistakable. The walking stick Thomas was never without, ribbons knotted at the end, was used to support the limp he claimed a riding accident had inflicted upon him. Much improved, Stuart noted, since the war had passed and men were no longer needed on the battlefield. Always the dandy, Thomas fluttered a handkerchief, scented, no doubt, as he spoke.

"You were right about an unsavory presence," Stuart muttered, indicating Thomas. "Who is he with?"

"A dead man."

He glanced sharply at Hettie. "The fellow's as plain as day and I cannot view the departed."

She looked as if she'd seen an apparition. "A close relative, then."

He didn't know whether to be afraid or annoyed. "What?"

She beckoned him nearer with a shaky hand and he bent his head until she pressed her lips to his ear. "In the dream your father showed me, this man, or one quite like him, lay dead in the coffin filled with goods. I have the same knot in the pit of my stomach I had when looking on him. Like viewing the devil's own."

"Devil or not, he can't be in two places, one deceased and the other entered into conversation with Thomas Vaughan. I suspect he must be related to—" Stuart paused. "Are you acquainted with the corpse's name?"

"Manley Collins." It escaped her in a reluctant hiss.

The dread she spoke of struck Stuart like a fist in the gut. He tightened his hold on her arm. "Collins? Tories with rumors of—"

"Witchcraft in some of the family," she finished for him, a shudder running through her. "I know. But no one else seems to take notice."

"No." Everyone went on eating and conversing normally. "What in hell is he doing here?" Stuart whispered.

"Scheming to get his treasure back, I should think. He's the source of darkness."

"Not Thomas?"

"Not as much. Perhaps this man has been in on the plotting from the start. Thomas and Davis may be in league with him."

"I'm certain Thomas is the architect of all evil." Stuart would bet his life on it.

Hettie was pensive. "I cannot yet say."

"Ask my father when next you see him."

"I haven't since the dream," she admitted.

Partly relieved that she approached normal, and

frustrated by the unwelcome discovery, Stuart swiveled to look back at the pair. Unlike Thomas Vaughan, this man had a taller more muscular build. There was nothing foppish about him. He had a stern demeanor. His suit wasn't black, but colorless enough, charcoal. His hair was his own, brown streaked with red, and pulled back at the neck.

Stuart couldn't clearly see his face, but his features were strong and square. Bulldoggish. He wasn't someone to trifle with.

He refused to be intimidated. "Let's go and greet them."

"Are you mad?" He met the disbelieving gaze she lifted to his.

"Best to know one's enemy."

"I should have brought a crucifix," she murmured. "And a stake to drive through his bloodless heart."

"You cannot simply attack him."

"There would be nothing simple about it. Have you heard of vampires?"

"Please do not ask me to believe such a foul creature sits before us." Stuart had indulged her enough.

"Perhaps not, but he's most foul."

"Agreed." Stuart gestured her ahead. "Shall we, dearest?"

"Certainly. I've seen worse."

"Where?"

"In the grave," she said quietly, walking beside him.

"I have more regard for the living than the dead."

"If by regard you mean fear, in this instance, you may be correct."

He guided her between crowded tables. Savory

scents of food rose along smells of unwashed men. "Stay close to me."

"As if I would stray."

Heads turned with the awareness of their presence. Stuart and Hettie became the objects of scrutiny from travelers passing through and neighbors alike. Chairs scraped as the gentlemanly males got to their feet and offered her a bow, others a nod. She returned the civility with a short curtsy or nod, ignoring the rude men who ogled her.

These, Stuart quelled with a glance. Any who knew him were acquainted with his temper and ready fists. Those not yet in possession of that knowledge, read it in his eyes.

Thomas glanced around. The astonishment in his face when he saw them was droll, if Stuart were in a mood to be humored.

He wasn't.

To give Thomas credit, he collected himself enough to shut his slack jaw and form his lips in the semblance of a smile. He almost fell over his ridiculous buckled shoes scrambling to his feet. Fortunate for him, he didn't topple to the floor.

"Miss Fairfax, what an unexpected pleasure." Leaning on his beribboned cane, Thomas tucked the handkerchief in his lace-edged cuff and extended his pale hand to Hettie.

She accepted the gesture with the fawn tips of her gloved fingers. "Mister Vaughan. How good to see you, after so many years. I understand you are residing with my family."

Those dark eyes highly praised by many scrutinized her, shifting back and forth to Stuart.

"Temporarily, thanks to the kindness of your generous relations."

The smile she rewarded him with radiated such sweetness it couldn't possibly be genuine. "How very like dear Uncle Ezra and Cousin Jonas to extend hospitality. Did they not take me in? A poor orphan girl."

"And you brighten their home immeasurably, I'm often told. I understood you to be convalescing at Thornton Hall, yet remarkably, here you are."

"My first outing. No doubt I shall be fatigued."

"I pray you do not overtire yourself, dear lady. Both Mister Ezra and Jonas Jones would be most distressed."

She squeezed Stuart's arm. "I shall be quite well. Captain Monroe takes excellent care of me."

"Indeed." Rather tight around the mouth, Thomas inclined his head at Stuart in greeting. "Captain Monroe."

Stuart stared right through him. "Yes?" he replied, as if anticipating further explanation.

He was.

Thomas indicated the grim man who'd reluctantly gained his feet. "Miss Fairfax, Captain Monroe, allow me to introduce Silas Collins." He didn't notice the intake of breath on Hettie's part, or Stuart's tension, as he continued. "Mister Collins is recently come to Halifax to work for Ezra Jones. Jonas, really. He hired him. To oversee unloading shipments at the dock and in the warehouse in place of Mister Davis. After the unfortunate affair with—"

Stuart broke in. "Enough said on that sorry subject, I believe. We don't want to upset Miss Fairfax, do we?"

"Certainly not. Forgive me," Thomas sputtered, coloring. Out came the handkerchief, and he fluttered it.

Hettie inclined her head graciously, belying the tremor in her grip on Stuart. She said not a word to Mister Collins.

Stuart was spared the awkwardness of refusal as Collins didn't attempt to offer his hand, but only gave the briefest nod. Stuart returned it with equal brevity. The look Mister Collins turned on Hettie could be termed dead eyed. There was a cold, fish like quality to his gray stare.

What on earth had she done to him, or was it what she inherently knew about both Collins' men that he despised? Whatever it was, the man seemed intent on unsettling her.

Stuart waited to see how she'd respond before he intervened. A balled up fist in that squat face would bring those dead eyes flashing to life, he'd bet.

Despite her quiver, she exuded a haughty, imperial air. Arching her chin, she surveyed Mister Collins with the regal regard of the duchess Stuart had compared her to. "Sir. Are you also residing with my family?"

"A short stay, Madame."

"Yes. I dare say it shall be. I'm certain you will make other arrangements."

He faltered. "Mister Jonas Jones said there was no rush."

She feigned a small laugh. "Dear Cousin Jonas doesn't understand how matters stand in the household. Uncle Ezra mustn't be put out. You won't put my uncle out, will you, Mister Collins?"

If she'd told him to leave at once, and watch his step, she couldn't have been plainer.

He squared his already quadrangle-shaped chin. "No, Ma'am."

"Good." Finished with him, she spoke to Stuart. "I fear I've lost my appetite. Will you see me back to Thornton, Captain Monroe?"

"Gladly."

"I bid you good day, gentlemen." She retook Thomas's hand, slighting Collins. Once more, she was all charm. "I trust we will meet again soon."

He brightened, and nearly snapped her a salute. "I look forward to it, Miss Fairfax."

"Give my fondest regards to dearest Uncle Ezra. How he adores me." This directed at Collins. "Not to neglect my devoted Cousin Jonas."

"Yes—I mean—no, indeed. I shall convey your regards to both gentlemen." The normally coherent Thomas blathered.

A parting smile for him. "Until then, Mister Vaughan." Snubbing Collins, she turned away.

Slightly baffled, but impressed by Hettie, Stuart grunted goodbye and turned with her. Clearly, she had no intention of remaining one second longer in Collins' presence. Any drink they imbibed would be supplied by the brandy in his flask, until they reached dinner at Thornton Hall.

"Why show such favor to Thomas Vaughan?" Stuart asked under his breath, assisting her through the congested room.

"To cause division."

Understanding dawned. Anything that could be done to kindle animosity among one's enemy was welcome. "Clever girl."

"I was frightened to death," she whispered.

"You never betrayed yourself for a moment."

"That's a mercy."

Stuart guided her through the door and down the steps into the cobbled yard. Horses whinnied in greeting from the stable. He spoke in her ear. "Which man do you believe is the mastermind now?"

"Thomas, when it comes to recovering the treasure. He hatched this scheme, but has no idea how vile his partner is."

Stuart was beginning to. With that awareness came a sobering realization of the challenge involved in defeating the pair. Not to mention Davis skulking in the shadows, licking his wounds, contriving his next move, and plotting revenge.

"Hettie, we have a formidable foe."

"And more help than you know."

Circling his arms around her, he whispered. "You mean my ghostly father and the wolf?"

"And my gift, or oddity, whatever you term it. I believe I can predict what they will do next."

"I'm listening."

"Lie in wait for you at the race, around one of the bends in the track. With you unhorsed and bound, they will come after me. If you will not reveal the site, they will force you to with threats to my life. Or, if Collins is as astute as I fear, he has seen that I also know the site."

"My father showed you?"

"All, in my dream. You can believe or disbelieve."

"I believe you see more than I realized."

Eyes searching, she gazed up at him, the chill breeze blowing lengths of black hair around her face. "Does this alter your feelings for me?"

He nodded, noting the dismay in her eyes. Then

hastened to amend his reply. Before passersby disturbed them, he held her to him and answered with all the passion his lips could deliver. "Whatever you are, dearest, you're a rare one. I love you all the more."

Tears wet her cheeks and dampened his as she kissed him back. She trembled in his arms. "You don't think me some sort of witch?"

"Possibly. But, if so, you are a good one."

"I have no powers," she protested against his mouth. "Only the sight."

"You're more powerful than you know. For caution's sake, we will speak no more of witches. Come now, we must go and make our plans to foil their schemes." He kissed her once more. "And a little love."

Chapter Eighteen

Midafternoon and the sun was already low in the steel blue sky when Hettie and Stuart trotted into the yard at Thornton Hall. Tangy smoke from the hearths promised warmth and food. Hettie was more than ready.

"Ho!" Stuart halted La Belle and sprang to the ground.

The more docile gelding stopped of his own accord, but Hettie wasn't as quick to depart Bryan. Stuart reached up to help her dismount. Feeling more like a bedraggled kitten than the stylish huntress of several hours ago, she tried to suppress a wince.

His perceptive gaze saw right through her. "Been an age since you tore around the countryside, hasn't it?"

She nodded. All this riding when she hadn't mounted a saddle in months, left her sorer than she cared to admit. Muscles she'd forgotten existed stridently asserted themselves. She knew from experience, this would only worsen.

Sympathy warmed his greenish eyes. "A soak in a hot bath for you. Go to the house and Mrs. Jenner's ministrations, sweetheart. I'll see to the horses."

An average ride for him had presented a major outing to Hettie. The impact on her reserves made her realize recovery wasn't won in a few days. She had some mending to do yet. Any fanciful thoughts she'd nurtured of nestling in his arms gave way to groans as she mounted the stairs to her bedchamber.

Mrs. Jenner met her in the hall at the top of the steps, her plump arms heaped with clean linen. She assessed Hettie at a glance. Clucking disapproval, she shook her head. "I feared it were too much, you taking off like a cat with a singed tail so soon after being laid flat on yer back."

She gestured at Minnie, traipsing beside her with the tea tray. "Leave that in Miss Fairfax's chamber and git Maddie to help you haul buckets of hot water up here. And tell yer Grandpa we'll need some willow and whatever else he's got fer this lady who's done herself no good galloping around every which where."

Still 'tch, tching,' the disgruntled woman ushered Hettie to her chamber. She laid the clean laundry on the trunk. Maddie deposited the tray with the floral china teapot, cups, and saucers, covered sugar bowl and cream pot on the washstand, and scuttled off.

Hettie sighed in anticipation. "I could do with a cup."

"Yer doting uncle refreshed the tea supplies, so you kin drink all you want. He even sent chocolate fer a hot drink."

"Dear Uncle Ezra."

"Fortunate fer you, and us all. Let's git you out of these clothes first and I'll pour you a cup." Rounding on her, Mrs. Jenner unbuttoned the fitted habit and peeled the skirted coat from her sore arms and shoulders.

Gasps and groans punctuated Hettie's struggles to escape her dress. Layers of clothing remained, and boots to unlace, stockings to unroll. She sagged on the bed, only to be routed back onto her aching legs as Mrs. Jenner removed her outer skirt and petticoats. The cloth diminished and she was left shivering in her shift from the draft blowing under the door, through the windows, and whistling down the chimney.

Mrs. Jenner wrapped her in a shawl and she sank into the armchair before the orange hearth while the wooden tub was dragged into place. A steaming cup of sweet, milky tea in hand, she sipped gratefully. Minnie and Maddie appeared carrying buckets of water. They upturned the steamy liquid into the tub.

Mrs. Jenner took a cheesecloth bag filled with fragrant leaves, tied at the top with twine, and suspended it in the hot water. The pleasant blend of minty oregano scented the chamber. Monarda, Hettie guessed, a favorite herb.

After a refreshing cup, she slid down into the soothing herbal bath before the fire. Mrs. Jenner poured a second cup and added a dollop of the tincture Ezekiel sent with Maddie to ease her aches. The sweetened brew disguised the bitterness of his remedy enough to consume it without grimacing.

More content than she'd been in a donkey's age, Hettie yawned, her eyes half shut. "I'll feed up this fire," she heard Mrs. Jenner say. "Another bucket of water each, girls," she admonished the two. "We best do yer hair whilst we're about it," she added, speaking to Hettie again. "We got company coming fer supper."

Nudged from her drowsiness, she blinked. "Who?"

"Mister Alston Brinkley, a friend of Captain Monroe's. He recently returned from the war. Fought years, same as our menfolk. Many of 'em alongside the captain."

"I recall the name, but don't believe I have ever made his acquaintance. Is he an amiable gentleman?"

Mrs. Jenner's mouth turned down at the corners. "Many declare him so. Judge fer yerself, if yer able to dine downstairs. Alston Brinkley is the nephew of our neighbor, Mister Ellis, and staying with the Ellis family. Mayhap permanently. He's to inherit after them."

Realization dawned as to the housekeeper's reluctance regarding their guest. "I hope he's not paying Thornton Hall a visit to urge Captain Monroe to sell his land and horses."

"Just what I hope, but you never know where Mister Brinkley's true loyalty lies."

"With Captain Monroe, I pray, but confess to knowing next to nothing about Mister Brinkley. Give me a bit to soak, then we'll tackle my hair. I intend to meet this *old friend* and see how true he is."

"Mister Monroe declares he's dining at the table this evening, and Miss Smith's to be included."

"Oh. My." Hettie especially wanted to make a good impression on Stuart's grandfather. She wished she wasn't quite so sore, but the herbal bath and Ezekiel's tonic was working its magic.

A thought crossed her mind. "Did Captain John approve of Alston Brinkley?"

Mrs. Jenner regarded her with a hint of condescension. "I couldn't say. Ask him yerself."

"He's not at my beck and call," Hettie tossed back.

"Next time you see him then."

Chapter Nineteen

Pride that Stuart had chosen her, wanted her, flooded Hettie in a warm tide, as did the near overpowering urge to fling her arms around his strong neck. Modest behavior must be observed, though, and her arms were sore. The bath and herbal potion had eased, not erased, her aches. She could at least walk in her gold shoes, the buckles sparkling, without hobbling. Her head held high, she swished by Stuart's side into the dining room.

He was bracingly handsome in a blue velvet coat, waistcoat, and sleek dove gray breeches. The white cravat knotted at his throat didn't draw undue attention, as with some fops. White stockings accentuated his athletic legs. Rather than the usual riding boots, he'd donned low-heeled black leather shoes with tasteful silver buckles.

His was an easy elegance, no frills, lace, or unnecessary adornment. The fashion suited his earthy masculinity. Shunning powder and wigs, he wore his streaked brown hair pulled back and tied with a black ribbon. She wished more gentlemen would emulate him. Thomas Jefferson did the same with his hair, and there were others, but many still sported the powdered wigs. Some appeared so effeminate, she wondered how they ever bedded a woman and sired offspring.

Not that ladies' fashion was a great deal better.

Thanks to her mass of hair, Hettie had adapted the high-flown style of the day into an attractive mound on her head without extra padding from animal hair, cloth, or framework. A gold ribbon, threaded by Maddie's deft fingers, wound through the artful tresses. Curling tendrils tumbled over her shoulders, and colorful feathers fluttered from the ornate comb tucked into the top of the arrangement.

For this special evening, she was attired in the greenish-gold taffeta gown from Uncle Ezra and the apricot silk shawl Jonas had given her. A teardrop topaz necklace glittered at her throat and matching earrings dangled from her ears, gifts from her late father. The burnished hues of her dress shimmered in the tapers winking from candelabras on the polished sideboard and high cabinet. The painted fan she clasped in one gloved hand had been her mother's.

Odd, Hettie might be, but not dowdy. Judging from the way Stuart looked at her, he applauded her efforts. The flame in his eyes sent desire flashing through her like heat lightning.

Tearing her eyes away from his compelling gaze, she directed her attention to the room. Overhead, the chandelier spilled light on them and the hearth added illumination. The sweet scent of beeswax from candles wafted alongside the spiciness of pomander balls.

The green paneled walls reminded her of holly leaves, the red chair railing of its berries. This lovely room was colored like Christmas. She longed to be married by Yuletide, but that hardly seemed possible. Much could go awry before then.

Two others were in the room before them. After what had transpired earlier in the week, Hettie cautiously surveyed Abigail Smith. Was she innocent of any actual transgression against her? Stuart believed so.

Hettie wasn't sure. She couldn't rely on that inner sense to guide her. Part of her excused Abigail's involvement in the poisoning, while the other did not.

The young woman had taken pains with her appearance. She wasn't so plain in the pale green gown, yellow skirt, and embroidered shawl, likely her own handiwork. Her soft brown hair was simply styled on her head beneath a small lace cap.

A black onyx brooch with a white flower pattern encircled by a narrow gold band secured the muslin kerchief at her bodice. This sole piece of jewelry was probably given to her by Stuart's aunt, Mrs. Peyton. She'd taken the girl in before she came to Thornton Hall. Although she was no great beauty, Abigail's fresh face, hazel eyes, and slender figure had undeniable appeal. If only Hettie didn't fear that murderous mask would transform her into the menace it had in her dream.

Also present, the elderly Mister Monroe. He'd been assisted into a chestnut colored coat, waistcoat, and fawn breeches. His silvery hair was combed loose around his shoulders. A beard of the same hue flowed down his front. He leaned on a brass-headed cane. His other hand gripped the back of a walnut splat-back chair, its seat cushioned in green damask that matched the drapes closed against the cold night. Identical chairs lined the table, spread with snowy damask linen and the best china, crystal, and silverware the household possessed.

A large porcelain punch bowl, the ivory hue embellished with a gold emblem on the sides, stood at the head of the table. The ladle had been in use, judging by the emptied glass at Mister Monroe's seat. He'd sampled the drink, possibly more than once.

Hettie hoped he wasn't too fuddled by drink. This was the first occasion she'd had of meeting him face-to-face. Normally, he kept to his chamber. She'd only caught a glimpse of him, but had heard plenty about this erratic old gentleman.

Stuart nodded at his relation. "Good evening, Grandfather. Allow me to introduce the enchanting Miss Hettie Fairfax."

The older man offered no immediate greeting. Rather, he drew bushy gray eyebrows together above his blue gaze. His craggy brow grew craggier as he scrutinized Hettie.

Should she address him, or curtsy? She hardly dared to breathe for fear of a misstep.

The intensity in his expression lessened and he seemed to come to a decision. He inclined his head, a bow beyond his stiff gait and grip on the cane and chair. "Good evening to you, Miss Fairfax. Mrs. Jenner tells me yer the provider of the feast."

Her cheeks warmed. Was he pleased or chagrinned by her uncle's generosity? She curtsied and met his close study. "Good evening, Mister Monroe. Uncle Ezra sent the gifts to thank you for your care as I convalesce at Thornton Hall."

"And charm m' grandson," the gruff man interjected, with a pitying glance at Abigail. "But no matter. This one hasn't two shillings to rub together. Having a grand lady sech as yerself among us is, indeed, a benefit."

Hettie hardly knew how to reply to such

outspokenness. While glad to be of use, she'd hoped to be valued beyond the goods that accompanied her presence in the house. And she felt sorry for poor, pink, flustered Abigail. No matter how well one was acquainted with the old gentleman, predicting his behavior must be quite impossible.

Accustomed to his elderly relation's eccentricity, Stuart gave Hettie a 'don't let it trouble you' look. "You're in fine mettle this evening, Grandfather."

"Humph," he grunted. "Suppose I am."

Stuart nodded at the blushing Abigail. "Good evening, Miss Smith. How charming you look this evening."

Murmuring her thanks, she inclined her head.

"Good evening." Hettie nodded distractedly to the young woman, who did the same.

Civilities exchanged, such as they were, Mister Monroe glanced around, annoyance in his eyes. "What's keeping young Master Brinkley? I'm needing m' supper. Bedtime afore long. Likely, that wily scamp is up to some mischievousness."

Hettie suspected a great many years had passed since Mister Brinkley resembled the rascally youth of the older man's memory.

Stuart interceded. "Let me assist you to your seat, sir, and I will have a word with Mrs. Jenner about bringing some dishes. It would seem we must begin without Brinkley."

"I don't much care for that notion," Mister Monroe muttered. "'Taint polite." As if anything he'd said thus far had been. "We don't want the Ellis clan getting word the Monroe's are lapse in their hospitality."

Before Hettie assured him of her discretion,

footsteps scuffled in the hall preceding Mrs. Jenner, who sailed into the room. "Mister Alston Brinkley," she announced, followed by the man himself. "I'll leave you folk to visit and fetch the victuals." She skirted out the door, while all eyes fell on the newcomer.

He swept the party a bow worthy of royalty, then raised his head. A smile enhanced his agreeable countenance, and he exuded goodwill. "Greetings gentlemen, fair ladies. I extend apologies for my tardiness. My mount lost a shoe and wanted attention."

What an amiable fellow. Hettie returned his smile and curtsied. Her admiring gaze took in his blond hair, the shade of his gold velvet coat, tidily pulled back. While shorter than Stuart and not quite as striking in appearance, he was wholly pleasing to look on, with handsome brown eyes beneath a smooth brow, comely nose and chin set in a congenial face that readily gained her notice. He held her gaze without igniting the blaze Stuart kindled in her.

She couldn't imagine such an affable gentleman fighting a war at all, let alone for so many years. But his lean figure conveyed a wiry strength, and it might be that grit hardened his eyes when challenged. Battle altered a man. And a woman, she'd discovered, when she was attacked by Davis.

Smiling broadly, Stuart held out his hand. "Welcome to Thornton Hall, Lieutenant. I cannot tell you how glad I am to see a fellow officer again."

Their guest wrung his hand heartily. "Nor I you." He stepped to Mister Monroe, gentling the grip with which he enfolded his aged fingers. "Good to see you again, sir. I trust you are keeping out of mischief." His brown eyes twinkled.

Hettie liked him all the more for his teasing, and his effect on the old gentleman was remarkable.

"Brinkley, you scallywag," Mister Monroe chided, with a rare grin. "Got to admit we've missed you. Have you taken up piracy and come to plunder our land and horses?"

"No, sir. I'm simply here to dine with my old friends and these lovely damsels, if someone will be so good as to introduce me. Or are you keeping the ladies to yourselves?"

Still smiling, Mister Monroe waved him aside. "Go on with you then, you rogue. My grandson will make the introductions."

Stuart indicated Hettie. "Brinkley, I'm delighted to present my intended, Miss Fairfax." He swept his hand at Abigail, who eyed the new arrival with interest. "This fair lady is Miss Abigail Smith, a faithful support to our family these past few years."

In one swift introduction, he'd made it quite clear which of the women present was available. Hettie was impressed. She smiled again at Brinkley, as Stuart referred to him, and nodded. Abigail did the same.

"I'm gratified to make the acquaintance of two such exquisite creatures." Brinkley extended his arm to Abigail. "Might I be permitted to escort you to the table?"

She flushed with pleasure and took his arm. "Thank you, sir. Do you prefer Lieutenant or Mister?"

"Please, call me Brinkley. Everyone does. The war's over, and we're all friends here, are we not?"

"Indeed." The happiness in Abigail's gaze enhanced her eyes, her best feature.

Perhaps there was hope for her yet. Hettie would

be vastly relieved if she turned her sights on their new neighbor.

Mister Monroe waved at the table. "Enough of this chatter. Let's be seated afore the cock crows. Sit where you like." He indicated a place at the table. "But leave that spot vacant fer John. He'll join us in a bit."

A palpable tension circled the gathering, and Abigail grimaced. Stuart walked to his grandfather and clasped his shoulder. "Papa's dead, sir. More than two years now since he fell."

The older man glowered at his grandson. "Nonsense. I see him as plain as I do you." He swiped a bony hand at the door. "Standing right there."

Stuart glanced from the empty doorway to Hettie. She looked closely where his grandfather gestured, but saw no one. Not even a hint of the blue coat and red vest that normally accompanied any sighting of Captain John.

Was she losing her gift, or was Mister Monroe confused? Perhaps she'd been more affected by the fever and potions than she realized.

Puzzled, she shrugged her lack of awareness at Stuart. The relief in his expression was undeniable. As she suspected, he wanted her to be *normal*.

Abigail shifted uncomfortably in the strain. Brinkley released her arm. "Allow me a moment, Miss Smith."

He strode to the agitated man and laid a hand on his other shoulder, so that he and Stuart were on either side of him. "We shall reserve John's place at the table, sir. Haven't I always had the highest regard for him?"

"That you have, Brinkley, m' boy." Mister Monroe appeared mollified.

"Then let us all be seated, sir. I'm eager to sample the delights of Sally's cooking."

"Aye. A sensible arrangement. That woman can cook."

Stuart considered his old friend with a glint of appreciation in his eyes, Abigail looked on with adoration, and Hettie concluded that in Brinkley, they had a potential ally—one whose assistance might well be required soon.

While Brinkley seated Mister Monroe and Stuart refilled his drink, an unconscious pull drew Hettie's gaze back to the doorway. There he was. She blinked to be certain. But no, she wasn't dreaming.

Captain John stood straight and tall in his regimentals, head bare, clean shaven, graying brown hair pulled back, a dress sword at his side. He considered her, his green gaze thoughtful, as if he knew her struggles. He tipped his gloved hand to her in greeting.

She swallowed hard. Stuart wouldn't approve. But how could she help what she saw?

Subtly, so Stuart wouldn't notice, she acknowledged the figure in the doorway with a nod. Glancing around, she noted Mister Monroe observing her. Approval warmed his eyes. So, this was the way to win him over, their shared insanity.

Would you really rather not see me? Captain John asked, in the way he had where no one else took heed.

Hettie couldn't honestly insist she'd rather surrender her sight. It was her gift. Hers alone. She doubted Mister Monroe was in the habit of seeing specters, only this one. Not that she'd seen a great many. And none like Captain John. He was special.

No, she admitted. *I wouldn't rather.*

Then make your peace, lass. You are what you are.

But Stuart—

Must accept you, or he's not for you.

Unaware of her inner turmoil, Stuart escorted her to the table. She swiveled away from his ghostly father to the man she desperately wanted to marry. The man she feared would think her mad.

"Here you are, sweetheart." Stuart seated her to the right of his grandfather in a rustle of skirts. Bending low, he pressed a kiss to her cheek.

Tingles ran through her. She didn't want to confess to him, but knew she must. His ear was in range of her whisper. "I see him now," she said under her breath.

Momentary silence from Stuart. Then he reasoned. "Maybe it's the lingering effects from belladonna."

"No. Not this time. I think he's really there."

She lifted her eyes to Stuart's. A shadow passed over their green depths. And darkness veiled her heart. It was as she'd feared. He didn't want to know the truth. Despite his assurances to the contrary, when it came right down to it, he wanted her to be like other women. And she never would be.

Blinking at the mist in her eyes, she slanted her gaze at the door. Captain John regarded her somberly. *I'm sorry, girl.*

Not as sorry as Hettie was.

Stuart took the seat beside her. Brinkley and Abigail settled in the chairs across from them. Mrs. Jenner and the attendants she'd commandeered arrived bearing platters of steaming food. All should be jolly, and Hettie made every effort to curve her lips into a smile. But she had no appetite. The tantalizing dishes tasted like grass.

Stuart was lost to her. To remain here any longer wasn't fair to him and would be torture for her. She must forfeit all hopes of a life with him and return to Uncle Ezra.

Marriage to another was out of the question. Her relations must accept her spinsterhood. She'd live simply, quietly, and offset her support when her inheritance came in.

If Stuart was bent on going to the cemetery, she'd assist him as best she could. More than this, she hadn't the heart to do. Never had she been so filled with despair. The one man she truly loved couldn't love her as she was, and she couldn't be anyone else.

Chapter Twenty

Brinkley prodded the coals in the grate with the poker, opening a ribbon of light in a reddish gray lump. "If you'll allow my observation, your Miss Fairfax is hauntingly beautiful."

Jarred from somber reflection, Stuart roused at his friend's utterance. They sat in armchairs before the fireside in the west parlor, a glass of brandy in hand. The others had retired to bed.

"Unusual choice of words, but fitting. She is, indeed." And Stuart would be haunted by Hettie for the rest of his days if he didn't make amends with her.

"There's an unearthly quality about the lady." Brinkley's voice was so low, no one could possibly overhear.

Shadows danced on the walls as Stuart debated whether or not to confide further revelations. "She's more connected to the next world."

Brinkley glanced around, concern in his eyes. "I trust not because she's crossing over anytime soon."

"I pray not. She's come all too near in the past few weeks." Stuart hated to think how close.

"She seems quite recovered in health. Though her spirits are low."

"Exceedingly." The glow had gone from Hettie's eyes this evening like a candle snuffed out, and with it, all light in Stuart's life. Being in love was exhilarating and terrifying, his fate intricately entwined with that of another.

Brinkley considered him in the way he had of assessing people and situations, intuition that had aided them during military campaigns. "You don't appear much better. What's troubling the pair of you? Something happened at supper."

"Yes." Still, Stuart pondered how much to confide. He took a swallow before speaking. "Brinkley, promise me not a word of this conversation will leave the room."

He set his glass on the side table and clasped Stuart's shoulder. "We've been through Hell and back together. Your confidence is safe with me. I swear it, by all that's sacred."

A sigh escaped Stuart. "Of course. You've always been a good friend, and the only one I trust. So, I turn to you now."

"Go on, then. What's bedeviling you?"

"Devil is the word. Strange things are happening at Thornton Hall."

"You mean apart from your grandfather seeing Captain John?"

"Grandfather's a bit tetched," Stuart reminded him.

"Granted." More poking at the fire, accompanied by popping and hissing wood, then Brinkley continued. "But not wrong in this instance, I think."

Stuart arched quizzical brows at his friend.

"Miss Fairfax also saw him, didn't she?" Brinkley persisted. "That's what came between you."

Damn his insights. Would others also take notice?

"If word gets out about Hettie, she could be branded odd, or mad. And shunned, even locked away."

"You needn't fear I'll repeat anything. I would never wish harm on such an exquisite creature."

The knot in Stuart's gut eased a little. He sagged on one elbow with his fingers pressed against his forehead. It had been a long day—week—two weeks. "I'm baffled by her, Brinkley. By all that's happening."

"There's something else you might consider, old man."

A jab at the two year difference between their ages. "What's that?"

"Your father is actually here."

Lifting his head, Stuart stared at his friend. "Do you truly believe that's possible?"

"Thought I glimpsed him myself out of the corner of my eye. The glint of his sword caught the light."

"His sword? That could have been a candlestick." Stuart shifted his astonished gaze from his friend and waved at the blue-gray walls hung with portraits. Most were painted by John Monroe. "Hettie declares this is my father's favorite room. Do you see him now?"

Brinkley eyed Stuart steadily. "No. I may never glimpse him again. Ghosts are unpredictable."

"How is it you know so much about them? Is this All Hallows' Eve that you must go wandering among the dead?"

Brinkley gave him a look. "I didn't realize I had ventured among them before learning the young woman I saw seated beside a dying soldier had passed two years earlier."

"When was this?" Stuart asked.

"In camp. During the bombardment of Yorktown."

"I saw nothing beyond the rain of hellfire."

"You weren't there that night. And I have no

explanation for what happened. I'm only reporting what I saw."

"Did anyone else see the woman?"

"One or two. The dying man spoke to her, called her by name, as if they were sweethearts. She seemed as real as you or me. Makes you think, doesn't it?"

"Yeah, makes me wonder how much you men had to drink to steady your nerves."

Brinkley crossed his heart with his right forefinger. "Not a lot. Rum ran low."

"Before or after you drained it?"

"*Touché*. But I'm telling you, something strange took place that night, and it cannot be explained."

Still skeptical, Stuart ran his eye over the familiar parlor, the worn gold couch, purring yellow tabby curled on a pillow, the books piled on a low table. He and Claire used to share private moments in this room, apart from their insane family. His dear sister wasn't here to advise him now.

He turned to Brinkley. "What do you make of all this, and me not seeing my father, if he's here?"

"Sometimes we only perceive what we wish and discount the rest. The real question isn't so much if Captain John has returned to Thornton, but why?"

"Now, you're getting to the heart of the matter. And don't let me forget to tell you about the wolf."

Brinkley closed his hand around the glass on the table beside him. "Are you referring to the black one I spotted in front of the house?"

"Good heavens, man. Is there anything here you haven't seen?"

"Don't know. What else have I missed? My uncle said you killed a panther."

Stuart nodded. "But no one is to shoot the wolf. Hettie insists he's been sent to protect us."

Brinkley shrugged good-naturedly. "Very well. The wolf is yours. But who do you need protecting from? I hear there's a manhunt out for some criminal named Davis."

"He's after us, for one." Stuart leaned in. "What do you know of a Loyalist by the name of Silas Collins?"

"Nothing good. For starts, his Tory brother, Manley, is dead."

"And?"

"Folk said their mother's a witch."

A chill ran down Stuart's spine. "A bad one, I'm guessing."

"The worst. If you can go by what people say." Brinkley seemed disinclined.

"You believe in ghosts, but not witches?"

He lifted one shoulder and let it drop. "Haven't decided for sure one way or the other."

Stuart had definite leanings. "What happened to the woman?"

"Did I say she was dead?"

****

A flickering candle to illuminate his way, Stuart crept up the steps. The hour was late, the night cold, and Brinkley had accepted his offer to bed down on the parlor couch under blankets.

Stuart trusted Mister and Mrs. Ellis would assume he'd remained at Thornton Hall. Brinkley had been through a lengthy war, so they couldn't fret over him unduly, despite their tendencies. Being childless, they doted on their nephew.

He left his friend lightly snoring. Brinkley could

sleep through cannon fire. And had. Stuart envied him his repose.

The household was still, apart from the clock chiming twelve. Hounds bayed in the distance. No wolf howled. He hadn't heard the creature in several days.

He slowed outside Hettie's chamber. Should he tap on the door and beg entry? He ached to slip inside and make amends, but didn't want to disturb her, nor did he know how to banish the hurt from her eyes. Praying tomorrow would shed light on his dilemma, he entered his room.

Thoughts churning, he unbuttoned his coat and waistcoat and laid them over the back of the maroon striped armchair before the hearth. He stirred up the fire, tossed on more kindling, and sank into the upholstery to pull off his boots. The crackle warmed his stocking feet.

Just his luck. Now, he had an actual witch to worry over, assuming he believed such a being existed. And possibly, even if he didn't.

Mrs. Jenner was zealous in her precautions. Surely, she'd covered him and the household in a protective blanket of sacred herbs, amulets, and incantations? The woman was practically a white witch herself.

If her efforts were insufficient, what more could be done? Brinkley wasn't certain if Mrs. Collins still dwelled in the Collins' homeplace in Eastern Virginia, or had been forced to move, only that her son, Manley, fell at the hand of Patriots—Captain John's party.

Even if Stuart discovered where the woman lived, he wasn't about to journey to her sinister fortress and demand she remove whatever curse she'd laid on the Monroe burial plot, assuming she even had. And why should she heed him? What could he offer to appease her wrath at the death of her son? Embittered witches didn't strike him as reasonable.

No. If the wealth amassed to bribe a Tory into revealing the whereabouts of Benedict Arnold was cursed, there was nothing Stuart could do about it.

Oh, this was madness! Mrs. Collins couldn't possess knowledge of the treasure, unless by divination.

Manley hadn't lived to tell the tale. His brother, Silas, must've gained whatever knowledge he'd come by through Thomas Vaughan. If they were aware of the secret location, the stash would already be gone. The curse must be attached to the treasure, wherever it lay.

Meanwhile, that traitor, Arnold, was safely in England, unaware of the goods collected to bring about his end and the havoc they'd wrought. He'd have a jolly sneer.

If the British ever returned to Halifax, a treasure awaited them. Major Vaughan said Tarleton knew of it, but he'd been defeated and sailed from America empty-handed. Vaughan and Claire had left the prize to Stuart, unaware of the accompanying dangers.

Bizarre. Stuart couldn't take it in. Admittedly, he didn't really want to. All this emphasis on dark forces made his skin crawl.

Getting to his feet, he unknotted the cravat at this throat and laid it aside. He left on his white shirt, opened midway down his chest. The hem reached to his thighs. He poured water into a basin and brushed his teeth, splashed his face, toweled off, then crawled into bed.

Sound sleep evaded him and he tossed as if onboard ship in a rough sea. Images of a wrathful she-devil rode alongside his torment over the abysmal way he'd left matters with Hettie. Better to stay awake than succumb to nightmares, but he was dog-tired. The clock struck two before he finally drifted off.

When Stuart first grew aware of the male voice speaking near his ear, he couldn't say. Through the fog hazing his mind, he heard, *Wake up*, over and over until he roused and opened heavy eyes.

No one was evident in his chamber, silvered in the gray early predawn light. But the ghostly summons sounded uncannily like his father. It couldn't be.

Go to her. Now.

Goosebumps flushed down his neck and back. The eeriness of the directive vied with immediate fear for Hettie.

His heart lurched. Had she been snatched? Must he chase after her in rescue?

Instantly alert, he leapt from bed. A glance at the window revealed the sky heavily misted. If she'd been taken, which way would he search?

Alarm tempted him to go as he was. But he'd not get far clothed only in his shirt. He pulled on leather riding breeches, fastening them with deft fingers. He thrust stocking feet into his boots. Leaving his shirt open at the neck, he grabbed his heavy brown coat from the hook on the wall. Shoving his arms into the sleeves, he sprinted out the door and across the hall to her chamber.

God, let her be there! The plea hammered with every breath.

If she wasn't, would his father guide him from beyond?

That seemed rather much to hope for, considering

he hadn't believed his father was remotely present in the house.

Praying he wasn't too late, Stuart pushed open the door. There she was. Relief left him weaker than pounding fear. "Hettie—thank the Lord."

She whirled around, shock etched on her face, lengths of black hair spilling to her waist. The fire burned low. The muted light made her appear even more ethereal than usual, as if she were from the other world.

His heart leapt with joy at finding her safely within her chamber. Then fell as he surveyed her condition. Something was amiss.

Discovering Hettie fully clothed before sunrise, meant she'd never completely undressed last evening. She couldn't manage the stays alone. And she wore travel garb, the navy blue jacket and skirt not readily spotted. Worse—she'd placed folded garments in her heaped trunk. She clutched the last petticoat.

He swept his gaze around the room, emptied of her belongings. She'd done all this unaided, or her hair would be dressed as well. She must've sent Minnie or Maddie away, so they'd not realize her intentions and sound the alarm.

Stuart had given orders that Hettie never be left unattended. Not certain which girl to scold, he stood where he'd halted inside the door. His father hadn't sent him a moment too soon.

Hurt needled him like shards of ice. "You're leaving?"

"How did you know to come?" Her voice a whisper.

"Father told me."

If possible, she paled even more. "You heard him?" Her voice shook, she shook.

Stuart nodded. "Seems he doesn't want you to go. Sent me to stop you. Not that I wouldn't have anyway, *had I known*."

He gestured at the window. "If I look below, will I find my coach ready to bear you back to Halifax, with Jim in attendance?"

She hung her head. "You might."

"I never thought you would slip away like this, Hettie. Did you even plan to bid me farewell?"

Her eyes mirrored the pain stabbing his heart. "I thought it better this way."

"For whom? Only yesterday, you promised to wed me."

"That was before I fully realized how difficult my seeing the departed was for you."

"So you were running away?" He threw his hands up. "Not one for marching into battle, are you?"

"I was returning home," she corrected him, indignation mingling with the wounded expression in her face.

He also preferred annoyance to heartache.

She hastened to justify herself. "I feared you would grow unhappy with me."

He crossed his arms over his chest. "I am. Exceedingly. At the moment."

"Not before?" she pressed.

"What? Discovering you about to depart like a thief in the night?"

"It's nearly dawn," she argued, but her cheeks colored.

He shook his head at her. "A moot point, given

your stealth. After all we've meant to each other, still mean, couldn't you allow me the chance I requested to prove myself?"

"I'm sorry, Stuart. I feared what your life might be when joined with me, given my *gift*."

"Dearest, I should have been more reassuring last evening at supper. I wasn't certain what to say, and for that, I apologize. But this?" He waved his hand at the room. "There's no cause for flight. My concern lies in protecting you from any who might wish you harm if word gets out about your *gift*."

She eyed him doubtfully. "You do not worry I may be mad?"

"I did. No longer."

So intent were her eyes, as if she tried to peer inside his soul. "Truly?"

"How can I worry over your potential madness when I'm here because my father's voice awoke me?"

Still, she hesitated.

Stuart decided for them both, a throwback to years of leadership. "I shall tell Jim to unharness the horses and put away the coach. If you still wish to leave, you may write your uncle. This allows you the opportunity to reflect on the vow you made me regarding our upcoming marriage. I suggest you order a pot of tea. I'm going for a ride."

Before she could argue, apologize again, or rush at him with an embrace, he pivoted and strode out the door.

To his satisfaction, he glimpsed truce in her eyes before he departed. But anger and disappointment drove him on.

Whatever Hettie saw, or thought she saw, didn't

matter nearly as much as his ability to trust her. He'd like to be able to say of his future wife, she's beautiful, a bit odd, perhaps, but faithful and true.

Chapter Twenty-One

A host of butterflies fluttered in Hettie's chest when Stuart strode into the dining room for breakfast. She straightened in her chair, where she'd sagged before his arrival, but refrained from springing to her feet. The early morning ride had heightened the vitality he exuded, and masculine energy filled the chamber like a burst of new wind. He smelled of horses, leather, and his own unique scent that stirred every sense within her.

Brinkley shouldered back in his seat. "Training for the big race without me, are you?" he queried, feigning reproach.

"You seem well attended. Like a cat with the cream," Stuart quipped.

Brinkley simply smiled. Mrs. Jenner had supplied him with fresh linen and foreseen his every need. Now that he'd made clear his alliance to the Monroes, he was her new favorite.

Hettie was grateful to him, too. He'd kept her company at the table, offering witty comments in between sips of fragrant tea. He amiably spooned hot porridge, waded through pumpkin pie, and apple tarts, and patiently bore with her less than charming presence.

Subdued from her predawn encounter with Stuart, she'd added little to the conversation. If Brinkley hadn't consumed hearty portions of whatever Mrs. Jenner trotted to the table, the avid woman would be most put out. Hettie had scarcely nibbled a thing.

The hours she'd spent in reflection resulted in black regret at her attempt to flee, even though she thought she'd been acting for the best. She'd misunderstood Stuart and cheated him of the opportunity he'd requested of her. How could she make amends?

She was thankful when Abigail had arrived in the dining room, smiling to outshine the sun. The blue ribbon in her hair and muslin tucker of the same hue at her bodice enhanced her eyes. Who knew they could appear blue or greenish depending on her choice of clothes? She'd mostly worn gray before.

More surprising than her attire, she wafted a spicy floral scent. The little Quaker was lightening her sobriety. And she hung on Brinkley's every word, gratifying to a male.

Now that Stuart had come, a mixture of relief and anxiety swelled inside Hettie. Was he still vexed with her? He had every right to be.

As gracious as ever, he nodded at the gathering and swept them a bow. "Ladies, Brinkley."

Hettie lifted hopeful eyes, but Stuart didn't single her out for any particular notice. His gaze didn't fall on her, and her alone. She tapped a pink silk slipper as he settled at the table beside her.

To signal her change of heart, she'd removed her navy blue attire and donned a frilly rose-colored gown with lacy white skirting, layered with flounces. A rosy bow and ribbons topped the lace on her head, gifts from her mother who'd loved frippery. The garnets at her ears and throat were from her late father, and the gold bracelet at her wrist a final remembrance from her grandmother. For added warmth, she'd wrapped in the lavender shawl from Uncle Ezra. Her family's adoration cloaked her from head to toe.

What of Stuart? Did he wax hot or cold?

Mrs. Jenner swept through the door. She set a heaped plate before him and a bowl of porridge beside that. "Here you are, Captain. Kept it warm fer you."

Minnie scurried behind the housekeeper with a steaming teapot. She poured the rich brew in a china cup and nestled it on the saucer at his place. Mrs. Jenner positioned the sugar and cream within reach, and waited at his elbow for refills. Maddie rushed in with new made cornbread and a pot of honey to set before him. He was as fawned over as a lord.

He waved them aside. "I'll tend to myself. We all can. You three go about your business. Excellent as always, Mrs. Jenner."

Bustling with pleasure, she ushered the girls away.

Even though Stuart sat by Hettie, and was outwardly hospitable, she'd failed to glean a real sense of his mood. She darted glances at him while he ate. Still, she gleaned nothing.

After a swallow of tea, he spoke to Brinkley. "You racing this year?"

"And go up against that mare of yours?" Brinkley shook his head. "I'll save my money."

Stuart gave a genial shrug. "Clever fellow."

He had yet to meet Hettie's eyes. He was taking his time revealing his true frame of mind. She had no idea how to convey hers, apart from the festive gown, and quivers running through her at the mere sight of him.

How many more moments would he keep her in suspense? It seemed an eternity.

He brushed her hand, the barest touch. Tingles prickled over her skin, and she lifted her eyes to his. He looked long and hard at her, then smiled. Warmth rushed through her, and she nearly choked on her tea.

Brinkley chuckled. Miss Smith glanced around to see what was so amusing. "I believe they've reconciled," he observed.

"Did they quarrel?" She seemed utterly unaware.

He pressed his lips to the tips of his fingers and saluted her. "We must work on your powers of perception."

They could explore whatever they liked, Hettie was engrossed in Stuart. She reveled in his smile. Craving more, she leaned in to whisper her gratitude. Perhaps they'd reached an understanding and there was hope for them yet.

"I will speak with you later," Stuart whispered back, but the earlier expression of betrayal had gone from his eyes.

Lips twitching, he glanced at Abigail. "Does my grandfather not require your services this morning?"

She'd made such a fuss over attending him daily. Hettie awaited her response.

A blush crept over her cheeks. "Mister Monroe has already breakfasted in his chamber and is reading the newspaper."

Stuart arched sandy-brown eyebrows. "To himself?"

"He has agreed to use the spectacles your sister, Claire, sent him from England."

"Last year," he reminded her. "But that is just as

well. I'm sure Brinkley values your company."

His friend nodded, a ready smile at his mouth.

"Good. Now listen closely." Stuart's voice dropped. He cast brevity aside like a borrowed cloak and beckoned the others to draw closer.

They inched their chairs nearer his. If thunder had rumbled beyond the glass with the threat of an impending storm, the mood couldn't have altered more abruptly.

He ran his eyes over the tight circle. "We are facing challenges that make even strong souls flinch."

A grave nod from Brinkley indicated his awareness.

Stuart continued in hushed tones. "If there is anything I should be made aware of by anyone present I would be most gratified if you would share that information with me at once." He scrutinized Abigail. "Miss Smith, have you anything else to impart regarding the notorious Mister Davis, who is not yet apprehended and a most dangerous man."

A shudder coursed through Hettie. Stuart squeezed her hand with his warm grip, while all eyes fixed on Abigail.

The flush deepened in her cheeks. "There is something. I'm not sure how much difference it makes."

"Go on," Stuart directed. "It well may."

The intensity in Brinkley's gaze belied his congeniality. Clearly, he was no fool.

The flustered young woman twisted the handkerchief in her lap. "When Mister Davis came to the house and asked after me, he offered me money."

"For what purpose?" Stuart demanded.

"To report your movements," she confessed in a small voice. "I refused."

"Did he approach anyone else in the household?"

"None I know of, sir—" she faltered. "Besides, I am the only one he felt he had a chance with."

"And still you added the potion he supplied you to Miss Fairfax's tea. Did you not think it strange the two requests coincided?" Stuart asked.

She dabbed at her eyes. "I thought as Davis worked for Mister Jones, who would never wish his niece harm, the potion was the tonic he declared it to be, and that Mister Jones must wish to know your whereabouts. Perhaps because of Miss Fairfax being in your care."

Given Abigail's naiveté, Hettie believed her.

Brinkley gave a low whistle. "Those powers of perception I referred to, let me amend that to *do not trust strange men who ask you to spy for them*."

The poor girl appeared thoroughly wretched.

Stuart raised a conciliatory hand. "At least, Miss Smith refused to cooperate with the villain."

"Which means, whoever is funding this venture may have sought elsewhere for their extra eyes," Brinkley remarked.

Rubbing a chin dusted with whiskers, Stuart nodded. "The devious circle includes Davis, Thomas Vaughan, Silas Collins, and possibly his mother?"

"Esther," Brinkley supplied, "who is reputed to be a heinous witch."

"And may have cursed us," Stuart muttered.

Hettie jerked at these tidings. Captain John had never revealed anything to her about a witch, unless she'd missed something. Was that the dark presence she'd sensed behind Silas at *Person's Ordinary*? Wild conjecture tumbling through her mind, she noted Abigail had gone deathly pale.

Brinkley reached out an arm to support her before she slumped on the floor. "Here, drink this," he encouraged, holding a glass of cider to her lips.

She sipped, and seemed steadier. Eyeing Stuart in dread, she wiped at her lips. "What manner of folk are we reckoning with, Captain?"

"The devil himself, quite possibly. His henchmen, at least." He gave her a moment to absorb this, then gestured at the circle. "I must be able to rely on each of you."

Every head nodded.

"Excellent. I have a race to win and may require help to defend myself against those lying in wait along the course."

A glint gleamed in Brinkley's brown eyes. He smoothed back blond hair. "Nothing I should enjoy more."

"Please allow me to be of help in some way. I am eager to make amends." Abigail's courage despite white-faced fear was moving.

Hettie turned to Stuart. "Have I not requested assistance in perfecting my shooting, sir?"

He rolled his eyes. "Perfect it? You scarcely know the first thing about shooting."

"I'll teach her," Brinkley interjected. "You condition the mare. As for Miss Smith, I welcome her assistance."

She shot him a grateful look.

Fingering his chin, Stuart considered. "As do I. There are tasks for all."

Hettie hesitated, then plunged ahead. "Regarding

the funding you spoke of earlier, is it possible Uncle Ezra is unintentionally providing it?"

Like a cat on the prowl, Stuart was instantly alert. "He's setting Thomas Vaughan up in business."

"He may be doing more than he realizes."

"Difficult to persuade your uncle of this, though. He has great confidence in Thomas."

"As does my uncle," Brinkley reminded them.

"Ah, yes." Hettie pushed ahead. "Then we must contrive some means to convince them both otherwise."

"First, let's get through this race." Stuart raised a glass. "To surviving the run and winning the purse."

"Hear. Hear." Brinkley lifted a glass, followed by Abigail, and Hettie. They clinked together in harmony.

Hettie glimpsed the blur of blue and red in the doorway, and the glint of a sword. Another raised an unseen glass.

Chapter Twenty-Two

Weather had no allegiance, nor were the heavens under any man or woman's control, but it seemed to Stuart as if the curse had spread beyond the cemetery. Ghostly whiteness veiled the horses and riders lining up at the edge of the track. Mist enveloped the distant reaches of the course encircling the wide field, and haze muted the trees and underbrush dotting the way.

Potential ambush lay at every bend, enhanced by the fog. Anyone could hide in this cover. And probably did.

Dark forces were at work, the odds against him. He and Hettie must prevail over the sinister threat stalking them, or they'd never be free—perpetual turmoil their lot, until they fell. On a smaller scale, their conflict mirrored the eternal battle between good and evil.

Not that Stuart was blameless, but he wasn't wicked. Those hunting him were. They would stop at nothing to achieve their end.

He had no powerful magic, just the will to fight, and a prayer in his soul. Now, he had a race to win.

Only gentlemen participated in the annual run. The race wasn't fraught with the rough sport common in wilder parts of the country—jabbing, knifing, gouging—whatever it took to win. Still, tensions ran high. Even so-called gentlemen weren't above elbowing other riders who got too close. An occasional crop came into play. Oaths were muttered.

Nickers and high-pitched whinnies carried above the rumble of men. The scent of horses, and some pungent riders, charged the cold air. Adjoining mounts sidestepped in the anticipation rippling through the assembly. Flared nostrils snorted white. Ears alternately pricked forward, and then laid back in a scowl at a restless neighbor crowding too near. Arched necks and quivering flanks bespoke their nervousness.

Checking excited horses was no small feat. Only superior riders possessed the expertise. Some participants shouldn't have entered. They fought for control over high-stepping mounts ratcheting into a frenzy.

One man nearly lost his seat as his roan gelding bolted into the fog. A second rider tumbled to the leaf-strewn turf. His horse galloped off without him, onlookers running in pursuit.

La Belle remained alert, but calm. Those months with Captain Vaughan and the British Legion had prepared the mare for the noise, press, and tumult of battle. Her high level of training reflected Vaughan's expertise. After all she'd experienced, a race was manageable. She snorted with eagerness, not explosive nerves.

The buzz of expectation hummed in the crowd milling around the backside of the course. Ladies and gentlemen dressed in an array of silk, satin, and the finest wool, contrasted with rustic country folk in plain linen, homespun, and dressed animal skins. Some slaves had been allowed to attend, and he spotted free Negroes in the swell. Children darted through the diverse gathering, their mothers shouting futile threats.

Abigail was a fetching sight in their midst, dressed like a highborn lady by Hettie and Mrs. Jenner. She inclined her head from beneath a wide brimmed hat encircled with blue ribbons, one tied beneath her chin, her figure draped in a blue cloak and floral gown. Her instructions were to mingle and glean information. She wasn't to converse with anyone apart from the safety of the group.

The honor of officiating belonged to Ezra Jones, the sponsor of the race. His son, Jonas, lacked the balls to mount the wooden block at one side of the restless stretch of horses and riders. Wearing a crimson cloak no eye could miss, Ezra assumed his position.

Stuart tried not to be distracted by Hettie in her flowing green, hooded cloak, mounted on Bryan a little way behind her uncle. She steadied the battle-hardened gelding with easy grace. She had no intention of participating in the race, but planned to join Brinkley and scout the perimeter for anyone lying in wait. Stuart balked at allowing her to undertake this risk, but she was nothing if not determined.

If Ezra had realized her intent, he'd forbid it outright. He thought her present only to look on, and riding the boundary good fun for a skilled equestrian. Nothing more.

The vapor partially shrouding Hettie enhanced the otherworldly quality she conveyed—enchanting, but rather unsettling. Stuart prayed her unique ability would aid her. And Brinkley had promised to keep watch.

She patted Bryan's neck and waved a gloved hand at Stuart. He lifted gloved fingers in return.

"Godspeed!" she called.

He nodded. Much was up to Providence. He could

but do his part.

A shrill whistle broke into his conjecture. Heads turned in Ezra's direction.

"Gentleman!" Gripping a pistol in one hand and a cane in the other, the older man scowled at the spirited cluster. He stabbed the walking stick at them—preferable to the pistol. "Straighten this line! I want to see an even row!"

A task better achieved by some than others. Dark chestnuts, like La Belle, lined up beside horses sporting varying shades of brown, and a few dappled grays. Bays with black manes and tails, and lighter bodies made a striking sight. Not all were cooperative.

Apparently satisfied they were as even as they were likely to get, and fast deteriorating, Ezra raised the pistol.

"At my shot, commence the race!"

A smoky blast, and they were off. La Belle could maintain her speed over a distance. Stuart didn't fear taxing her, and gave the mare her head.

She stretched out long legs. Clumps of greenish brown turf and dry leaves flew up beneath her hooves. Other riders tore over the ground, minus those who'd tumbled from the saddle. One or two free horses galloped riderless in the race.

Stuart had already weighed the competition. A mahogany bay mare and reddish-brown gelding were said to be the swiftest, and proving that claim. These were out in front with La Belle. Winning this race wouldn't be easy, but he enjoyed a challenge, so did the mare. As if the horse sensed what was at stake, she gave her all. Spurting ahead, she passed the fastest mounts.

Crouched low in the saddle, Stuart forgot everything except maintaining the lead. Riding was second nature to him. He'd done it all his life. Years with the light dragoons had strengthened his horsemanship. Out here, in the brisk air, surrounded by pounding hooves, he was in his element.

The drum of an approaching rider caught his ear. He glanced back. Long, powerful legs churned the turf. The reddish gelding, Diamond, so-called from the white mark on its chiseled face, was closing the gap between them. Over sixteen hands high, he stood taller than La Belle, his confirmation perfect. The lean rider was a master of the saddle, but not more than Stuart.

He urged La Belle on. She flew as if he'd whispered magic in her ears. They left the gelding and mahogany bay mare behind, legs outstretched, straining to catch up. Both were outstanding horses, but lacked heart, a quality La Belle had in abundance.

When Silas Collins appeared ahead of him in the mist, Stuart wasn't certain. One moment, nothing but the hazy course—the next—Silas seated astride a gray mount. The gelding was big, possibly part draft horse, but fleet. Most of all, its color blended in with the whiteness.

What a fraud. Collins hadn't even entered the race. He couldn't possibly hope to win. Everyone knew he didn't belong. Then it occurred to Stuart that Silas was here for him.

Damn and blast. He could drop back, letting others pass him by. And forfeit the race. Or proceed and run into Lord only knows what.

"Foul cheat!" He drew his pistol and charged ahead.

Silas shot a glance over his shoulder.

Was the dead-eyed toad actually grinning?

Anger seared him. He was tempted to lodge a bullet in Collins' back here and now, though he'd likely swing for it. No one else was acquainted with the scoundrel in the way Stuart was.

Prodding La Belle to an even faster pace, he tore up behind man and horse. Nearer and nearer. La Belle was on his tail. She narrowed the distance until they rode abreast. If Collins had some vile scheme in mind, this was the time he'd attempt it.

That maddening sneer! Stuart wanted to punch the smirk from his face and send him skidding sideways.

A woman shrieked from the trees to his right. He knew that cry anywhere. *Hettie*!

Thudding in his chest accompanied the ghastly realization. If he deterred from the track to go in pursuit of her, the race was lost. Collins would follow on his heels with a barrel or blade. The promise was written in his leer.

"Go on, Captain!"

The shout came from Brinkley. He must have the situation in hand. Even if someone put a gun to Brinkley's head, he'd not urge Stuart ahead if Hettie wasn't safe.

Trusting his friend to care for her, Stuart ripped past Silas. He glimpsed the shock in his face. Finally, an emotion he approved of in those fish eyes.

As a parting volley, Stuart turned in the saddle and shot the bastard in the shoulder. He toppled to the ground with a bellow, rolling over and over in the turf. That should keep him at bay for a time. He'd be fortunate if the riders pelting up behind them didn't trample him where he lay.

They'd all heard the shot. Bound to have. But no one could see a thing in this mist.

There'd be questions later. Who would folk believe? Stuart, legitimately entered in the race, or Silas Collins, an outsider where he didn't belong, who'd threatened him?

One of Collins' henchman must've alarmed Hettie. It wouldn't have been Thomas Vaughan. He'd not sully his hands, but Davis might have turned up.

His chest still thudding, Stuart rode on. By heaven, he was winning this and then getting to Hettie as fast as was humanly possible.

He strained to hear another volley suggesting Brinkley had laid the outlaw low.

He never expected the enraged snarls.

Holy Mother of God. The wolf.

Chapter Twenty-Three

"You're safe. I've got you."

"Brinkley—thank God." He pulled Hettie, panting, to her feet, and circled a steadying arm around her shoulders. His other hand gripped the pistol he'd trained on Davis.

She'd heard him shout to Stuart, and an answering shot—not sure at who. Then the black wolf sprang from the misty undergrowth in an arching leap—the image forever branded on her mind. Davis gaped open-mouthed as the creature hurtled at him, knocking him on his back.

Hettie was winded from slamming onto the ground when he'd ripped her from Bryan. She'd unleashed a shriek as she went down—hard—but not after. Gasping for air, she'd crouched in the leaves, the woodsy scent of humus in her nose. Davis was advancing on her with a length of rope when the wolf sprang at him.

His cries rose against the snapping and snarls. The creature latched onto his arm. Both assaults occurred so fast, she could hardly take it in. Bryan backed away. To his credit, the stout horse didn't bolt.

She stared at Davis and the wolf in horror and amazement. Hadn't he endured enough punishment the last time he'd attempted to grab her? His upper arm couldn't yet be healed from the gunshot wound Mrs. Jenner had inflicted, and he must still suffer from wolf bites. He suffered more now—rolling convulsively, his face a howling blur.

Did he want that accursed treasure so badly he was willing to risk all to gain it, or was he so confident of finding her unprotected he hadn't considered the danger?

Vile, foolish man.

When Brinkley arrived on the scene, she wasn't sure. He hadn't been far ahead of her to begin with and must've swiftly doubled back. She hadn't meant to ignore his warning to keep up, and had lingered for a glimpse of the race through the partings in the trees. She'd seen Stuart charge ahead. Then Silas Collins rode out from cover to harass him.

Wondering what that scoundrel's intentions were and how to help Stuart held her focus. She'd made an easy target for Davis, or so he'd thought.

"Who in hell has a wolf protecting her?" he hurled at Hettie in between screams. "You must be some sort of—"

Before he spat out 'witch' Brinkley put a bullet in his heart. The wolf whipped around at the blast and sprang into the haze, vanishing like a shadow.

"We don't want that ugly name bandied about." Brinkley was so calm.

Hettie lifted dazed eyes to his steely gaze. "But why—"

"Shoot him? None need hear his accusations. Davis was intent on snatching, even killing, you. This was his third assault. He'd have hung for sure. Though possibly not before he'd sullied your honor in the community."

So, he'd killed Davis to protect her. Stuart would have done the same, she didn't doubt. Even so. As much as she loathed the man, seeing him lying there with that dead-eyed glare was more than she could stomach.

Her gut churned. Trembling started at her knees and spread through her entire body. Even her teeth chattered.

"Come on. I'll take you back on my mount, and lead Bryan behind. Your uncle's home is the nearest refuge." They were several miles outside of Halifax, between the town and Thornton Hall.

"Say nothing of the wolf, or it will come under attack. If any ask, say only it was a dog," he added, in a whisper.

She nodded, vaguely aware of Brinkley boosting her up on his steady charcoal gelding. People were rushing onto the site as he closed an arm around Hettie to keep her from toppling senseless to the ground. The entire affair had transpired in minutes, but it would take her some time to recover.

Brinkley waved at the fast-gathering crowd. "Make way, folk! The poor lady's come under attack by the black-hearted criminal who lies dead by my hand."

Agog at the startling tidings, they parted to let him pass with Hettie and Bryan. Behind them, curious onlookers made a mad dash—falling over each other— to goggle at the fallen man. Exclamations and cheers broke out.

"Got the bugger!" a man crowed, as if he owned the triumph.

"One down. Maybe two," Brinkley muttered. He prodded his gelding into a brisk trot, Bryan jogging at the rear.

Hettie wondered again who Stuart may have fired

on. "You think he shot Collins?"

"That would be my guess."

"Can he do that?"

"Stuart Monroe can do the outrageous and get away with it." Brinkley's admiration was heartening.

"On his own, Thomas Vaughan poses little threat. He works through others," Brinkley added.

Relief flowed alongside the tremor racking Hettie. She was too muzzy headed to think clearly. But it seemed to her there was something—or someone—important she'd forgotten.

Chapter Twenty-Four

"You carried the day, my boys! Won the race and felled Davis!"

Ezra was in high spirits this evening, the grin stretching his angular face a sight Stuart never thought to see. At least, not on his account. To his astonishment, the older man capered about the parlor, particularly comical with his thin legs and knobby knees. Crimson lengths of the scarf wound at his skinny neck flew.

Even Jonas arranged his squat features into the semblance of a smile. And both father and son had turned their favorite armchairs away from the hearth to visit with guests. Normally, they hugged the blaze like bloodless reptiles.

Remarkable. Though in Ezra's case, drink had something to do with his altered state, as evidenced by the rosiness in his bulbous nose. The monk-like Jonas exercised more restraint when imbibing strong spirits, and in everything else, as well.

Ezra paused unsteadily by his seat. Waving his glass, he sloshed wine onto the floral carpet. "What a ride you had! Never seen the like before. The late Captain Monroe would be proud of you, Stuart, m' lad!"

"Hear. Hear." Brinkley managed a hoarse cheer, the most enthusiasm he could muster after all the ale he'd consumed earlier at the tavern. He was about to sag in a heap on the floor.

Stuart nodded his appreciation from where he sat on the couch beside Hettie. The fruity aroma of wine in their glasses blended with her violet perfume. "Thank you, sir. No doubt, my father would be well pleased." And possibly already was. "Is he here?" Stuart whispered to her.

She shook her head. "I believe he remains within Thornton," she said under her breath.

"Is he bound to the house, or can he move about?"

"I'm not certain."

"When he completes his mission will he return to heaven, or did he never cross over to begin with?"

Hesitancy in her eyes, she shrugged.

"You are not as acquainted with the departed as you assert, dear heart," Stuart challenged in a low voice.

Adorably flustered, she argued. "I never said I—"

"What are you two murmuring over there?" Ezra broke in.

"Soft nothings." Brinkley answered for them.

Hettie smiled, Stuart chuckled, and Abigail tittered. Ezra guffawed, swayed, and plopped down into his seat. At his insistence, the couple sat on *the courting couch*, as he'd termed it.

Considering they were beyond simple courting and betrothed to be wed, Stuart was taken aback by the reference. He might need to be firmer with her stubborn relation about the upcoming nuptials. After all, the banns were posted.

Ezra could be as erratic as his grandfather at times. It seemed Stuart's lot in life to have eccentric relations, making it difficult to assess where one stood with them at any given moment. They blew with the wind. Clearly, this evening, Ezra held him in high regard.

Laughter echoed in the room Stuart had visited not many days ago, and left after a terse exchange. The quarrel between them seemingly forgotten, Ezra exuded good will. Not only was Stuart toasted by Hettie's uncle, but proclaimed a town hero, closely followed by Brinkley. This afternoon, they'd been hoisted on men's shoulders and carried through the streets.

After a rowdy celebration at *The Sign of the Thistle*, Stuart was eager to disentangle himself from the crowd and find Hettie. Brinkley offered no protest at escaping the throng of sweaty men. A stiff wind chased away the mist and the first stars shone when they staggered, arm in arm, to the Jones' home.

Hettie rushed at Stuart upon his return, and nestled against him on the couch as if she couldn't sit near enough. Much as this thrilled him, he knew she was still shaken from events of the morning. At least, she'd had the afternoon to rest in her former bedchamber, ministered to by the adoring household and Miss Smith, who'd proved a Godsend.

Abigail sat demurely on an upholstered chair as near to Brinkley as she could arrange without appearing unladylike. He'd sunk into an armchair midway between the couch and the hearth. His blond hair was disarrayed, eyes bloodshot, and his coat reeked of tobacco smoke and ale. Stuart hadn't fared much better. Both could do with hot water, soap, fresh clothes, and sound sleep.

Brinkley was in no state now to return Abigail's marked favor. Whether or not he eventually chose to do so, resided solely with him. Thank heavens, it wouldn't be Stuart's fault if her hopes were dashed a second time.

He gestured at his friend. "I couldn't have prevailed today without Brinkley intervening for Hettie, else I would have had to abandon the race and speed to her defense."

"So you would." Ezra dwelt devotedly on his niece, then turned his exalted gaze to Brinkley. "We shall forever be in your debt. Bravo, I say. Bravo!"

An answering salute from Brinkley, who neglected all mention of any assistance from the wolf. Stuart had agreed it was best not to dwell on the near mystical creature.

"Your devoted servant, sir," he offered instead.

Abigail gazed at him adoringly, and Hettie, with a mix of gratitude and somber reckoning.

Flushed from wine, Ezra raised his glass. Otis, the footman, had refilled his goblet. "Your Uncle Ellis must swell with satisfaction, Brinkley. You are the son he never had. Both you boys do us proud."

"Indeed. To Monroe and Brinkley." Jonas toasted them with his good arm.

Stuart had consumed more than enough at the tavern, and Brinkley was barely conscious. Out of regard for their merry host, though, they raised their glasses and swigged yet another round. The fine wine could be swamp water for all Stuart cared at this point. Hettie and Abigail sipped decorously. Ladies weren't pressed to imbibe endless spirits.

A serving girl arrived with small cakes, confections, and cheese neatly arranged on the large china platter. Otis took the plate from her. He served while she sped away. Again, Stuart and Brinkley exerted themselves to partake of Ezra's hospitality. They'd eaten plenty at the tavern, too. Stuart hoped he and Brinkley weren't sick on this expensive carpet.

The door opened again. Rather than the girl with more provisions, Thomas Vaughan appeared in the entryway. Stuart bristled, and Hettie stiffened against him. What was that conniving snake up to now?

Ezra spotted Thomas and gave a jovial wave. "Come in, man, and join the celebration."

Apparently, he'd conveniently forgotten Stuart's antagonism toward the former turncoat/traitor/British spy, who was plotting his demise, and quite possibly Hettie's as well. Thomas had been conspicuous among the throng at the tavern only by his absence. Presumably, he was preoccupied seeing to Collins' injury and hushing him up.

Strangely, not a word had passed the wounded man's lips regarding Stuart. The anticipated charge never arose, and he hadn't needed to justify himself. The rumor circulating town was that Collins had been struck by a stray bullet from the trees fired by that criminal, Davis, before he fell. No mention was made as to why Collins had been on the race course at the time. Folk were satisfied with the explanation.

Stuart couldn't fathom Collins' silence. Granted, he was glad to be heralded for his superior run. La Belle won by a respectable lead, the best time of any horse— ever. Still, he was baffled by the lack of complaint.

Why did Collins keep quiet? Something sinister was at work, probably Thomas. Perhaps if he kept Collins muzzled, they could continue their plot without contriving alterations.

Whatever lay behind the secrecy, Stuart didn't trust

Thomas and shifted edgily at his coming. Hettie paled. Brinkley roused from his stupor as if dashed with cold water. Stuart had witnessed his friend snap to life in this manner during the war. He never counted Brinkley out. Abigail widened her eyes and the four of them regarded Thomas closely.

The thought of sharing this house with that scoundrel was insufferable. Thank God, they were traveling to Thornton Hall tomorrow, the gentlemen by horse, and the ladies by carriage. Jim and his brother Joseph were camped out in the stable with the horses. La Belle was to be particularly well-guarded. The sight of Thomas made Stuart want to leave at once.

Elegant as ever, he minced into the room, tapping his cane knotted with lavender ribbons. How he'd acquired the parrot green suit he wore, Stuart couldn't imagine. His business couldn't possibly be that prosperous yet. Likely, he owed Ezra money.

Distaste crossed Jonas's close set gaze behind his spectacles. Thomas must've thinned his welcome in that quarter. Jonas abhorred unnecessary expenditure, and Thomas was no true kin. Jonas was already stretched doing his duty to Hettie, and he liked her—as much as this dispassionate scholar was capable of caring for anyone. Plainly, Thomas fell short in his estimation.

If it were up to Jonas, he'd likely boot the ne'er-do-well from the house, and he didn't know the half of it. But Jonas wouldn't readily oppose his father. Nor did he surrender his seat to the usurper, offering a chill nod, instead.

Otis selected a less comfortable seat from along the wall beside the glass front cabinet overflowing with china and figurines. He set the wooden chair in the center of the room. "Here you go, Mister Vaughan."

Did Stuart detect a hint of disdain in the look Otis cast Thomas? Highly unusual for a footman.

Thomas behaved as if he were oblivious of the frost in the room. The only one truly unaware was Ezra, who ought to be ushered to bed. With a ducal bow to the ladies, nods for the gentlemen, and 'good evenings' all around, Thomas sat in the hard seat. Accepting a glass of wine and piece of cake from Otis, he surveyed the group between cagey eyes as he nibbled.

The hush in the chamber reminded Stuart of the stillness before a breaking storm. Ezra looked about him, bushy brows arched. "What's this? You lot have gone quiet. Come now, let's have some cheer. Who will oblige me with a song?"

Not Stuart or Brinkley, though both could sing when they chose.

Abigail rose and curtsied to Ezra. "I should be glad to oblige you, sir."

"That would be most welcome, Miss Smith. Will you join her and make it a duet, Hettie, dear?"

"If you like, Uncle."

"Very much." He waited expectantly.

She exchanged glances with Stuart. He pressed her fingers, and she rose reluctantly to her feet, swishing to the center of the room beside Abigail. What a striking pair they made, Hettie with her dark looks and deep green grown and Abigail with her lighter coloring and blue floral dress.

The two conferred on their choice and broke into a lovely rendition of *Greensleeves*, sung in a round.

The beauty was lost on Stuart. His hackles rising,

he trained every sense on Thomas. A guard dog couldn't do better.

Brinkley did the same, with the added element excessive drink gave him, when he no longer gave a damn about propriety. He wasn't mean, just unpredictable. Highly so.

Stuart ought to extract his friend from the room, get them all out and away from Halifax. But Ezra wouldn't hear of their leaving before the morrow.

Heedless of the volatile mood, their giddy host enjoyed the tune and applauded. The ladies obliged him with another song. Jonas shifted his nervous gaze between the men. Unlike his father, he was aware of the mounting tension.

With an air of contempt, Thomas plucked a scented handkerchief from his lace-edged sleeve and waved it beneath his nose as if to mask a noxious odor. Then he removed a small gilded snuff box from his pocket, bright flowers embellishing the enamel, and inhaled the pinch of vanilla-scented powder. It wasn't Thomas's use of snuff that offended Stuart, many enjoyed smokeless tobacco in various flavors, but his manner of warding off pestilence in doing so.

The implication couldn't be plainer. Was he challenging them, angry they'd shot two of his fellows and killed one?

Normally, Thomas was more judicious. Now, he taunted them as one might a maddened bull. *Unwise.*

Stuart rose to the bait. "How fares Mister Collins? Brinkley and I have been most concerned."

"Indeed. Perhaps we ought to pay him a visit." Brinkley didn't add, *and finish him off,* but the threat was clear.

Thomas flicked a speck from his immaculate coat. "Mister Collins is of no particular importance to me."

"No? You seemed quite friendly at the Ordinary the other day." Stuart reminded him of the meeting he'd witnessed between them.

Thomas was unaffected. "Not in the least. But as you are both solicitous for the gentleman's welfare, let me assure you, he's not far removed."

"Indeed?" Stuart pressed.

Triumph hinted in those black-brown eyes. "He lies in a back chamber."

"In this house?" Stuart nearly choked on his cake.

A smile flitted over Thomas's smug face. "At Mister Jones insistence. He was borne here after the surgeon at *Dudley's Tavern* removed the lead from his shoulder and dressed the wound."

"Why was he not left to recover in a room at the tavern?"

Thomas wore the gloat of a man about to win at cards. "Mister Jones insists on him being tended properly. He felt it his duty after hearing Collins was wounded by a bullet from his former employee, Mister Davis."

"We both know that's not the way it was," Stuart hissed.

"Will you inform Mister Jones or shall I?" Thomas countered.

Brinkley shifted his chair closer so Thomas didn't miss his growl. "Perhaps we'll just shoot you and be done with it."

"No doubt you would, after your days' work."

Stuart bent near Thomas to assure him. "We both would."

The rash usurper had the sense to blanch a little. "Now, gentlemen. The war is over. We live in a society of laws."

"Indeed? These laws you speak of have been broken a lot of late," Stuart tossed back.

Restoring the snuff box, Thomas attempted another tack. "Not by my doing. I wish only for peace between us, Captain."

"Much blood was shed before the Treaty of Paris was signed. We saw. We were there."

Brinkley grunted agreement. "Unlike some."

"Will you scorn the afflicted?" Thomas asked, piteously.

"Not the truly afflicted. No." Stuart nodded at Jonas. "Hear me well. If you or anyone associated with you threatens Miss Fairfax or any of us again, it will be the last time."

Thomas inclined his head at Stuart's ultimatum, but his flinty gaze promised otherwise. This wasn't over.

Stuart barely refrained from attacking him then and there. No wonder Hettie was so skittish. The enemy were among them, and Collins only winged. She must have Abigail stay in her chamber tonight and sleep with the pistol under her pillow. Stuart and Brinkley would keep watch down here.

There'd be scant rest and patrols to conduct. Stuart couldn't get Hettie back to Thornton fast enough. If Ezra kicked up a fuss, he was taking her anyway, and wedding her at his first opportunity. This he must make clear.

Hettie and Abigail concluded their next song and the room quieted. Ezra burst into applause. "Oh, well done."

Jonas clapped warmly. "Never better."

A smattering of applause from Thomas, who stifled a yawn.

Stuart wanted to punch him in the mouth as he brought his hands together. "Charming, ladies."

"Utterly," Brinkley assured them.

He rose, a trifle unsteadily, and bowed to the lovely pair, then reached out a hand and shoved Thomas off his chair. His drink sloshed over his new suit as he careened to the floor, and he may have squashed what was left of the cake beneath him.

Stuart blinked, but was only mildly surprised. He should've seen this coming. A gasp circled the assembly and everyone stared from the man scuffling on the floor to Brinkley. Otis smothered a smile behind his hand.

Brinkley shrugged. "I fear I'm a little wobbly from all the celebrating."

"Of course. Perfectly understandable," Jonas murmured.

"Certainly," Ezra agreed. "I'm a bit shaky myself."

The fury in Thomas's slitted gaze would scorch a normal man. Brinkley didn't flinch. But the danger had ratcheted up several notches.

Stuart was torn between laughing hysterically and getting the hell out of Halifax. Who knew what forces of evil Thomas would summon next?

****

What in heaven's name was Brinkley thinking? And it was he who'd said Stuart got away with doing outrageous things!

"Otis, bring a cloth and some water for Mister

Vaughan." Hettie jerked up her skirts and dashed to the man sprawled on the floor, his face mottled, eyes firing daggers at Brinkley.

Kneeling beside him, she patted his arm. "There, now. Just a small tumble. We'll soon have you tidied," she crooned, as if soothing a five-year-old, though this enraged *child* was anything but harmless.

Otis dipped a cloth into the basin on the stand in the corner, wrung it out, and passed her the dampened linen. "Here, Miss."

"Thank you." She blotted at Thomas's stained coat. "Good as new. You'll see."

"I am perfectly capable of tending to myself, Miss Fairfax, and certainly do not require *your* aid. Of all the impertinence." Jerking from her hand, as though from a beggar's claw, he clambered to his feet.

She gasped, a breathless knot in her middle.

Not that Thomas gave her a second thought. His tight gaze flashed to her uncle. "If you will be so good as to send a manservant to my chamber to assist me, Mister Jones."

Uncle Ezra eyed the infuriated man like one piecing together a puzzle while half asleep.

Not Jonas. "My father is fatigued and retiring to his chamber," he replied shortly. "You shall have to make do this evening. As you are *capable*, that should prove no difficulty." Ice in his tone, he flung Thomas's words back at him.

Hettie never thought to see Jonas come to her defense. And so bold. Thomas appeared equally stunned.

When Stuart got to his feet, she wasn't sure. He helped her rise and nudged her toward the couch. "Wait there. You, too, Miss Smith." They scurried aside in a rustle of taffeta.

Rounding on Thomas, he blocked his way as he attempted to stride from the room. "You owe Miss Fairfax an apology." She scarcely recognized the low growl.

"M-M-Me?" Sputtering wrath, Thomas drew himself up to his full height, still a head shorter than Stuart. "It's that scoundrel, Brinkley, who owes me one."

Brinkley trapped Thomas between Stuart and himself. "Did you refer to me as a scoundrel?" Menacing calm underlay the query.

Jonas gestured from his seat before the hearth. "Gentlemen, please. We want no dueling in this house."

Thomas swiveled gaping eyes from one man to the other. "D-D-Duel? I never said anything about a duel."

Stuart crossed both arms over his chest. "What did you expect would follow? You insulted Miss Fairfax."

"And slurred my name," Brinkley muttered.

"You cast me on the floor—"

Rapping intruded. Heads turned at Uncle Ezra pounding his cane. Fire lit his gaze. "Mister Vaughan you have thoroughly spoilt our party."

A grievous offence, Hettie knew.

He attempted an apology, engulfed in the ensuing tirade.

"I cannot countenance the discourteous treatment of my niece. 'Tisn't she who tipped you from your chair, but knelt by you in Christian charity. She sullied her skirts in your aid. A lady, grubbing on the floor! Unheard of."

"Please forgive—"

Uncle Ezra overrode Thomas's next attempt. "And did Brinkley not rescue dear Hettie from that foul Davis? He cannot be held to account for upsetting you, as he imbibed too freely in the resulting celebration. You must let the matter rest. Such fuss over a trifle. Will you declare war?"

"No, indeed."

"It appears so to me. Such commotion I never saw since the British went through Halifax." Uncle Ezra was nearly apoplectic.

Jonas regarded him in alarm, as did Hettie. "Father, do not vex yourself so."

"I cannot abide to see our darling Hettie suffer."

"I am shaken, but tolerable, and do most heartily thank you for your tender care, Uncle," she assured him.

Abigail trembled at her side. "Please, take some rest, sir. You are overwrought."

The older man seemed slightly calmer.

Stuart and Brinkley relaxed their aggressive posture and stepped back from Thomas. Stuart swept his hand at the door. He was free to go.

But Thomas remained to battle for forgiveness from his patron. "I'm abjectly repentant, Mister Jones. There are no words to express my contrite spirit."

"I fear you've displayed your true colors."

"Please, sir. I was caught off guard and gave into my deplorable temper. My worst fault. It will not happen again."

"See that it doesn't, Mister Vaughan. I think it fair to say Brinkley's uncle, Mister Ellis, will not be pleased to hear of this hostility. You may lay to rest any hopes of conducting business with that gentleman."

Thomas stared at him mutely.

"And now, I really must retire to my bed and bid you all goodnight." Ezra lifted a hand to the gathering.

Nods and bows returned his farewell. Hettie snatched up her skirts and rushed to his side. "Dearest Uncle."

She gave him an embrace, heartily returned, then Otis assisted the frailer looking man from the room. The day had taken a toll on him, and it grieved her.

Stuart gestured again at the doorway. "Pray, do not let us detain you, Mister Vaughan. We bid you a good evening."

The look Thomas shot him and Brinkley could roast them to cinders. He nodded curtly to Jonas and strode across the room.

Jonas cleared his throat. "Once more, you neglect to show the proper courtesy to my cousin and her fair friend, Miss Smith. You will be gone from this house on the morrow, sir."

Thomas drew up. "But the senior Mister Jones—"

"Will heed me. I am finished with your impertinence, sir. Remove yourself to your home directly after breakfast. We must consider whether to continue to foster your establishment."

Thomas eyed Jonas as if seeing him for the first time. "What of Mister Collins?"

Suspicion crossed the pale eyes behind the spectacles. "Remove him with you on the morrow. He is no longer our employee. We will draw from local workers."

Hettie had never witnessed this forthright side of her cousin and regretted her earlier, unkind opinion. Stuart and Brinkley regarded him with newfound respect, as did Abigail.

Turning on his haunches with evident disinclination, Thomas scraped a bow. "Ladies, gentlemen, I bid you *adieu*." With that farewell, uttered through clenched teeth, he stormed out the door. On his backside—the squashed cake.

Whatever move he made next, no doubt he'd attempt it with the help of Collins and his satanic mother. God help them all.

Chapter Twenty-Five

Hettie. The low summons repeated, calling her from a hazy place of forgotten dreams.

Captain John? She stirred drowsily in her bed at Thornton Hall. The hall clock downstairs struck 3:00 as she opened heavy eyes to seek for him.

There. Instead of sitting in the chair by her bed, he stood at the window.

Bright moonlight spilled through the parting in the heavy damask drapes to reveal him staring out the glass, both arms crossed behind his straight back. The celestial beams poured over his gray-streaked hair, neatly tied with a black ribbon, and his blue coat faced with red.

He turned and she took in the white waistcoat, the red officer's sash at his waist, the sword by his side, the cream-colored breeches and high black riding boots. In all the times he'd appeared to her, he'd never worn a hat, perhaps because he was always indoors. And she'd never seen him so clearly.

Was she dreaming?

With a sense of unreality, she slipped from beneath her warm covers and crept beside him in her white shift and bare feet. The cold floor was real enough, as was the chill in the room. The fire burned low.

Wood smoke mingled with spice from the pomander ball. A whiff of pipe tobacco emanated from

Captain John. She hadn't noticed that about him before.

She sensed he was disturbed, and tilted her head at him. "What is it?"

The pearly sheen illuminated his greenish eyes. *There is something you must do for me.*

"Anything, if I'm able."

Fondness warmed his gaze. *So like my darling Claire.*

"Would you like me to write her about you?" Hettie found herself offering.

He shook his head. *Her role in this scheme is done. As to my love for Claire, she knows.*

"You are here on account of Stuart," Hettie determined.

I am. He must abandon his intent to dig up that accursed treasure. You must convince him.

A weighty directive, but she nodded. "I will do my utmost. He's beginning to believe in you."

Though not entirely persuaded.

"No. And he frets over clearing his debts, and will not allow me to use my inheritance to help him."

He is proud.

"Too proud. He sorely vexes me. We quarreled earlier today." She'd retired to bed troubled.

Captain John laid a gloved hand lightly on her shoulder, also a first. *Be patient, yet persistent. And tell him, upon my word, his debt shall be paid.*

"Without the treasure? Even the generous purse from the race wasn't enough."

All will be settled. He must trust in Divine Providence, as does General Washington. You both must. Or evil shall befall you.

Dread overshadowed Captain John's commission

to have faith.

This is why I am come, to prevent your ruin.

"I will exert my all to make Stuart hear me."

There is more. Not easy to hear.

"Nothing has been." Taut with suspense, she waited.

Thomas Vaughan has learned where the treasure is hidden.

"How?"

Esther Collins.

"The witch mother? She divined the site?"

He inclined his head. *After many dark spells. And sent word to Silas Collins.*

"How do you know this?" Hettie asked, then caught herself. How did he know anything?

He didn't bother to reply to her question. *Listen well. Tomorrow night, Thomas Vaughan, Silas Collins, and one other will unearth the grave.*

"What of Esther?"

She is crippled and cannot leave her home.

"Thank God for that," Hettie said in relief, then amended her exhalation. "Not that I rejoice in her infirmity."

She has lost much and will soon lose more.

"Why?"

The treasure is cursed, he repeated, as though Hettie had missed the obvious.

She stared blankly at him. "I thought Esther is the one who cursed it."

Beyond her. Manley.

"Oh. I see." But she didn't really. She had difficulty following an exchange that seemed more and more dreamlike.

Do not allow the treasure to fall into innocent hands. It jeopardizes all. Tomorrow, journey to the graveyard and watch in secret.

"For what?"

You will see. Remember, the treasure must be restored.

"Back in the grave?" Hettie felt as dense as stone.

Yes. Leave it and Manley in peace...as near to peace as that wretched soul can come.

"What of your peace?"

My fate depends on you and Stuart.

Did she detect sadness in his reply? "Must you remain here until all is made right?"

I choose to remain until then.

"I vow to do my all to fulfill your charge, so you may go where you belong. What if Stuart won't believe me?"

Make him see. This may help.

He walked across her chamber and stopped before the fireplace. Taking the sword from his side, he laid it on the mantel. Flecks of silver glinted in the orange glow cast by the low flames.

If this were real, and not a dream, the sword would still be there come morning. "What if Stuart says I found it in the house?"

Captain John turned from the hearth toward her. *My sword was not in this house.*

"You mean, it was buried with you?"

No. It was lost. And now, is found. Meant for my son.

If she could persuade Stuart of that.

Ready yourself for tomorrow night. Much depends on the outcome. Your very lives. Have great care.

"We shall." A thought occurred in her dazed state. "Tomorrow night is the ball at Uncle Ezra's."

Then you will already be in Halifax, near the cemetery.

"Won't people be suspicious of the activity in the graveyard?"

They will be too preoccupied with the dancing and merriment to notice.

"Maybe that's why Thomas and Collins chose this night to undertake their dark deed."

Yes. If all goes as we wish, you may not see me again.

A strange sadness came over her. "I will miss you."

We shall meet again on the other side. Live and prosper, dear lady. Love my son well.

"I will. If he doesn't drive me to distraction."

His lips curved in a brief smile. *Cherish each moment together.*

Was that his way of warning her they didn't have many left? She prayed not.

He lifted his hand in farewell. Then his form grew fainter, fading into the smoky whiteness by the hearth.

She didn't want him to go. "Wait. Can you come to the cemetery with us?"

No. The wolf can.

She hadn't seen the wolf since the race five days ago.

Adieu, Hettie. Only Captain John's voice floated in her head, no glimpse of him remained.

"*Adieu,*" she repeated, sobered to her core. He'd sounded the call; the quest rested with her now.

Shivering set in and chills shook her. She stepped into her slippers. Gathering a coverlet around her, she closed it around her shoulders. She must go to Stuart.

Whether awake or dreaming, she was on her feet and had to go to him at once.

****

Like a melody gently playing, Stuart gradually became aware of Hettie whispering his name, her breath warm in his ear. The scent of violets beckoned to him in sensuous sweetness. A hand on his shoulder gave him a shake.

"Please wake up. I need you."

Everything in him longed for her. He struggled to reach her through the veils of sleep weighing him down. It seemed to him there was some discord between them, though he couldn't think what it was. Nothing mattered now except Hettie.

Had he been given a sleep potion? What a battle to open his eyes. He surveyed her groggily through blurry slits.

Was she actually in his chamber in the middle of the night? Probably not for the seductive reason he hoped.

"Stuart, you must promise me something."

Anything, for a kiss from those beguiling lips.

In that ethereal way Hettie had, she stood by his bed dusted in starlight and moonbeams. Angelic or ghostly, he wasn't sure, but utterly enchanting. Black hair tumbled down over her shoulders to her waist, and she clutched a blanket around her slender figure. The coverlet didn't prevent tremors from coursing through her.

Was she cold or frightened? Possibly both. But the urgency in her demeanor spoke to the latter.

Years of war had taught him to shake off sleep like

a mantle. He sat upright in his shirt, opened down the front. "What is it? What's happened?"

Firelight dappled her as she lowered herself onto the edge of his bed. "Your father—"

He groaned wearily. "Not another vision." He'd feared they were under attack.

"Visitation," she corrected, the wounded tone reflected in her reproachful gaze. "His last, he says."

"Why that? This isn't like him." At least, not like Hettie to let go of the late captain.

"We are nearing the end of his reason for being here."

That was a step in the right direction. "How so?"

Puckers creased her forehead, the corners of her eyes, and her mouth. "He came to warn us. If we fail to do as he says, we shall perish and join him on the other side. Unless, we're forever cursed. I'm not certain which it was."

"Sounds dire either way."

"I thought so." Hurt still edged her tone.

Stuart smoothed back the tendrils from her troubled face. If he wasn't getting anymore sleep tonight, he could envision better ways to pass the hours than agonizing over his father's forewarning, but she was in dead earnest.

"Forgive me, sweetheart. I'm listening. What's the alternative to this hellish fate?"

"Do as Captain John directs and he shall depart in peace. Although..." she trailed off, hesitancy in her voice.

He cupped her cold cheek. She was chilled through. "What?"

"I'm not certain we shall survive that either."

"Ah. Unfavorable odds?"

"Rather."

He slid his hand from her face and drew her trembling into his arms. How soft she was against him, and pleasingly curved. "My father sent you to tell me we're doomed?"

She burrowed closer and laid her head on his shoulder. "No. He says all will be well if we heed him. 'Tis difficult to believe."

"Quite. Anything else?" It was bizarrely like receiving a report from a scout who'd gone ahead to survey the enemy before battle.

"There's a dig at the graveyard tomorrow night."

"I thought there might be."

"How?" She tilted her face at him.

He shrugged. "Collins is on the mend and Thomas anxious to proceed now that his business connections are faltering. I assume they'll dupe some simple soul into doing the hard work."

"How did you know?" Wonder tinged her voice.

"I'm no seer. It only stands to reason, dear heart. Are they digging up the entire cemetery or have they figured out where the goods are hidden?"

"Collin's mother did, with some sort of spell. We're to watch from cover and then restore the treasure."

"We'll need a spell of our own for that. Thomas and Collins won't simply surrender the stash. And if we're looking on in secret, they won't even know we're there."

"That's the idea, as I understood it. What will follow, I cannot say, only that we're to do as Captain John says. Or perish."

"He always was a man of decided opinions."

Hettie tensed at Stuart's observation. "This goes well beyond that. Warning us is his sole purpose for being here. Promise me we'll abide by his sacred charge."

"Is that how you view it?"

"How else? We are entrusted with this task, and if we do not carry it out, all is lost."

Stuart brushed his lips over her satiny cheek. "And if we do?"

"All may be well."

"You don't sound persuaded."

"No. Only certain we must try. Will you promise me?"

Savoring the richness of Hettie in his arms, he pondered. "I didn't like being told what to do by my father when he was alive, let alone taking direction from his spirit. But I have to admit, John Monroe was a good and wise man."

"He still is," she whispered.

"Perhaps so." Whether his father truly spoke to Hettie from beyond, he didn't know, but she believed he had. If Stuart refused to cooperate, it would crush her spirit.

"You are worth a wealth of treasure. Yes, sweetheart, I relinquish all claim on this hidden wealth. We will do as you request and he directs."

"Thank God." She breathed out as if a heavy burden had been lifted from her.

With Hettie relaxed deliciously against him, Stuart hated to point out an impediment. But must.

"There's a slight hindrance to this scheme, dearest. You do recall the ball tomorrow evening at your uncle's? I hate to spoil yet another of his parties."

"As would I. Perhaps Brinkley might keep watch for a time, and let us know what's happening. We'll be close by."

"Oh, Brinkley would love that. Nothing he enjoys more than a haunted cemetery, cursed treasure, and grave robbers."

"Stuart," she chided.

"Here's a thought. If they're unearthing stuff that's not meant for us, why don't we just let them have it?"

"Captain John was adamant this trove isn't meant for any living soul. The curse will overtake them. We're to restore everything and hide it away. Forever."

"As long as we're not caught in the crossfire."

"That is my concern," she confided.

"A valid one." He buried his lips in the inviting curve of her neck. "If we may perish tomorrow, let's make the most of the few hours we have left now."

If the quivers running through her resulted from more than fear and cold, he had his answer.

Exquisite tingles shimmered over every inch of Hettie, the opposite of the racking tremors accompanying her arrival in Stuart's bedchamber. It was enough that he'd heard and agreed with her. What happened tomorrow was for God to determine. For now, she relished the wondrous sensations rippling through her at Stuart's touch.

Her coverlet fell away. The shift slipped from her under his hands and was tossed on the floor. To her surprise, she didn't balk at her nakedness before him as she'd thought she would. He'd already peered into her soul, and the muted light in here was more forgiving than full revelation beneath the radiance of a crystal chandelier.

The admiration in Stuart's gaze eased any hesitancy she might've had. He slowly kissed over her shivery shoulders and her breasts, small by any standard, as she was slender.

"I fear I'm not buxom," she whispered, gasping as he lightly suckled a pert nipple.

He chuckled against her skin, flushed with goosebumps. "If I desired a woman overflowing her bodice like a swollen stream, I should wed the barmaid."

She giggled at the absurd image he painted.

"You are perfection," he assured her.

"But odd," she managed, between inhalations of air.

"Only a foolish man runs from a beautiful woman because she sees what no one else does."

"Almost no one," she corrected, waves of delight coursing through her.

"Even this I shall concede. Content now?"

"Supremely."

He discarded his shirt, baring his muscled chest. She could scarcely breathe. "You are glorious, dear one."

A grin split his handsome face.

"I mean it."

"I know." His mouth sought hers and covered her tremulous lips.

She returned his heated kiss. For a sublime moment, there was only Stuart, the crackle of the fire, and moonbeams.

Circling his arms around her, he drew her down beneath the covers. "Lest you grow chill."

She savored the feel of his hard chest against hers, of Stuart finally lying with her as she'd longed for him to do. "Can we do this often?"

He laughed softly. "You may change your mind when all is said and done."

"No." Not even the ripe evidence of masculine desire intimidated her.

Rolling with her in his arms, he bent over her, his hair brushing her cheek. "If we survive tomorrow night."

"How shall we do that?"

"Duck any curses flying about."

As fearful as she was of what lay ahead, she convulsed into laughter.

"Shhh," he chuckled, pressing his fingers to her lips to muffle her outburst. "You'll waken the household. If you had any hopes of our rendezvous remaining secret."

"None." She gave herself up to merriment and to him.

Celestial chords beat in her heart. Even the presence of angels couldn't heighten the sacredness of their union.

He was all tenderness. Only a small gasp escaped her as he slide inside her ready flesh, rocking her with a rhythm as ancient as the sea.

Chapter Twenty-Six

What a merry assembly. Gladness imbued the gathering at Uncle Ezra's. Punch flowed freely, borne in cups on trays by Otis and two other Negro footmen in red and black livery.

Gaiety curved the lips of dancers in the wide hall running through the center of the luxurious home. The hard-fought war was won, the treaty with Great Britain signed, and they'd come ready to celebrate their lives in this fledgling nation. Surely, prosperous times lay ahead for Halifax. The spirit of hope was palpable in the heady crowd.

Outside the windows, snowflakes laced the black sky. Coaches lined the white dusted yard and the street in front of the house. The stable overflowed with horses and kept stable boys rushing to tend the mounts. Inside, all was warmth and light.

Candles glowed with the sweet scent of beeswax and the chandelier overhead shone like the evening star. Two of these light fixtures were suspended in dazzling splendor in the house. One illuminated the front hall, another the dining room. These were in addition to the candles in holders on stands and alight on the tops of tables, chests, cabinets... Uncle Ezra adored an extravagant light display, and Jonas hadn't stinted tonight.

Furniture had been pushed back against walls or

rearranged to leave the hall free for dancing. The bird eggs were tucked away. Another tribute from Jonas, to remove his prized collection.

Laughter rose alongside the music. Men's low guffaws contrasted with the high titters of women. Men with high-pitched twitters were also in evidence, their company avoided by Hettie.

Hair piled atop their heads, artful tresses dangling over their shoulders, a colorful array of ladies in taffeta, silk, and velvet gowns swirled to the lively strains from the harpsichord. Two energetic fiddlers also plied their bows and a flutist trilled in accompaniment. Feathers waving in their coiffures, the women flitted in and out of the dance like so many butterflies in a cloud of floral perfume.

Gentlemen with their natural hair dressed in queues, or concealed beneath powdered wigs, wore suits ranging from somber to flamboyant hues. Many waistcoats were embellished by embroidery, as were the panels and stomachers of ladies' gowns, including the fanciful display at Hettie's midriff. Candles revealed the painstaking work of skilled seamstresses.

All this, Hettie took in at a glance, her focus on the steps. Gentlemen swung their partners as men and women came together in the English country dance and whirled away again. Stepping, circling, clapping couples wove their way down the rows, alternately changing gloved hands with other ladies and gentlemen in the pairing. How jolly it all was.

Cousin Jonas looked on from the side, a pleased expression on his chubby countenance, his cane tapping to the music. His infirmity didn't allow him to dance, but he entered into the gaiety of the evening, even humming along. Hettie nodded at him in passing and he returned the gesture, seeming more congenial than she could recall. It gladdened her heart. And Uncle Ezra was in grand form.

"I'm stepping lively with the merry widow, Niece!" he called to her.

"So you are, Uncle," she smiled.

He partnered the giggling matron, as wide as she was tall, given the breadth of her reddish brown skirts and the big bustle at her rear. The thin man and rotund woman made a comical couple. What a relief to see he'd recovered from his previous upset and was enjoying himself.

If Thomas Vaughan wondered at his lack of an invitation to the ball, he need seek no farther than the distress he'd occasioned last week. Wagging tongues, likely instigated by Otis, had spread an account of the incident, referred to as *the affair of the chair*, or more crudely, *cake up his arse*, all over town, causing much jocularity.

Brinkley received claps on the back for the escapade, and Stuart was praised for defending his lady. Jonas and Uncle Ezra were also lauded. Thomas, however, had dipped in public opinion. If he deported himself genially, he might recover his credibility, but his petulant attitude hadn't endeared him to anybody.

Hettie didn't mind so much being the subject of gossip in this instance. And she loved dancing. She would've enjoyed the occasion immensely had she not been on edge.

As it was, she admired Stuart in the deep blue coat and breeches that fitted his tall figure flawlessly, and vowed to ply her needle to his unadorned waistcoat.

Above all, she vowed to be alone with him every possible moment, and quivered at the slightest touch of his hand as he circled with her. If they were still standing at the end of the evening, she intended to visit his chamber again, or invite him to hers.

Memories of their passionate exchange in the wee hours sent heat blazing through her. The thought that her cheeks might betray her unladylike desire, made her blush all the more.

Stuart smiled, as if he knew, and likely did. The wink he flicked her heightened the heat flooding her face.

He bowed his head to whisper in her ear. "Are you free for a rendezvous later tonight?"

Nearly undone, it was all she could do not to fumble her steps. Fortunately, the dance was fairly simple. She wasn't at liberty to pause and fan herself, while gulping in air.

Instead, she shook her head at him in mock scolding. What female would object to the ardent attention of Stuart Monroe?

"Such a man," Hettie overhead one young lady sigh, her eyes on Stuart.

Bosoms heaved from more than physical activity as unmarried women, and some wed, gazed wistfully at him, though not Abigail. Her eyes were all for Brinkley, elegant in his hunter green coat and breeches, his waistcoat worked in silver thread, blond hair shining. She'd claimed him as her partner before another had the chance, not that he put up a fuss.

Brinkley, Stuart, and Hettie each wore colors that would least catch the eye out of doors. So dusky was Hettie's plum silk, the hue would fade into shadows and the cloth didn't rustle like taffeta. Instead of feathers, ribbons and lace fluttered in her hair, and she'd don her black cloak when the time came, as would the men.

For Abigail's protection, she'd been told as little as possible of the night's anticipated event. "The fewer aware, the better," Stuart had said.

And Brinkley agreed. "The girl's happier in her ignorance."

True. She seemed so pretty and carefree stepping along in her yellow gown, Hettie hated to spoil the ball for her.

At the moment, the *highly trusted Jim,* as Stuart referred to the young Negro, stood watch behind a tree near the cemetery with instructions to alert him or Brinkley at the first sign of the grave diggers.

Considering the ball was being held in Stuart and Hettie's honor by her beaming uncle, slipping away from the affair required thought. Leaving undetected in the crush of dancers might be easier than later, during the supper planned for after the ball. None of these options held great promise.

Brinkley smiled at her as she and Stuart promenaded past him and Abigail. "How fare you this merry evening, dear lady?"

Behind his unruffled veneer she sensed keen watchfulness. If he were inquiring whether she felt near to swooning, he was close to the mark.

"She's delightful," Stuart replied for her, "and delectable," he added for Hettie's ear only, sending a thrill through her.

He conveyed the same demeanor as Brinkley, confident, charming, and alert. Like herd dogs intent on driving sheep, little escaped their notice. If they suffered from the strain, they hid it well. Facing battle as often as they had over the years must've hardened them, and attuned their senses.

They knew who was where in the room, and maneuvered in the dance so that one of them was often at the front of the hall near the door, in the event Jim stuck his head around the entryway. Both awaited a tap on their shoulder, should either man not spy him. And Hettie continually swiveled her head in that direction, while pretending nonchalance.

What would transpire when Thomas Vaughan, Silas Collins, and whatever poor soul they'd pressed into service arrived, she had no idea. Watch and wait for the opportunity to act, was all she'd gleaned from Captain John.

Outwardly, she entered into the festivity of the evening, all the while praying they'd live to see the morrow.

As long as that witch mother remained at home, they stood a chance. If only Captain John could be with them.

****

The hour Hettie dreaded was upon them. Through trees brushed by lightly falling snow, she spied the trio bent over a grave. The smoky lantern Thomas held revealed the men's dark shapes. Here and there, raised stone table tombs enshrined the remains of the wealthier occupants of the cemetery. However, the site commanding their focus was not an ornate memorial, but a simple headstone. She didn't recognize the fellow in the rough attire of a worker. He wielded a shovel while the other two urged him on in gruff syllables.

"Poor fool will bear the blame for this if he's

detected," Stuart whispered.

"Even if he's not perceived," Brinkley hissed.

Hettie nodded beneath her hood. That man's fate was sealed before he arrived. God only knew what awaited the rest of them.

How strange to be so near and yet removed from the festivity taking place across the street in the house glittering like a jewel. Oblivious of what transpired beyond their snug walls, folk danced on and guzzled more punch. Here, in the bleak cemetery, she and Stuart hid behind an old tree with a wide girth, its gnarled trunk white where snow clung.

Brinkley had taken cover behind a tree near theirs. "Like fighting Indian style," he muttered.

"How we're to battle at all, remains to be seen," Stuart muttered in turn.

"Watch and wait." Hettie was at a loss herself.

"We are," Stuart said shortly. "But if we're attacked, we're fighting back."

"Agreed." She was acutely aware of the precarious trust he'd placed in her abilities. Well, she'd been proven right thus far. The dig was underway, as Captain John had predicted.

In order to reach this accursed spot, she'd made her excuses to Uncle Ezra, promising to return from her chamber after a brief respite. There, she'd exchanged her silk slippers for ankle high leather shoes and wrapped in the black mantle. No one in the lively throng noted her glide downstairs and hover by the door any more than they might've a shadow.

Rather than using stealth, Stuart and Brinkley had declared their intent of visiting the stable with the assurance of soon returning. Brinkley hushed Abigail's protest by kissing her pink cheek. The glow in her eyes promised forgiveness. Hettie hoped he wasn't merely trifling with the girl—she'd heard he had something of a reputation, charming, but difficult to pin down—but couldn't fret over that now.

She'd slipped out with the men, as though accompanying them for a breath of fresh air, should any ask. Once outside, the dark cloaks each wore, and black tricorns atop the men's heads, shielded them from sight and the raw chill.

Minutes passed as they looked on from behind the trees, through softly swirling snow. Despite the finger numbing cold that penetrated Hettie's gloves, the hole the worker dug rapidly deepened. The ground wasn't too frozen to yield its sought after riches.

Thank God, Stuart wasn't the one with his boot on that shovel. Everything in her screamed, *Stop*!

What form might the curse take? Would demons fly up from the pit forming in the ground with a ghostly cackle?

She shrank against Stuart. He closed a supportive arm around her shoulders, and she knew he'd fight to the death for her. But how were they to battle evil?

Shouting warnings at those consumed by greed would avail nothing. Thomas Vaughan and Silas Collins each bore arms, as did Stuart and Brinkley. Firing on one another, or clashing swords, would draw onlookers.

This treasure was meant to remain a secret, and Captain John hadn't said anything about killing anyone. The realm they waged war in was a spiritual one. She prayed for direction. Turning these mantles into cloaks of invisibility would also be welcome.

The buzz of excitement from the men up ahead caught her attention. His breath white against snowflakes drifting like goose down, Thomas gave a nod and the wiry laborer scrambled into the hole. The thud of a shovel carried through the still trees. He must be clearing dirt from the sides of the coffin to free it from the ground. Thomas directed the lamp so the light beamed below. Silas Collins peered into the pit, gesturing with beefy gloved hands and grunting direction.

Still nothing earthshaking occurred. She'd expected flashes of lightning, shrieking ghouls, men stricken with leprosy. Anything terrible. Not this quiet. Only muffled merriment in the background sounded apart from the rumble of voices and the clunk of the shovel.

Apparently satisfied with the progress made, Silas Collins reached into a lumpy knapsack and withdrew two stout lengths of rope. He flung them to the man below. Oaths issued from the grave while the worker struggled to secure the twine around the wooden box, then tossed up the lengths to the men hovering above ground.

Stuart and Brinkley were silent, waiting, as was Hettie, wondering what would occur when the coffin was lifted.

Maybe nothing. Maybe she'd dreamed that last encounter with Captain John. But the grave robbers were here, and she sensed something more in store for them.

Thomas set the lamp down beside the hole. He and Silas grasped a line and heaved, while the unseen man hoisted from below. Their efforts were rewarded when the coffin appeared. The box tilted precariously to the left, then the right, but was swiftly straightened.

Muffled cheers from the worker snapped off at Thomas's rebuke. He didn't want to be detected now.

He reclaimed the lamp and lit the way while Collins and the rustic, who emerged slaked in mud, raised the coffin onto their shoulders. Thomas lent his free hand for stability, though the bulk of the heavy lifting resided with the other two. No sign of a limp was in evidence as Thomas climbed with them over the iron fence around the plot—awkward while balancing the coffin. The trio trudged through the powdery snow to the wagon left on the path in the cemetery as near to the site as possible. Headstones and trees prevented the wagon from waiting alongside the grave.

The patient team of horses perked up at their coming, likely hopeful of feed and stabling out of the weather. A last heave, more oaths, and the coffin rested in the wagon bed. The worker scrambled inside and covered it with a blanket.

Still nothing magnanimous transpired. Stuart must wonder if she'd misunderstood.

"Looks like they're making off with the goods," Brinkley whispered.

"Appearances can be deceptive," Hettie hissed.

The final vote rested with Stuart. "Either we let them take the stuff, or intervene." He didn't add, *because nothing and no one is waylaying them*, but that was implied. "What do you say, Hettie?"

"Let them go." If she was wrong, she was wrong.

Still, a strong foreboding suggested otherwise.

Chapter Twenty-Seven

Stuart battled divergent emotions. He wanted to believe Hettie, he truly did, but the wagon rolled over the snowy path, seemingly bound for the road. Meanwhile, he and Brinkley, both experienced officers, stood by helpless to intervene. At least, according to her. They'd even fought in the Battle of the Hook, shortly before the British Surrender at Yorktown, with a picked battalion of grenadiers chosen for their strength, skill, and resilience.

He and Brinkley could easily halt that wagon, and why shouldn't they? The three commandeering it were all former Tories, the very men they'd battled bitterly all those years. Collins might prove an able opponent, but the workman was unarmed, and Thomas relied on deceit. Cunning would avail him little now. Stuart and Brinkley had the advantage.

None of that mattered, though. Adhering to the promise he'd made Hettie last night, and honoring her current request, Stuart restrained himself from taking action. Brinkley dutifully followed his lead, as he had in battle, except on those occasions when he'd put forth a better proposal. Apparently, he had none.

Collins drove on, the reins in his hands. Thomas held the lantern and bounced at his side on the seat. The filthy worker crouched in the wagon gripping the coffin. The haversack, shovel, crowbar, and other paraphernalia jounced around the bed. Curses emanated from the fellow, probably as a result of encountering the metal implements.

The gleeful yokel had lit into the coffin with the crowbar and pried open one corner before Thomas put a stop to it. "We'll examine the trove later, far from potential onlookers."

Collins had grudgingly agreed, and the worker gave in. He was fortunate to still live. They'd dispatch the poor beggar when they saw no further need for his services.

To appease Thomas, he'd looped rope around the wooden box, and off they went with the treasure, no evil befalling them. It rankled Stuart, but he didn't want to make Hettie feel any worse than she already did. And he'd never been easy in his mind about digging up the grave anyway, even if the stash had been put there as a result of his father.

This was it, then. They might as well head back inside and enjoy the party—

Wait. Did he detect a high, thin howl?

There it was again.

He'd forgotten something in his calculations—the wolf. Sharp memory returned when the bristling beast appeared in front of the wagon, barring its way. Feathery snow powdered its black coat. Canine eyes glowed red in the lamplight, jaws gaping in toothy snarls.

High-pitched whinnies tore from the formerly docile horses. Heads jerked up. Front legs danced. They were about to bolt.

Collins hauled on the reins. "Get away, damn you!" he cursed the wolf. "Shoot it, you fool!" he yelled at Thomas.

Even Collins couldn't strong-arm the spooked team and shoot at the same time. "God damn you, fire!"

But Thomas was useless. By the bobbing light, he was visible clinging to the seat and goggling at the beast. He made no move to reach for his pistol.

More growls erupted. They seemed to come from everywhere at once. Snarls were thick in the air. Added wolves were closing in. But Stuart saw only the one incensed creature. The others must be hidden by the darkness and swirling snow.

The lone wolf had incited alarm. A pack was enough to derange the horses. The team reared. Hooves scrabbled in the whiteness, as if they sought to climb an invisible hill. The wagon lurched, its front wheels lifting off the ground.

The man in the bed was hurled head over heels and pinned between the back of the wagon and the coffin. He cried out, the terrified horses neighed, and curses flew. All the while, snarls, snapping, and growls broke loose on every side. Yet there was only one wolf in sight.

If the music and gaiety in the Jones' house hadn't been so raucous, the guests would surely grow aware of the commotion outside. Still, none came running to see. Nor did nearby townsfolk, also attending the festivity.

"Must be the curse!" Hettie shouted to make herself heard.

Granted, the wolf and its unseen pack were highly unusual. Unearthly, even. Halifax hadn't been overrun by wolves since the early settlement days. And black ones were extremely rare. If this was what his father's spirit had summoned them to witness, there was plenty to view.

Brinkley gaped in amazement. "Holy—"

The frenzied horses cut him off. Slamming their hooves back to the ground, they fought to tear free. Then swung to the right. The wolf blocked their way. They reared again in a thrashing of legs, tearing wildly to escape their bonds. The wagon bucked like a live thing. The bed rocked back and forth. The team broke loose and the wagon careened onto its side. Still wearing their collars and what remained of the harness, the horses galloped off into the white veil of night.

Stuart hoped no hapless soul stood in their way. They'd run for miles, trampling all, before some farmer found them.

He returned his gaze to the garish scene. How the lamp still shone, he couldn't imagine, but it landed upright in the snow. The circle of light revealed the wreckage.

Thomas had been thrown free and sprawled, moaning, on the path. Collins was pinned under a wheel and one side of the splintered wagon, his cries piteous. No sound came from the ill-fated man who'd done the digging. He'd landed headfirst against a tombstone, his blood reddening the snow. He'd not rise again.

The already damaged coffin cracked open in the crash. Silver bowls and plates, mixed with jewelry and a hodgepodge of valuables, spilled forth. Rather like pirate treasure, without the gold doubloons. Although they might be somewhere in the cache.

Not all the goods had spewed onto the ground. Some were still contained by the ornate coverlet they'd been wrapped inside before placement in the coffin, a sort of sack.

The small band of Patriots whom Stuart's father had lead, badly wanted to bribe a Loyalist into revealing the whereabouts of Benedict Arnold so he might be taken and hung. If the traitor hadn't fled Virginia when he did, this trove would've been all the persuasion many Tories needed to turn on him. That was the intent behind collecting the goods, but the stash had gone well beyond Arnold.

Every single member of the original band had fallen. And it wasn't treasure, alone, strewn over the ground. A skeleton lay amid the jumble, its mouth open in a voiceless scream, its eye sockets empty, as if crows had pecked his eyes out. They hadn't, but it was a spine-chilling sight.

Two and a half years had failed to complete the decomposition process. Hair hung in patches from the scalp. Bone showed in spots there and on the eroded face. A similar effect was evident in the hands. The suit of clothes was mostly intact.

Hettie sucked in her breath. "Manley."

"What remains of him." She'd declared him buried along with the goods after her dream. Eerily enough, here he was. If the mayhem was related to him, that was one wrathful spirit.

Stuart thought the wolf and its mates might tear into the survivors. But they didn't. The creature vanished into the night on noiseless paws, taking his invisible pack with him. Apparently, his work was done.

"Do we act now?" Brinkley asked.

Hettie nodded. "Have great care. The curse remains until all is restored."

Without waiting for Stuart and Brinkley to take the

lead, she sprang from behind the tree and ran at the wreckage. *Impulsive girl.*

Stuart took off after her. "Watch out for the graves!" She was a fleet little thing and might collide with a headstone disguised by snow.

Brinkley sprinted behind them. "Don't fall over a stone table!"

"Those are a bit more obvious," Stuart shot back, knowing Brinkley used sarcasm as a defense against the ghoulish.

They weren't far from the wagon and reached it in moments. Collins howled lustily. If the wolves hadn't departed, he'd attract every predator within earshot.

Stuart and Brinkley pried off the wheel and the portion of wagon lying atop him. They heaved the heavy wood aside. Hettie knelt by Collins, with Stuart standing guard. Brinkley took position by Thomas.

"Where in hell did those wolves come from?" Collins panted. He eyed Hettie, a belligerent gleam in his pain-glazed stare. "You do this, witch?"

Never mind he was injured, Stuart struck him across the mouth. "No. And refrain from using that term."

Collins wiped at the blood trickling down his unshaven chin. "Gonna shoot me again if I don't."

"Sure am. But only once."

His leg was twisted in an unnatural shape, most likely broken. Stuart leaned in. "Do you really prefer death? Give up this futile pursuit of treasure and allow a physician to tend you. Then get on home where you belong. It's not here."

The injured man sat in the snow, shaking from cold and shock. Still, he argued. "Some of that stuff's mine.

271

Belongs to the family."

Hettie gestured at the skeleton. "Your brother doesn't agree."

Turning his head as if seeing the remains for the first time, Collins grunted. "That's Manley?"

"Yes. Didn't your mother tell you?" she pressed.

"No. Mama only said he was dead. Rebels killed him."

"You'll follow him in death, Mister Collins, if you don't see sense."

"What you gonna do, Miss high and mighty? Keep all for yourself and these two?" He waved at Stuart and Brinkley.

She shook her hooded head. "We can't, even if we wanted to. It's all cursed."

"What do you mean?"

"Just what I said."

Thomas roused at this, and struggled weakly to sit. "Miss Fairfax is spinning tales."

"Are you thick in the head?" Stuart countered. "It wasn't the lady who sent the wolf and that pack with him. Something mighty peculiar is going on here."

"Or hadn't you noticed?" Brinkley interjected. "We've got to get all this stuff, and him—" He waved at the skeleton. "Back into that grave before the next blow falls."

Thomas clambered to his feet and staggered a few paces. "Why not divide the spoils among us? Plenty here for all."

"No!"

Ignoring Hettie's protest, he bent down and picked up a silver plate. A moment's satisfaction crossed his face, then he screeched and dropped his prize in the snow. "What the—Blasted thing's hot!"

"I was afraid of that. Or something like it," she sighed.

Thomas rounded on her. "Makes no sense. Did your spell go awry, Missy?"

"It's not her, you lout." Stuart seized Thomas by the shoulders. Lifting him off the ground, he gave him a shake. Then roughly set him down. He swayed unsteadily.

Stuart eyed Hettie. "Now what?"

"Tend to Mister Collins, while I attempt to commune with his brother. Brinkley, see Mister Vaughan doesn't burn himself again."

"Gladly." Brinkley stood guard by an irate, unstable Thomas.

Stuart fished the blanket from the wreckage they'd used to cover the coffin and wrapped it around Collins. Then he eased the battered man, groaning, onto what was left of the wagon seat to shield him from further wet. "As soon as we're finished here, we'll fetch a surgeon."

"Thank you, I suppose," he said through chattering teeth.

"Would you rather join your brother? We can arrange that, if you'd prefer," Stuart suggested.

"Reckon not. Mama wants me home." Each word escaped him in gasps. "She'll be angry, my returning empty-handed. Said she'd spell the treasure, so we could get it."

Thomas glared at him. "What in blazes? Your mother's a bloody witch?"

"What of it? If I weren't down with a broken leg, I'd knock your teeth out," Collins growled.

"I do not consort with witches," Thomas fired back.

Collins glowered at him. "She's not a bad sort, *Mister don't want to dirty your hands*."

Bad enough. But Stuart forbore to speak that aloud.

"We'd not have gotten this far without her," Collins thrust at his infuriated partner.

Thomas waved at the wreckage. "Look where we are, you idiot."

Ignoring him and his insults, Collins turned to Hettie. "Whatever Mama did, failed. You got a counter spell?"

"No. Because *I'm not a witch*," she emphasized, as if for the slow in thought. "But if you will all keep still, I can try and speak with Manley."

"How?" Collins wiped his beaded nose on the blanket. "You daft?"

"I can communicate with the dead, if they wish it."

He glanced around blankly. "Can you see them too?"

"Yes. Unfortunately, with him."

"Manley never was much to look at," he sniffed.

"You resemble each other."

Thomas gave a ragged laugh.

"Quiet, now," she rapped.

"Or I'm gagging you both," Stuart threatened.

The assembly grew still, apart from the groans escaping Collins.

Stuart watched in wonder, sensing Brinkley do the same, as Hettie poised, eyes closed, trancelike, snowflakes floating past her cloak. The hood fell back, and she raised her face to the heavens. No wind stirred the falling snow. She could have been a beautiful sculpture, an angel in this place of death.

In the hush of trees and snow, she spoke. "Manley, I am sent to help you regain what is taken."

Silence. Unless, Hettie heard a reply.

"Mister Vaughan will not touch a thing," she promised the unseen presence. "The other two gentlemen and I will restore your possessions and body to the grave. Do you understand?"

Again, Stuart heard nothing, saw nothing. But she must have, judging by her frown.

"If you do not allow us to pick up what is fallen and return these valuables to the earth, they will remain strewn here, and your bones spread over this cemetery by wild animals. I know who sent the wolf and can summon him again."

Muffling a low whistle, Stuart exchanged glances with Brinkley. Sweet Hettie was getting tough. How she had the nerve to face this malevolent spirit, he didn't know. His respect for her tripled.

He'd refrained from looking into the sightless stare of the skeleton for fear it would blink—worse—speak audibly. Yet, she remained as she was. True courage.

"If you are in agreement, all shall be returned, including your remains," she bargained.

Stuart strained to hear the reply but couldn't detect a word. Apparently, the voice sounded only in her head. Judging by the others, none of them heard either.

"Very well." She seemed satisfied.

Thank God. Battling this sort of enemy was beyond him.

Hettie continued. "Your brother, Silas, is here and injured. Your mother in need. If there is anything you will spare them, show me now."

Stuart couldn't imagine this grasping spirit would share a piece of straw, let alone anything of value.

Evidently, she received a favorable reply. Rather than speaking to the unseen presence, she walked to the pile of goods spilled from the broken coffin. Some lay outside the coverlet worked in gold thread, others within. Bending down, she reached into the hidden wealth and withdrew a small leather pouch. It jingled when she shook it.

"This?" She remained as she was, seemingly awaiting affirmation. "I shall give it to him."

The cloak floating about her, she made her way to an incredulous Collins. She passed the pouch into his trembling hands. "'Tis enough to pay a doctor to tend you, and get you home, and purchase provisions for winter. The rest, your brother insists must remain with him."

A vacant nod from Collins. For a man whose mother was a purported witch, he seemed taken aback by these peculiar doings; that dead-eyed stare gone from his eyes.

Thomas exploded. "What? Nothing for me?"

"Manley doesn't favor you," she said.

He stabbed a finger at her. "Miss Fairfax conjured this whole affair. And the three of you will return to this spot at your leisure and take what you please."

Hettie shook her head at him. "You are doomed, Mister Vaughan, if you truly believe that. Between the two of you, I never expected it would be Mister Collins who was spared."

Thomas closed his mouth, but fury emanated from him.

"If you remove one single item, or speak of this

treasure to a living soul, you will surely perish." With that dire warning, she waved him away. "Leave now. We have work to be about. The others will ask after us."

"You mean, I can go?" Thomas faltered.

Brinkley gave him a suggestive push. "I should prefer to shoot you and have done with it, but we've enough vindictive spirits to contend with at present."

"Make yourself useful and send a surgeon for Collins," Stuart directed. "And if you cease to be such an ass, you might find your place in this town," he added, though that seemed remote. "Make no mistake, sir. This is your final chance for redemption. We've allowed you to go, twice. There won't be a third time."

Disheveled and not at all his immaculate self, Thomas stumbled off into the night. Like a cat, he always landed on his feet. And no doubt, would again.

Stuart would also have preferred to dispatch him on the spot. Accounting for his action might not be so easy. The war, as folk incessantly reminded him, was over. And he had no proof regarding Thomas's foul play. The man bore watching. But not now.

The present situation demanded Stuart's attention. Uncertain how to proceed, he asked Hettie. "What first?"

"The reburial."

"Yes. Let's get that eyesore out of view."

"There's ugly and there's *ugly*," Brinkley muttered.

The coffin was beyond hasty repairs. There was nothing for it other than to remove the long coat from the dead worker and wrap the skeleton in it. Then Stuart and Brinkley bore him back to the grave and laid him to rest at the bottom.

"May God rest your black soul," Stuart said under his breath.

"Amen." Brinkley turned and scaled the fence. "I'm burning these gloves when we're finished here."

"Too costly for me. Mrs. Jenner will cleanse mine with some sacred herb."

They returned to find Hettie scooping valuables into the coverlet. Not a finger singed. Manley must not object to her handling his things. They let her finish, then each took a corner. Stuart grasped two ends, and Brinkley the other two.

Between them, they carried the makeshift sack, sagging awkwardly under its weight, and lowered it, clanking, into the hole. They took turns with the shovel and soon had the gap filled in. Together, they stomped the earth in place. Stuart rather enjoyed this bit, like dancing on Manley's grave.

"Cover it with stones, so none disturb his resting place," Hettie suggested, with more solemnity.

Loose rocks were piled on the site to conceal the recent dig. Brinkley swiped an arm across his heated forehead. "What about the broken cart and corpse?"

"Leave the poor beggar with the cart. He'll be found," Stuart determined. "Let's get back to the house. We've delayed long enough and could all do with a wash."

"Hear. Hear," Brinkley resounded.

"My, yes—"

Collins broke into Hettie's response. "Wait—what about me? You can't just leave me out here."

"We shall report sighting an overturned wagon in the cemetery. Help will be along shortly." Stuart wanted to return to the house before curious onlookers arrived.

"But it'll look like we robbed a grave with that broken coffin lying there," Collis pointed out.

"You did!" Stuart was losing patience. "But we don't want questions asked. Best set it ablaze."

With Brinkley's help, he stacked the broken wood closely enough to warm Collins without turning him into a funeral pyre. Then he took the lamp and used it to set the remains of the coffin afire. He nodded approvingly.

"There. That should keep you toasty."

The wounded man grunted his appreciation. "One last question. Who sent the wolf?"

Hettie didn't hesitate. "Captain John Monroe."

"But he's dead."

"Yes."

"What of the others in the pack, Miss?"

She shrugged. "Echoes."

They left Collins muttering to himself, likely half out of his head with pain. But he'd live, and no one would believe a word he said.

Whether or not sparing his life was wise, Stuart couldn't say. Killing him didn't seem right, and Hettie had wielded extraordinary influence with the man. Maybe some of her goodness would stick.

Stuart's love for her was already boundless. If possible, it deepened. She walked over the white ground between him and Brinkley, her arms hooked with theirs.

Pondering her last reply, Stuart repeated, "Echoes?"

"I honestly don't know where those added howls came from. Perhaps it was Manley's curse. Or some other ghost who didn't want Silas and Thomas here."

"One malignant soul is enough."

"More than adequate," Brinkley concurred.

Hettie seemed pensive. They were nearly to the house before she spoke again. "It might be best to build something over that spot."

"Like what?" Stuart asked.

"Something sacred to sanctify the ground."

"Not an altar, surely. I'm not reenacting scenes from the Old Testament with burnt sacrifices."

"Any nearer that bonfire and Collins would be one. How about a church?" Brinkley suggested. "Seems a suitable site."

Stuart agreed. "A sound idea."

"Oh Brinkley, it's perfect." Hettie freed her arms and clapped her hands together. "I'll mention it to Jonas. He's the religious sort. And Uncle Ezra has the influence in town to gets things done."

"I have no argument with that, so long as what Ezra achieves in the near future is his blessing at our nuptials." Stuart stopped at the base of the steps. "Hettie Louise, I adore you."

"We know, we know," Brinkley intoned.

"Marry me?" Stuart asked, wrapping her in his arms.

"This instant. Though Uncle Ezra will still accuse you of lacking sufficient funds."

"Indeed, he will. Now that the answer to my financial woes is forever buried, I must find another way of meeting my obligations." He angled his head at Brinkley. "Suppose, I ought to discuss the sale of a portion of my land with you. And maybe my prize mare."

"That'll keep for a few days, old man. Let's clean up and get back to the ball. Ought to be supper time soon. All that work in a haunted graveyard sure gave me an appetite."

"Indeed. I'm happy to frolic and feast with Hettie by my side until the wee hours. But postponing our wedding is out of the question." Especially a bride who might be with child.

Hettie clasped his arm. "Stuart, your father says all will be well."

He groaned. "Enough of him for one night, sweetheart."

Chapter Twenty-Eight

Sunshine gilded the elegant dining room in Thornton Hall, and the aroma of corn fritters, sausage, porridge, and stewed apples mingled with wood smoke from the hearth. Hettie sat to the left of Mister Monroe, sipping hot milky tea. Despite her fatigue, she offered the old gentleman her warmest smile.

"I'm glad you are well enough to join us at breakfast this morning, sir, in your rightful place." He sat at the head of the table.

His pale blue eyes were bright and he smiled benignly at her. "'Tis happy I am to have you three back from town. Too dull here by half with Stuart's mama, and that scamp William, off in England. Don't see how they abide that chill land." He shuddered, his opinion of the Mother Country still rather low since the war. "Ought to come on home, the pair of them."

"I dare say they might, at some point," Hettie ventured.

Stuart wore his haunted look, and she knew it arose from the awareness that he could ill afford the return of his relations. She hoped she hadn't erred in offering the older man encouragement.

Glancing up from his plate, Stuart blotted his mouth with the napkin. "I shall write Mama, if you like, sir, and invite her to return. Though William must complete his schooling."

"See that you do." Mister Monroe waved his thin hand at the vacant seat at the other end of the table. "Her spot still awaits her. I miss Mavis, wife to my John all those years."

"As do I, my dear mother."

"William could get proper schooling here," his grandfather argued. "Don't want the lad growing up a Tory."

Stuart frowned. "Claire would never allow that, sir."

"She mightn't be able to prevent it." Mister Monroe appeared askance at the thought.

"I shall write them both at my first opportunity," Stuart assured him and exchanged glances with Hettie.

Perhaps his grandfather would cease to be so adamant on the subject when his erratic mind wandered to another. If he persisted, she supposed Mrs. Monroe and William could decline Stuart's invitation until Stuart possessed the funds to support them. They were accustomed to living in grand style with Lord and Lady Vaughan on their palatial estate.

Hettie understood Major Vaughan and Claire made every effort for Mrs. Monroe's comfort and William's education. That wouldn't be possible here for some time. Possibly, not ever.

Lines etched Stuart's brow beneath the sun-streaked brown hair. Several lengths had worked free from where he'd pulled it back and fell across the sides of his face. She wanted to smooth his hair and cares away. The wedding was only days from now, and he still had sizable debt to clear. That meant selling off vital Monroe land to Mister Ellis, and his champion mare, too. La Belle would fetch a rare price.

At least Brinkley would ultimately inherit everything from his uncle, but it still cut deep to part with precious acreage and his beloved horse. Nor had Stuart yet broached the sore subject with his grandfather.

All this, he'd proclaimed his willingness to do for Hettie, but he didn't seem in particularly good spirits today. Nor did Abigail, somber over Brinkley's lack of a proposal. He was as cordial as ever in her presence, though not besotted. Likely, she also fretted over her future.

"Yer as bonnie as a rose in May, m' dear." Mister Monroe broke into Hettie's conjecture and favored her with another smile. "I'm pleased yer to be a Monroe lady."

"Thank you, sir." After initial disapproval, he was finally accepting of her.

"Such a fine gown. Mavis would fancy it."

"I trust Mrs. Monroe shall see it before many months," Hettie said, to placate him.

Knowing the older man's enjoyment of color, she wore her lacy rose-colored gown and lavender shawl, ribbons in her hair, and garnets at her ears and throat. Her cheeks were pinkened and lips reddened from ceramic pots of makeup. Powder hid the inky smudges under her eyes. She'd labored over her toilette this morning.

The ordeal in the cemetery two nights ago had taken its toll. Any brightness she exuded, was forced. They'd only returned last evening, after a lengthy coach ride.

She'd seen no hint of Captain John since his last dreamlike visit. Thomas was holed up in his house, and

Collins would soon head home. It seemed this bizarre episode in their lives was at an end.

Mrs. Jenner swooped into the room in a flurry of petticoats. How fast the woman moved, given her girth. She wasn't bearing yet more food, as Hettie expected, but a silver tray holding a letter.

She paused beside Mister Monroe. "All the way from Williamsburg, sir." The awe in her voice was akin to announcing it hailed from Paris. She hovered nearby, likely hoping to overhear the contents.

He took the folded paper, and shooed her away. "If there be tidings to share you shall hear them, m' good woman."

"As you like, sir." She pivoted with evident reluctance and skirted out the door.

She'd not stray far, Hettie wagered.

Abigail looked around with a spark of interest in her hazel eyes. "Is it from Mrs. Peyton, sir?"

Hettie understood her to be Stuart's aunt and Abigail's guardian before she came to Thornton Hall.

Mister Monroe shook his silver head. "Nae. 'Tis from her spinster cousin, Ethel Beale. That woman must be nigh on a hundred by now." He pulled his spectacles from his waistcoat pocket and affixed them on his nose. Then broke the red seal on the letter and opened the parchment.

From her vantage point, Hettie noted the script was penned in a shaky scrawl. She'd offer to read aloud, but words often behaved peculiarly on the page for her.

Abigail extended her hand. "Perhaps I might read it for you, sir?"

"Not needed, lass. I'm able." His demeanor that of one fearing to be informed he'd lost every person and possession dear to him, Mister Monroe scanned the lines. The intensity in his gaze lessened as he neared the bottom of the page.

Stroking his beard, he reread the missive again. "'Tis what it says, aright, and no mistake."

By now, Hettie, Stuart, and Abigail all peered at him. "Well, then," Stuart prompted.

Mister Monroe laid the letter down. "Millicent's gone to meet her maker."

Alarm tolled in Hettie. "Who has?"

"Why, Mrs. Peyton, of course." He was matter-of-fact about the woman's passing.

Abigail clasped her small hands together on the table. "Oh my. I trust she had a peaceful end, sir."

"So Miss Beale informs me. Says she died in her sleep. We should all hope for such an end."

"I'm glad she didn't suffer," Stuart offered, though he didn't seem particularly affected one way or the other.

His grandfather's gaze took on a distant look. "Aye. She was an old besom, was Millicent, but she treated our Claire right enough when she stayed with her during the war. Toward the end, you remember, Miss Smith?"

"Yes, I do. Mrs. Peyton did, indeed, assure her safety," affirmed Abigail, who'd lived in Williamsburg at the time.

Stuart pushed back the loose hair from his face. "I'll grant her that. Claire wasn't happy being confined indoors, but Aunt Millicent kept her safe in those turbulent months."

Apparently that was all he had to contribute regarding the deceased, or anyone else. Millicent

Peyton hadn't stirred great fondness in any breast present at the table.

An unexpected smile lit Mister Monroe's face. "While grieved by her loss," he said, appearing anything but. "I expect you will take comfort in knowing what she's left you."

Stuart drew his bows together. "I thought she willed all to her cousin."

"Nae. Miss Beale has sufficient provision fer her remaining days, such as they are."

To Hettie's astonishment, Mister Monroe actually chuckled and slapped his thigh. She wouldn't have been surprised to see him leap to his feet and jig if his joints allowed.

The jubilant man grinned as if at the most marvelous secret. "You, sir, are the heir she names, of her home in Williamsburg and its contents, and her land in the country. She inherited a fine plantation on the James, you recall, and has run it with the help of her steward these many years."

Stuart eyed him wonderingly. "So she has."

Mister Monroe clapped him on the back with such force he was thrown forward. "Must be over three hundred acres, with a house, stables, and plenteous outbuildings. Bonnie horses, great fields of tobacco. Sell up, rent, do as you like. 'Tis all yers, m' boy."

"Mine? I had no notion Aunt Millicent held me in such high esteem."

Another hearty clap nearly sent Stuart into his plate. "Yer a hero, Captain Monroe! Like yer father before you."

Stuart couldn't seem to take it in. "I suppose so."

"No *suppose* about it, sir. You toiled and fought all

those years fer this country, our United States, our America. High time someone gave you yer rightful dues. Millicent was that proud of you. Said so in her letters." His grandfather couldn't have appeared more gratified.

Relief welled in Hettie, and a twinge of guilt that the unfortunate woman's death was cause for such rejoicing.

Mister Monroe indicated the dispirited girl at the table. "You, Miss Smith, are also left a generous bequest."

"Truly?" She gazed dazedly at him.

"Aye. Yer faithful service is remembered. You shall have enough to wed where you like and not where you dislike."

Color returned to her pale face. "I have a dowry? Oh, that is good news, sir."

"Aye." He banged his spoon on the table. "Sally forth, Mrs. Jenner! We have much to celebrate!"

He needn't have shouted. As Hettie predicted, she practically fell in the door where she'd been listening.

"Great God Almighty! It's a miracle." Her naturally florid hue flushed a deeper red, and a broad grin stretched her round face.

If anyone thought this woman had been unaware of the financial woes in the house, they were mightily mistaken. Mister Monroe must also have known, no matter what he'd pretended to Stuart. Likely, they all did.

Bringing her plump hands together, Mrs. Jenner called out. "Minnie, Maddie, run tell yer mama and Aunt Beulah we've got some feasting to do!" Her fond eye fell on Hettie. "And a Yuletide wedding to ready fer. You'll have the nuptials here, will you not?"

Warmth rushed through Hettie. "There's nowhere I should rather be wed and live out my days."

With a whoop, Mrs. Jenner lifted her skirts and capered about the room humming *God Rest Ye Merry Gentlemen.* "We'll bring in greens and holly. Have warm fires and candles all over the house. Decorate Thornton Hall for Christmas like we've never done before. There will be feasting and dancing. Gift giving."

"Carols sung," added a smiling Abigail.

"Aplenty," Mrs. Jenner proclaimed.

"And figgy pudding, mince pies, meat roasting. A stuffed goose. Spirits flowing." Mister Monroe was not to be outdone.

Hettie was flushed with happiness. At last, she'd found the husband and home she'd sought. If only her mother and father could witness her joy. Somehow, she expected they knew.

Shifting her eyes to the doorway, she caught a glimpse of the blue and red uniform, and a gloved hand raised in silent farewell. Captain John could go to his proper home now.

She met Stuart's adoring gaze. This might be the moment to tell him. While Mister Monroe, Abigail, and Mrs. Jenner excitedly made plans, Hettie confided. "Your father left his sword on the mantel in my chamber—for you." Her voice hitched with the emotion swelling inside.

Rather than chiding or reasoning with her, as he might have done before, Stuart smiled. The sheen in his eyes mirrored her sentiment. "I shall be proud to wear it, at our wedding."

Author's Note:

In 1793 a church was erected over an old grave in the Halifax town cemetery. Some say it's because the graveyard was too crowded to find adequate space for the structure without covering the grave. Others seek a different reason. The church collapsed in 1911 and has since been torn down. What happened to the grave?

Thank you for purchasing
this publication of The Wild Rose Press, Inc.

If you enjoyed the story, we would appreciate your
letting others know by leaving a review.

For other wonderful stories,
please visit our on-line bookstore at
www.thewildrosepress.com.

For questions or more information
contact us at
info@thewildrosepress.com.

The Wild Rose Press, Inc.
www.thewildrosepress.com

Stay current with The Wild Rose Press, Inc.

Like us on Facebook

https://www.facebook.com/TheWildRosePress

And Follow us on Twitter
https://twitter.com/WildRosePress